Highway One

Highway One

A Vietnam War Story

James E. Davidson

Writer's Showcase
San Jose New York Lincoln Shanghai

Highway One
A Vietnam War Story

Writer's Showcase
an imprint of iUniverse, Inc.

For information address:
iUniverse, Inc.
5220 S. 16th St., Suite 200
Lincoln, NE 68512
www.iuniverse.com

ISBN: 0-595-19654-3

Printed in the United States of America

To our South Vietnamese counterparts, who patiently put up with us.

Epigraph

"His lies were quite unimportant lies and consisted in attributing to himself things other men had seen, done or heard of, and stating as facts certain apocryphal incidents familiar to all soldiers."

Soldier's Home
- Ernest Hemingway

Introduction

There is a small village about halfway between Hue and Quang Tri in the Socialist Republic of Vietnam, where Highway One crosses the Song O Lau River. There is nothing really special about this village, assuming it is still there today, and there was nothing really special about the village when the Americans were there.

The only thing you need to know about the village is that in 1968 this small village served as the seat of the Phong Dien district government, in the province of Thua Thien, in the sovereign state of South Vietnam. This meant that the day-to-day affairs of the people of that little farming village were watched over, regulated, and complicated by the local district government and its American advisors.

If you recall, either from memory or history, during that American war martial law was in effect throughout South Vietnam. The top administrator at the local levels of government was the District Chief. He was usually not an elected official, but an officer of the South Vietnamese Regular Army. He was often a wealthy, educated man from Saigon, which was what Ho Chi Minh City was called back then, and a man who looked upon his assignment as District Chief as an irritating, yet required step in his military career.

In addition to looking after the civil affairs of the people, the District Chief was also the senior military commander of the local Popular Forces, somewhat condescendingly nicknamed the Ruff Puffs by their American Advisors. This paramilitary organization got this label from the combination of the first letters from their official designation: Regional Forces/Popular Forces. This force was started by the French and was known as the People's Self-defense Force. The name was changed to "Regional Forces/Popular Forces" by the Americans in an attempt to apply a "systems" approach to the war, much like it was done at the Ford Motor Company.

This local militia force was usually made up of good, law-abiding Vietnamese citizens, but often their ranks contained a fair number of petty criminals and men who were too old for South Vietnam's military draft. This local militia was also a relatively safe haven for local merchants and sons of wealthy families that bought their way out of the draft for the ARVN forces, or the regular Army of the Republic of South Vietnam. By joining these local paramilitary units of the Popular Forces, these men could stay close to home and often avoid combat.

It was a system not unlike the one being used in the United States at that time by the fortunate sons of the elite. A system where well-to-do white men, having used up their college deferment in graduate and divinity schools, obtained coveted spots in the National Guard and Reserve in order to avoid the draft and risk the chance of being sent to Vietnam.

Since the Popular Forces were recruited from their own community, the soldiers of the average Ruff Puff platoon would be representative of their community's politics. So each platoon contained about the same percentage of Viet Cong as the local population. In the district of Phong Dien, that was about fifty percent.

The mission of the Ruff Puffs, in general, was to protect their own district. The mission of the Ruff Puffs at Phong Dien, specifically, was to protect the bridge over the Song O Lau River on Highway One. This bridge was at the north end of the village and approximately halfway between Hue and Quang Tri on Highway One. Therefore, it was a very important strategic link in the supply line between the two cities.

In those days, the wise District Chiefs who rotated in and out of Phong Dien would seclude themselves in the yellow administration building inside the military compound located at the southern edge of the village and try not to make waves. Most believed their task was to run an efficient, do-nothing local government until some other luckless staff officer in Saigon screwed up and was ordered from that beautiful city to become the new District Chief at Phong Dien.

However, the foolish District Chiefs, usually upon the urging of their American advisors, would leave the sanctuary of the yellow administration building and attempt to bring change to the district in accordance with some plan or policy written thousands of miles away inside the Washington DC beltway. These new plans and policies arrived with regularity, and were forced upon the South Vietnamese District Chiefs as the right thing to do. Usually these great ideas were generated so the District Chiefs could win the hearts and minds of their own people.

It was always a variation of the same theme. District Chiefs would receive "recommendations" from American advisors to implement some grand plan to curb the influence of the Viet Cong Infrastructure. Or at least give the impression to the media of the Western World that South Vietnam and its Southeast Treaty Organization allies were winning the war. The wise District Chiefs ignored their American counterparts, and politely stonewalled the ideas arriving almost weekly from Washington. The foolish District Chiefs listened to their American advisors. The foolish District Chiefs always seemed to get people killed.

So the problem was, in this little village, at least, and perhaps throughout the entire country of South Vietnam in those days, not so much the Viet Cong and their guerilla war, but the American advisors and their advice. These Americans weren't necessarily incompetent, although there were plenty of incompetents involved in the war at all levels in those days, it was just that the American advisors were almost always career military officers who were sent to South Vietnam for only a one-year tour of duty. For these career officers, this was a year that would often determine their future in the military. This was a year for them to demonstrate their capabilities to their superior officers. This was a year for career officers to "punch their tickets", a term which was never, ever, clearly defined.

In other words, the advisors and everyone else in the American chain-of-command had one short year to make a difference. But, by not understanding the traditional Asian view of the relationship between time and war, the American advisors always felt like they had to do something. And that was the problem.

October 7, 1968

Major General H.M.S. Cooley squinted through his bifocals at an audience he could not see. He tried to adjust the glare of the reading light on the lectern, but only managed to light up his face like a Halloween pumpkin. The General licked his lips, then spoke slowly and deliberately into the microphone, signaling that the end of his speech was near.

"Remember the Roman soldiers of Caesar's army," the General said, "and walk out of here a professional warrior." The General looked slowly around the room at each soldier in the audience. "And if you should fail in your mission...If you should fall in the line of duty for your country...Let your comrades-in-arms carry you back on your shield like a noble Centurion."

The General paused for effect.

"Thank you gents," he continued, "and good luck in your new assignment as advisors to the Regional Forces and Popular Forces of South Vietnam. The time to Vietnamize this damn war is now! And you gents are the tip of the sword in this valiant crusade."

In the middle of the last row of the auditorium, First Lieutenant David Ruland, Infantry, United States Army Reserve, opened his eyes slowly, and sat up straight. He leaned over to the fellow junior officer sitting next to him.

"What did he say about being carried back on a shield?"

The artillery Captain sitting next to Ruland didn't answer. He was sleeping.

Suddenly, a weathered sergeant major appeared from the wings of the stage and marched slowly and solemnly to a spot in front of the lectern. He looked condescendingly down his nose at the junior officers, mostly reservists whom he considered draft-dodgers, and barked out at them.

"Gentlemens...Ten-hut!"

The men who were still awake jumped to their feet as one, forgetting that enlisted men didn't call officers to attention. They watched in silence as General H.M.S. Cooley slowly folded his glasses and put them in the right breast pocket of his neatly pressed jungle fatigues. The General then took two steps in the wrong direction before a fuzzy-faced second lieutenant caught him by the arm and pushed him to the exit at stage left.

When the General had disappeared into the wings, the ancient sergeant major carefully scrutinized the junior officers in front of him, barely holding back his distaste for the Army of the 1960s. After a slow survey of all the rows of the auditorium as a display of his position and power, the sergeant major released the men.

"Carry on, gentlemens," the sergeant major commanded.

Ruland carefully stepped over the sleeping artillery captain and shuffled toward the exit with the other junior officers. When he stepped outside, the heat of Southeast Asia stopped Ruland in his tracks. He put his hand to his forehead, staggered slightly, and took a quick breath to clear the sudden rush of hot, humid air.

The air conditioning in the auditorium was set at exactly seventy-five degrees. This was the temperature decreed by the Pentagon as the correct temperature for all the air-conditioned American military office buildings in Vietnam. It was rumored that this particular temperature was selected based on an extensive study done at the University of Minnesota under a lucrative Pentagon contract.

The contract was awarded to the university to determine the comfort range of Americans in Southeast Asia. The research was done on University of Minnesota college sophomores during February. It proved, with a reliability requirement clearly stipulated in the contract, that seventy-five degrees was the most cost-efficient temperature to cool a building for the maximum comfort and productivity of the average 20-year old Minnesota sophomore in February.

And in the manner of all the contracts supporting the war, research was immediately implemented in Vietnam without question. So when Ruland stepped from the auditorium into the noonday temperature of 101 degrees and 99 percent humidity, the hot heavy air smacked his head like a steam towel.

Lieutenant David Ruland had two weeks left to serve in the Army. And the Army, determined to get the last ounce of the pound of flesh Ruland owed it, had one last assignment for the young lieutenant. He was assigned to the Military Assistance Command Vietnam, identified early in the war as MACV, and pronounced MAC VEE. It was also known as Pentagon East, because it was the clearinghouse for all the new programs designed to "win the hearts and minds of the people". MACV ordered Ruland to report to a new advisory force called Mobile Advisory Teams, or MAT Teams.

The Mobile Advisory Teams were scattered throughout Vietnam in small villages and hamlets believed to be near Viet Cong strongholds. The concept was that these MAT teams would live off the local economy and work directly with the local Popular Forces. MAT Teams consisted of two officers and two or three noncommissioned officers, all with combat experience, and who were usually serving the last six months of their year-long tour. The primary mission of the MAT Team was to teach the Ruff Puffs modern infantry techniques and to show these local part-time soldiers how to use the new weapons and equipment they would be receiving from the United States.

These Mobile Advisory Teams were another new plan from Washington. The teams were to be an integral part of the Vietnamization program the Pentagon was pushing. If the Vietnamese were more involved in the war, the Pentagon planners reckoned, the South Vietnamese would fight their own war and the Americans could leave. Hence, the Vietnamization of the war would get the United States untangled from a political and unpopular mess. Vietnamization replaced the earlier philosophy of "pacification", a term which lost all meaning when the Chief of the South Vietnamese National Police blew the brains out of an alleged Viet Cong suspect on national television as Americans were eating their evening meal.

Ruland was assigned to the Mobile Advisory Team in the district of Phong Dien. The district was located in the northern province of Thuy Thien, the second province south of the DMZ. Highway One ran through Phong Dien district.

Much to his surprise and displeasure, Ruland was selected to become the OIC, or officer-in-charge, of the Mobile Advisory Team at Phong Dien. Even though he had only fourteen days left in the Army, he would become the senior member of the team, and with that seniority came the OIC title and the responsibility of leadership. Ruland really didn't want any more positions of responsibility or leadership. He just wanted out of the Army and out of Vietnam.

But the Army's plans for Lieutenant Ruland's last 14 days were a bit less grand and a lot more practical. Ruland's assignment was to build a rifle range. As an integral part of the Vietnamization effort, the Ruff Puffs throughout South Vietnam were scheduled to receive new M-16 rifles to replace the old M-1 rifles and M-30 carbines supplied by the United States earlier in the war. The Popular Forces soldiers needed to be taught how to use these weapons and to qualify on a firing range as soon as possible after receiving these new weapons.

Just as a matter of bad luck for Ruland, he had worked on a rifle range for two weeks during his first year in the Army at Fort Hood, so some computer in the Pentagon spotted this on his permanent record, and Ruland's card fell out of the machine.

Just three weeks before this day, Ruland was the Executive Officer of an infantry company of the Fourth Infantry Division operating in the Central Highlands. His tour had been pretty routine up to this point.

He had served his first six months in Vietnam in the triple-canopied highland jungle as a platoon leader. Ruland's company patrolled the Central Highlands along the Cambodian-Laotian border trying to intercept North Vietnamese Regulars as they entered South Vietnam from the Ho Chi Minh Trail. This was the real infantry, and an experience that Ruland looked back on with satisfaction. He didn't screw up and get anyone in his platoon killed.

After that six months of very interesting hiking and camping along the border, Ruland got the executive officer's desk job back at base camp in Pleiku. His job was to go to the field once a month to pay the troops and administer military justice to the dopeheads of the company who were caught smoking marijuana purchased from local Montagnard tribes. Ruland figured he had it made when he became the XO, and that the war was over for him. All he had to do was put in his time back at base camp and go home.

The six-months-in-the-field-deal was standard operating procedure for Army combat officers in Vietnam. Combat arms officers would serve six months in the bush and six months as a staff officer at base camp, then go home. However, the career Army officers, or the lifers as they were called by the drafted enlisted men, usually sought out another combat assignment with some unit of the Vietnamese Regular Army for the second half of their tour. The lifers figured it was a good career move to follow-up an initial combat assignment with another combat unit, even as an advisor. It was another punch of their ticket.

But the draftee reserve officers, like Ruland, just needed to endure their final six months somewhere safe in an air-conditioned building, not too far from a decent massage parlor. Of course, for the enlisted infantrymen, there was no such six-month good deal. They spent the entire year in the field, if they were lucky.

Still, six-month deal or not, MACV needed a rifle range for the Ruff Puffs at Phong Dien, and Ruland was chosen to get it built. The district was scheduled to receive new M-16s within a month, and the Ruff Puff soldiers needed a place to qualify with their new weapons. The Ruff Puffs were using surplus weapons from the Korean War. They had a collection of M-1 Garands, 30 caliber carbines, and a few old Browning Automatic Rifles. The M-1 and BAR weapons were old, yet reliable, but heavy and over-sized for the diminutive Vietnamese soldiers. The carbines were just the right size for these soldiers, and were battle-proven weapons in use since World War II. However, the M-16s were a status symbol among Vietnamese forces and were already showing up in Ruff Puff units through black market connections. So it was important for morale of the South Vietnamese soldiers and the Vietnamization of the war that all South Vietnamese units received M-16s just like their American counterparts.

So on this graduation day from the ten-day MACV Advisor School outside of Saigon, Lieutenant David Ruland completed what the Army called "intensive instruction" on how to be an advisor to the South Vietnamese Popular Forces. Ruland sat through rudimentary Vietnamese language instruction in the morning, and trained on the Korean War surplus weapons in the afternoon so he knew what the troops would be using. At night, Ruland and the other officers sat through informational sessions about the culture of Vietnam, so they would know a little about the people they would soon be living with.

After graduating from the school, Ruland would soon be on his way to the district of Phong Dien. His task was to build a rifle range so the Ruff Puffs could meet minimum marksmanship standards with their new M-16s, as directed by the Pentagon. And if everything went without a hitch, Ruland figured, he would soon be on a flight back to the United States and be discharged from the Army immediately upon arriving at the Oakland Army Terminal in California.

So when the graduation ceremony ended, Ruland gathered his belongings from the student officer barracks and waited outside the building for his ride to the airport. All of the junior officers who had just finished the ten-day school milled around the front of the building not speaking to each other. Whenever it came time for soldiers to leave their unit in the Army, nobody ever talked. So now all the men just milled around, making designs in the sand with the toes of their jungle boots.

Ruland rode a dark blue Air Force bus to the sprawling Tan Son Nhut airport outside of Saigon. The bus was not air-conditioned and the dark blue paint absorbed the mid-day sun like the walls of an oven. The windows of the bus had heavy metal grates over them so the soldiers couldn't throw candy out and the street children couldn't throw hand grenades in. Despite the heat in the bus, Ruland enjoyed the ride through the streets of Saigon. He was amazed at how European the city looked. Except for the red dust of the dry monsoon season and constant yelling of the children as they drove by, Ruland figured he could have been riding through a Paris neighborhood.

The airport at Tan Son Nhut was always busy. Men who had just arrived from the Oakland Army Terminal on one of the chartered civilian airlines mixed with the men who had just finished their one-year tour of duty. The men who just arrived were asking the men who were about to leave what it was like. The men who were about to leave couldn't give a straight answer. They all said something like, "It was all right," or "It ain't that bad." A few would say, "It sucks." They all felt uncomfortable with the small talk. They couldn't put the experience of the past year in a clever phrase, so it was easier to avoid it all together.

The departing veterans would board the same airplanes that just unloaded the new arrivals from what was called the Real World. However, the returnees who boarded the chartered planes would soon find out that the hometowns and college campuses they left 12 months earlier would not be the same. In the years to come, the soldiers would talk about how badly they were treated when they returned home. They would tell stories of how protestors would spit on them as they got off the plane. But these stories, like most war stories, would be based on hearsay. If anything, the returning veterans would experience a world of indifference. Upon their return home to a day-to-day existence, many of the soldiers would soon find out that Vietnam would be the only Real World they would ever know.

When the group of junior officers who had been classmates and drinking buddies at the club for the past ten days quietly got off the bus at the Ton Son Nhut terminal they scattered in all directions without saying a word. A chalkboard hung on the front of a Quonset hut that looked like some sort of an official place, so that's where everybody started to re-group. The chalkboard listed the day's shuttle departures to all parts of Vietnam. Ruland scanned the board and saw there was a flight to Danang at noon. That was the first leg of Ruland's trip north.

An Air Force sergeant emerged from the Quonset hut tightly holding a clipboard with both hands and surveyed the men standing in front of him. The sergeant had large turquoise rings on each little finger and a matching turquoise tint to the lenses of his eyeglasses. Ruland told the sergeant he was supposed to go to Danang that day. He held up the official MACV tan envelope that contained his orders to give some impact to his statement.

"I'm on special orders from MACV, Sergeant," Ruland said.

"Is that so? Aren't we all, Lieutenant," the sergeant said with a slight lisp.

"That's so, Sergeant," Ruland responded, unable to come up with anything more clever.

"What's your special job?" asked the Air Force sergeant, peeking over the top of his tinted blue glasses.

"I can't tell you. It's all in here," Ruland said as he tapped the tan envelope.

"And I suppose I don't have the security clearance to see what's inside that envelope, right Lieutenant?" The sergeant leaned forward and made a "V" with his hands, slowly resting his chin in the crotch of his hands and wiggling both bejeweled little fingers.

"You got it," Ruland said. "If I told you I would have to spank you."

The Air Force sergeant let out a high-pitched giggle and winked at Ruland.

"You young lieutenants are too much. I'd love to serve under you someday," he said, winking at Ruland. "Oh well, sign here Lieutenant, and I'll get you on the plane."

The sergeant handed the clipboard to Ruland and delicately pointed a polished, ringed finger to the spot where Ruland was to sign. Ruland signed his name and serial number on the manifest for the Danang flight and winked at the sergeant. The sergeant pointed to an Air Force C-130 warming up on the tarmac about fifty yards from the terminal.

"That's your plane, Lieutenant. Come back and see me sometime."

Ruland grabbed his suitcase and walked out to the C-130 and climbed on board. He picked a spot on one of the canvas seats that ran alongside of the cargo bay and settled in for the ride.

The camouflaged airplane left exactly at noon. When the plane was airborne, the crew chief announced there would be a brief stop at Cam Ranh Bay to deliver parts for some colonel's refrigerator. Since it was a short hop to Cam Ranh Bay, Ruland decided not to try and sleep on the plane. Ruland got airsick very easily. The only way he knew how to prevent airsickness was to get very drunk before a long flight and fall asleep as soon as possible after takeoff. He didn't have time to get drunk before today's flight.

The plane was loaded almost entirely with cargo, so Ruland was able to get a section of the canvas passenger seats all to himself. The other passengers on the plane sat on the canvas seats opposite Ruland on the other side of the aircraft. A Navy public information officer was escorting three Red Cross workers to Danang. The three Donut Dollies were all suffering from sunburn. It was the sure sign of a newcomer in Vietnam. All newly arrived Donut Dollies tried to get a tan their first week in-country so they could look like veterans as soon as possible.

When the plane made its stopover at Cam Ranh Bay the crew chief opened the side door as the plane was taxiing up to the terminal. He took a small box of parts and handed the box to some disinterested private on the ground who threw the box in the back of a shiny jeep. In exchange for the small box of parts a civilian with a black plastic briefcase got on the plane.

The man was wearing a plaid sport coat, a pink shirt, and a black knit tie. He was sweating heavily. His forehead was peeling from a recent sunburn, and he kept reaching up to pick off small pieces of dead skin and flick the fragments between his legs. Ruland figured the new passenger was a Department of Defense employee or some sort of civilian contractor on a boondoggle.

Ruland knew the man was probably receiving some sort of civilian combat pay equivalent for attending a drawn-out plans and policy conference in an air-conditioned room at the Cam Ranh Bay Officers' Club. The civilian looked at Ruland, decided he didn't want to sit on that side of the airplane, and selected a spot on the canvas seat opposite from Ruland, next to the Donut Dollies.

The C-130 took off before the man in the plaid sport coat could buckle his seatbelt. The plane climbed slowly and flew north along the coast of the South China Sea. The pilots were apparently navigating along Highway One, which stretched out below them. Ruland watched the scenery pass slowly below as the green and brown airplane flew over Nha Trang. He continued to look out the small porthole at the thin white strip of beach separating the blue sea from the dark green land until some low clouds blocked his view.

Ruland then laid down on the canvas seat and turned his attention to the Donut Dollies, deciding to study them for a while as he waited for the low drone of the plane's engines to put him to sleep. The women were already starting to get a little tired. As they began to nod off their knees began to inch apart slowly. Suddenly Ruland wasn't tired anymore.

Ruland confirmed his suspicion that the women were new arrivals. Not only did they have their telltale sunburn from the first few days on

China Beach, but they also wore white panties under their short, brown, Red Cross uniform dresses. The women would soon learn that white underwear was too hard to keep clean in Vietnam. In two or three weeks they would write home to their mothers back in Wisconsin or Kansas. And much to their mothers' despair, fearing that their daughters were starting to dress like Times Square hookers, the girls would ask that some black nylon panties and bras be sent immediately in their next CARE package from home.

After a while the girls started to get a little nervous with Ruland laying flat out on the long strip of canvas seat staring up their dresses, so they put their knees together and sat up straight. About this time Ruland also lost interest in the game, so he decided it was a good time to take a nap. Tuy Hoa, Qui Nhon, and Quang Ngai passed underneath the green and brown airplane as Ruland slept.

The plane hit some rough weather as it began to descend into Danang. This woke Ruland up, but he continued to lie on the canvas and stare at the wires and tubes overhead. The plane landed with a bounce and one long, graceful arc, coming to a complete stop just before the end of the runway.

The C-130 taxied to a stop next to a fuel truck, about a hundred yards from a hangar. A four-door pickup soon arrived for the Navy officer and the Donut Dollies. The driver of the pickup truck told Ruland the MACV headquarters was next to the Navy compound in Danang. Ruland asked the Navy officer if he could get a lift to the MACV headquarters. The officer had watched Ruland looking up the dresses of the Donut Dollies and didn't trust him, but wanted to be a team player in the war effort, so he agreed to let Ruland ride in the back of the pickup with some bags of empty beer cans.

The administration office at MACV headquarters was just being locked up when Ruland arrived. The NCO at the desk gave Ruland a mimeographed map showing the location of the transient officer's quarters and told Ruland to check back in the morning for in-processing. The sergeant told Ruland the hours of the headquarters were seven to five, with two hours off for lunch.

He smiled at Ruland and said, "That's when we take a nap to get out of the heat."

The transient officer's quarters were only two blocks from the MACV headquarters in what was once a comfortable, middle-class neighborhood of Danang. The area now served as cheap housing for lower class Vietnamese who worked the menial cleaning jobs for the Americans living there. Like other neighborhoods in Vietnam near American facilities, the area also had its fair share of whorehouses and massage parlors.

Ruland checked in at the transient officer's quarters' front desk and received the traditional two sheets and green blanket from the traditionally arrogant supply clerk. The transient quarters was a relatively new building in the neighborhood constructed by the Americans when they first arrived. It was a two-story building made out of concrete blocks with a ten-foot high fence around it. A six-foot high wall of sandbags was between the walls of the building and the barbed wire fence. There were no windows to the outside, designed to prevent sappers from throwing things in, but each room did open up to a large area in the center of the building which provided ventilation. There were two bunks in Ruland's room. He hoped no one else would check in that night and be assigned the same room.

After he made his bed, Ruland showered and shaved and put on a clean set of fatigues. He hadn't eaten since breakfast and wasn't sure where he could eat, but figured there had to be a café or some military club nearby. The Marine Corps sentry at the entrance to the transient quarters told Ruland that a Navy shuttle bus would be passing by the building in a few minutes and that the bus stopped at the Stone Elephant. Ruland asked what the Stone Elephant was and the Marine told him it was the name of the officers club at the Navy compound.

"Sir, it's supposed to be good food, sir," the Marine shouted while standing at attention and looking over Ruland's left shoulder. "And begging the Lieutenant's pardon, sir, they got hostesses there, too, sir, if the Lieutenant knows what I mean, sir."

Ruland decided to take the Marine's advice. He saluted the Marine and waited for the shuttle bus to the Stone Elephant.

A gray Navy bus came along in a few minutes just like the Marine guard said it would. The driver of the bus told Ruland he would signal him when they got to the Stone Elephant. After a short ride through the city, the bus pulled up in front of a neatly manicured lawn in front of a concrete building. The bus driver looked in his mirror back at Ruland and pointed at the building.

The club was another American-made building constructed by the Navy during the early days of the war. The Navy wanted to make sure they had a decent club if they had to be on land with the Army. A small, white elephant made of concrete stood in front of the building in the middle of a flowerbed.

Ruland walked in the front door and shivered when the seventy-five degree air hit him. He heard his sinuses crack inside his head. After wandering around for a while, he found the dining room and sat down in the far corner so he could watch the entrance to the room. He didn't like to sit with his back to the door.

Ruland ordered a steak and two beers from the Vietnamese waitress. She was a beautiful girl who only spoke menu-English. Ruland drank the first beer before the steak arrived and drank the other beer with the meal.

All during the meal a civilian woman at another table watched Ruland over the rim of a glass of white wine she kept pressed against the tip of her nose. The woman wore a denim skirt and a white Mexican peasant blouse unbuttoned to just below her nipple line. When she noticed Ruland had glanced at her she lightly ran her finger down the front of the blouse. Ruland tried to ignore her because he was tired and didn't feel in the mood to talk to anyone, especially with the distraction of an open blouse.

When he paid for his meal, the Vietnamese waitress handed Ruland a ticket for one free drink in the lounge and pointed to the two large louvered doors at the end of the dining room. Ruland hadn't planned on staying at the club. He wanted to get something to eat and have a couple of beers, then go back to his room and get some sleep. But he figured he would see what the lounge was like as long as he was getting a free drink.

Ruland walked into the lounge and sat alone at the end of the bar, facing the entrance to the lounge. Since his days in the infantry, he always felt uncomfortable with his back to the crowd. He thought about getting some exotic, expensive concoction for his free drink, but ended up ordering another beer. The Navy Chief Petty Officer tending bar was disappointed because Ruland didn't order the exotic Creme Danang, the specialty of the house. The bartender opened a can of Ballantines and poured it in a frosted mug.

"Haven't you got any other brands?" Ruland asked.

"Not this far north," the bartender answered. "The black market doesn't let premium brands get up this far…unless you find some Special Forces or MACV advisors and buy it from them."

Ruland took a sip of his beer and sat it down on the bar. He turned toward the dance floor just as the woman with the open blouse who was watching him in the dining room walked up and sat down next to him on the barstool.

"Kate Maddock-Smythe, Bold Challenge magazine," the woman said as she stuck her hand out. "Mind if I share the bar with you?"

Ruland took another sip of beer to give him time to think.

"No. I don't mind," Ruland said reluctantly. He really didn't want to talk to anybody.

Kate Maddock-Smythe smiled at Ruland. She was an attractive woman in her mid-twenties whose face was prematurely starting to wrinkle from too much time outdoors in the sun.

"Let me get straight to the point, Lieutenant. I'd like to talk to you about the war."

"Which war you talking about?" Ruland answered, taking a long sip of beer.

"I belong to an organization dedicated to world peace through social interaction. The name of the magazine that represents this organization is called Bold Challenge. Now don't get excited, we're authorized to be here. I have press credentials if you would like to see them."

"Bold Challenge…Your magazine sounds like a laundry detergent," Ruland commented.

This time the woman laughed and motioned to the bartender. The Navy Chief walked over to the couple and poured a glass of white wine without speaking to the woman, then placed the glass on a napkin in front of her.

"Here you go Kate," the bartender said. "Take it easy on this young lieutenant here."

Kate Maddock-Smythe smiled at the bartender, then turned toward Ruland. She crossed her legs like a man, exposing the inside of her thighs. Ruland noticed she was wearing black panties.

"A veteran," Ruland thought to himself.

"Here's to you, Lieutenant…"

She raised her glass and waited for Ruland to respond.

"Ruland…David Ruland."

"Here's to you, Lieutenant David Ruland."

Ruland and the magazine reporter/crusader clinked glasses and sipped their drinks. Kate unfolded her legs and moved her barstool closer to Ruland so her legs were between his. Ruland knew he couldn't escape so he decided to relax and talk with the woman. Ruland hoped she wouldn't ask him about the war. He didn't like to talk about it. People always wanted him to commit himself and explain why he was there. It always seemed to sound strange when he would tell them he was there because he wasn't doing anything special at the time he was drafted.

The Korean band in the lounge finished a series of songs that sounded a little like a Beatles' medley. They followed with a slow song to give their two flat-chested go-go girls a chance to catch their breath. Kate looked at Ruland and smiled, then took him by his index finger and led him out to the dance floor. The dance floor was full of Navy and Marine Corps officers dancing with tiny Vietnamese girls who were hired as hostesses.

The piano player began to sing about how he "reft his heart in San Francisco" as Kate pressed herself against Ruland and put both arms around his neck. She was not wearing a bra, and hadn't worn one since her freshman year at Brown. She slowly moved her upper body back and forth against Ruland in time with the music. This caused Kate's blouse to partially uncover a breast every fourth beat.

"What do you do?" she asked, pulling back to look at Ruland.

"What do you mean, 'do'?" Ruland countered.

"In the war, man. What do you do in the war?"

"Oh, you mean this war. Well…" Ruland said reluctantly, knowing that this was what she was after and what he really didn't want to do was talk about the war.

"I'm between jobs at the moment."

"You mean you're unemployed?" Kate said, smiling.

"No, not that," Ruland sighed, resigning himself to the fact he was going to have to make conversation. "I'm in sort of a strange situation. I just got a couple of weeks left in-country before I get out of the Army. My DEROS is exactly 14 days."

DEROS was a magic word for American troops. It was the acronym for Date of Estimated Return Overseas. It told other soldiers how much time you had left in-country, and was a point of pride for draftees. DEROS was a statement of experience. If your DEROS date was coming up sooner than another soldier, it meant you had some degree of generally accepted seniority, regardless of your rank.

Ruland waited for a response from Kate, but she just nodded like a good reporter, waiting for Ruland to continue.

"Believe me, I'm not a lifer," Ruland went on. "I was drafted the day I got out of college and did the OCS route because my brother told me I would have a cushy job as a staff officer. But I ended up in the infantry and came over here as a platoon leader. Now I'm ready to go home and get out, but the Army's not going to let me go easy. I'm supposed to go up north to build a rifle range for some Popular Forces outfit. But I'm not there yet, so I'm in-between jobs. What do you do in the war, Kate?"

Kate put her head on Ruland's chest and closed her eyes.

"This is it," she said.

"I suppose every little bit helps stem the red tide of communism," Ruland said.

Kate looked up at Ruland and smiled, then put her head back on his chest. She hung on Ruland and rubbed her legs against his. He nearly stumbled, but managed to catch his balance by leaning against a huge Marine with a shaved head who had enveloped a tiny Vietnamese hostess. The Marine growled at Ruland.

When the dance ended Kate led Ruland to a small table in the darkest corner of the lounge. She sat Ruland down and placed her hand on his thigh as the waitress approached. Kate ordered a beer for Ruland and another glass of white wine for herself. Ruland had four beers already and was getting a little uncomfortable.

"Wait right here," Ruland ordered. "I gotta visit the restroom." Kate smiled and moved her hand back and forth on Ruland's thigh.

"Don't worry. I'm not going anywhere."

Ruland made his way past the bald Marine crushing the hostess, through the other dancers, and found the men's room on the far side of the lounge. He walked in the white tile room and stepped up to the urinal and unbuttoned his fatigue pants. Just as he prepared to relieve himself the door swung open and Kate walked in. She closed the door behind her and pulled the trashcan in front of the door so no one else could enter.

"You know that you really don't have to go, David," she said.

"Yes I do," Ruland said, looking down at the urinal.

"I mean you don't have to go up north...You don't have to build that rifle range."

"Oh that," Ruland said. "I think I do. But it's not that bad. It's only for a couple of weeks."

Ruland was unable to urinate with the woman standing next to him.

"You can stay here. I'll find you a place to stay in Saigon until we get you to Hong Kong. You can work for me."

"What would I do for you?" Ruland asked, trying to make small talk to get his mind off the fact he was trying to piss with a woman standing next to him.

"Just talk to people on R and R. And if the Army comes after you, I can get you to Canada. The system's in place. I don't think you're really part of this war. It's the war of the military-industrial complex...a war of the establishment. It's an illegal, heinous war in a new age of love and understanding. The power is in peace. Stay with me and make love, not war."

Ruland looked straight ahead and took a deep breath to relax. He was never sure how to pronounce the word "heinous" so he figured that if he said it quietly to himself it might help him urinate.

"It'll be alright, Kate. I'm just going to help build a simple rifle range and then get out of the Army. You can continue the crusade without me."

Kate stepped closer and whispered in Ruland's ear.

"I want you to think very carefully about what you are doing," she said, taking a piece of paper from her blouse and putting it deep in Ruland's front pocket. She kept her hand in his pocket.

Ruland closed his eyes and tried to concentrate, but it didn't help. He still couldn't piss.

"Read my message and think very hard about your decision," she said.

"Think of war and love and peace. Promise me you will think."

She began to move her hand slowly around in Ruland's pocket.

"I promise, Kate. I'll think about it," Ruland said, his voice a little higher than usual.

"Just remember," Kate said as she ran her tongue in Ruland's ear. "It's an illegal war. The future of these people is in your hands."

"I know," Ruland said, raising his eyes to the ceiling. "But right now the future isn't working."

Just then the bartender swung the restroom door open and knocked the trashcan over. He held the door open so all the people in the lounge turned to look.

"OK, Katie dear," the bartender said. "Lighten up on the young lieutenant. Keep your peace and love crusade out of the men's room."

The table next to the restroom was full of DOD contractors from Grumman Aerospace Corporation dressed in matching tan blazers with some sort of crest on their left pockets. They looked in and saw Ruland standing at the urinal with Kate next to him with her hand in his pocket. Kate turned and saw the people looking in at them and smiling. She put her hands over her ears and screamed at them.

"My God. You are all fools. Don't you know? Don't any of you know? This is an internal struggle! It's not your war! The people will decide this peacefully if you will just leave!"

Kate stomped out of the restroom and across the dance floor. She knocked the tray out of the hands of a frightened waitress as she left the lounge. The bartender continued to hold the door open as he watched Kate march out. People on the dance floor looked in at Ruland, still standing at the urinal. A Donut Dolly on the dance floor took a step closer, put her glasses on, and peeked in at Ruland. The crowd waited for Ruland's next move. Then slowly, just a trickle at first, Ruland began to urinate.

"I'm saved," he said softly to himself, ignoring the spectators all focused on him.

He took a few small steps backward, away from the urinal. The Vietnamese waitress trying to clean up the spilled drinks looked up and gasped. Ruland pissed a graceful arc into the wall urinal while leaning against the far wall. The Grumman contractors cheered. The Navy Chief muttered something about officers and closed the door to the restroom.

When he finished, Ruland walked out of the restroom and the people applauded. The Donut Dolly smiled and raised her eyebrows before a Marine colonel pulled her back to his table. Ruland waved his hand to acknowledge the applause. He walked back to the bar and sat down. The bartender gave him another beer and told him it was on the house. When the crowd lost interest in him, Ruland took the piece of paper out of his pocket that Kate had given him and unfolded it.

Across the top of the paper the word SECRET was written in red ink like a classified document. The letterhead on the paper said: American Mobilization Committee. The paper listed names and addresses of people in Danang who would help soldiers find passage on freighters to Canada and jobs in Vancouver. Ruland read the paper and stuffed it back in his pocket. He had done what Kate had asked him to do. He had thought about it. But since he was now on his fifth beer, Ruland probably didn't give it his best shot.

"Besides," Ruland said to himself, "it would be too much of a hassle. I only got a couple weeks. What could happen in a couple of weeks?"

Ruland finished his beer and walked back to the transient officer's quarters. On the way back, a jeep with two MPs slowed down to look him over, then drove on. The Marine guard at the gate asked Ruland if he was interested in some grass or a girl for the night. Ruland shook his head, thanked the Marine for thinking of him, and walked past the guard and into the building. He was lucky. No roommate had checked in. He had the room all to himself.

October 8, 1968

Early the next morning Ruland checked in at the MACV headquarters. He was issued an M-16, one empty clip, and no ammunition. The supply clerk told Ruland that it was SOP, standard operating procedure, not to issue ammunition to new people until they got to their unit. Ruland asked what he was supposed to do if he needed to defend himself. The clerk said there was plenty of ammunition available in the small cigarette shops tucked in-between the cafes. According to the clerk, you could get 20 rounds of M-16 ammo for a dollar.

The staff sergeant in the administration office had arranged for Ruland to catch an early courier flight to Hue on a Marine helicopter. He told Ruland that "another helo" would take him to the Phong Dien district headquarters. The sergeant hustled Ruland through the paperwork to get him out of his hair. Ruland didn't have time for breakfast. He hated to miss a meal before flying because it usually made him airsick. After Ruland filled out a form listing people who should be notified in case the plane crashed and burned, a clerk in the administration office took him to the helicopter pad near the MACV compound.

The Marine helicopter that would take Ruland to Hue was an hour late. When it finally arrived, the crew chief told Ruland how one of the black boxes caught fire on the flight to Danang and the pilots had to set down on a dike in the middle of a rice paddy to take the smoking box out of the control panel. The crew chief thought this story was hilarious. It only made Ruland more nervous about the flight. He just couldn't get used to flying in aircraft built by the lowest bidder.

Ruland and three teenage Marine replacements on their way to Quang Tri were the only passengers. All four men got on the large green helo and listened to the routine safety briefing given by the bored crew chief. The pilots took off without shutting down the engines; apparently they were afraid they couldn't get the helicopter started again. Ruland was hung over and hungry. He knew it was going to be a rough ride. It didn't take much to make Ruland airsick, and he didn't want to get sick in front of the young Marines.

The helicopter flew north along Highway One toward Hue. Although it is one of the most beautiful stretches of the South China Sea coastline, Ruland spent the trip sitting on the floor of the helo fighting off airsickness from too much beer the night before. One of the young Marines was chewing tobacco and smiling at Ruland the entire trip. Every once in a while the young Marine would spit his tobacco juice into an empty 7-Up can. It was a miserable flight for Ruland.

The helicopter landed in the center of a soccer field, next to a river, in the center of Hue. The aircraft hovered for a while above the treetops before it landed and Ruland could see the ancient walled city off in the distance. The wall was scarred from the Tet Offensive earlier that year. A few destroyed tanks and vehicles were still sitting near the wall. The flag of South Vietnam flew on a flagpole near the middle of the wall. The flag was only attached at the top so it hung on the pole like a yellow dishrag.

As soon as the helo landed, a truck rumbled out from the tree line. It stopped next to the helo in the middle of the soccer field. The three young Marines got off the helo and climbed on the truck quickly. The truck left immediately. Ruland got out of the aircraft and lifted his gray suitcase from under the canvas seats just as the helo was lifting off. The helo hovered again about seventy-five feet off the ground, then disappeared over the trees. Neither the helicopter crew nor the truck driver was concerned about leaving Ruland behind.

Ruland was left alone in the middle of the soccer field waiting for this "other helo" that had been arranged for him. He sat down on his suitcase and lit a cigarette. He felt a little uncomfortable sitting alone in the middle of the field and thought about moving to the cover of the tree line, but decided to stay where he was so whatever was supposed to pick him up could easily spot him. He didn't want some edgy pilot to fly over the landing zone and then fly off because his passenger wasn't in sight.

Ruland looked at his watch, then opened his gray suitcase and took out a portable radio. He turned it on, shook it twice to activate the batteries, and began to scan through the Vietnamese stations until he found the U.S. Armed Forces Radio Network. The radio crackled as an hourly newscast was just ending. The announcer was reporting on a recent press conference by President Johnson telling how well things were going.

The American disc jockey chimed in at the end of the newscast in his best imitation of President Johnson's Texas drawl. "My fellow Americans, it won't be long now and your boys will be home." Then there was a brief silence.

"Gooooooooood morning, Vietnam! This is Army Specialist Fourth Class Freddy "Mad Dog" Ackley on Armed Forces Radio welcoming you to another beautiful day in scenic Vietnam, the vacation land of the poor and the drafted. I have part two of the morning show and it's October the eighth for all you short-timers out there. So keep your head down and your radio up and you'll be on that big silver bird and back in the real world before you can say 'Viet-nam-i-za-tion'. Meanwhile, here is the number one song today in Indianapolis, Indiana. Here's my main man, Otis Redding, still sittin' on a dock. Check it out, all you trained killers."

Otis just began singing about the morning sun when Ruland heard a helicopter. He turned the radio off and put it back in his suitcase. He stood up and listened again for the helo, but wasn't sure he heard anything, so he sat back down on his suitcase. In the distance he could hear the sound of "H and I" artillery firing from some firebase off in the distance.

The sound of “harassing and intermittent” artillery was second nature to Ruland at this point in his tour. The random shelling of “free fire zones” was supposed to keep the Viet Cong and North Vietnamese off-guard as they moved about the countryside. Ruland figured it only served to use up stockpiles of old Korean War artillery shells to make room for new shells being churned out by the arms manufacturers.

Then, suddenly, Ruland heard the sound of a helicopter just over the tree line. Ruland looked in the direction of the wap-wap-wap sound for the dark green nose of an aircraft to appear. But to his surprise, a silver helo appeared over the tops of the trees at the far end of the field. It was an Air America bird.

Ruland wasn’t sure what Air America was, or what they were doing in Vietnam. He’d heard from some Marine in Saigon that Air America was some CIA deal and flew a lot of missions for Special Forces. The helo paused briefly at the tree line, its nose pointed toward Ruland. It then moved slowly toward Ruland like a giant, flying insect as if cautiously checking its prey. The silver aircraft landed just in front of Ruland, apparently studying him.

The crew appeared to be civilians so Ruland figured the Marine was right about the CIA business. There were all sorts of strange operations going on in Vietnam in 1968, but Ruland wasn’t interested and didn’t really care enough to get involved.

Ruland picked up his gray suitcase and walked toward the side door of the helo as the two pilots studied him. The dark sun shields of their flight helmets hid the faces of the two pilots. Their heads turned as one like twin robots. Both robot-heads watched Ruland walk toward the helo. The civilian crew chief standing in the doorway wore blue jeans and a flowered Hawaiian shirt. He pointed at Ruland’s rifle and motioned for him to clear the chamber. Ruland removed the empty magazine, and then pulled the t-handle back on the M-16 to make sure the chamber was clear. Ruland then showed the crew chief the empty chamber. Ruland bent over and shuffled below the helicopter's rotating blades to the door of the helo where the civilian crew chief was waiting.

"Are you the guys who are supposed to take me to Phong Dien?" Ruland asked.

"That depends," the civilian said. "Who are you?"

"Lieutenant Ruland…I'm assigned to the MAT Team at Phong Dien."

"Ya, you're the one for the Ruff Puffs," the civilian nodded. "Get your ass on board so we can get the hell out of here."

Ruland climbed aboard the helo and tapped one of the pilots on the shoulder.

"How long does it take to get there?" Ruland asked.

The pilot shook his head and pointed to the bulge in his flight helmet where his ear should be, then shook his head indicating he couldn't hear. Ruland cupped his hands and shouted.

"Fine war we're having, isn't it?"

The pilot nodded his head and gave Ruland the thumbs-up sign as the co-pilot began flicking switches on the control panel.

"Asshole," Ruland said to himself as he sat down on the floor of the helo.

Ruland put his gray suitcase against the back wall of the passenger area and sat on the deck of the helo. That was how he used to ride in the infantry. The helo lifted off the grass slowly, then dropped its nose and gained speed as it moved toward the river. When the helicopter was over the river the pilot suddenly banked sharply to the right, pressing Ruland against the floor so Ruland looked straight down into the water. The co-pilot looked back at Ruland pinned helplessly against the floor by centrifugal force. He keyed his mike and said something to the pilot on the inter-com. The other pilot's head jerked back in laughter as the helo straightened its course and snaked its way up the river a few feet above the surface of the water, frightening a family fishing in a shallow boat near the riverbank.

Suddenly the helo jumped upward, pressing Ruland harder against the deck. A bridge passed underneath the landing skids as the helo turned sharply to the north, leaving the crew chief dangling by a canvas harness on the starboard side of the aircraft. The crew chief was taking pictures of the people on the road below. The two pilots gave each other the thumbs-up sign, apparently pleased with their aerobatic maneuvers. They finally settled back in their seats as the helo straightened its course and slowly began to gain altitude.

Below, on both sides of Highway One, Ruland could see people moving in two single files, one on each side of the highway. Some military vehicles and an occasional civilian bus passed underneath as the helicopter continued north. Ruland watched the string of people below as one line moved south toward the city of Hue and the other line moved north. Groups of two and three would break away from the northbound file as the farmers returned to their fields and small hamlets.

As the helo steadily climbed, the lines of people blended into the shoulders of the road. The helo reached its cruising altitude and leveled off. Ruland leaned back on his gray suitcase and looked out at the dark green mountains to the west and then at the deep blue waters of the South China Sea to the east. He stared at the horizon and thought of how his year was almost over, and how he would soon be going home.

After about twenty minutes, the crew chief tapped Ruland on the shoulder, bringing him back to reality. Ruland jumped when the man's hand touched him. The crew chief gave Ruland the peace sign with his gloved hand, and pointed to the west of the highway.

"That's Camp Evans!" the crew chief yelled over the roar of the engines. "That's the 1st Cavalry!"

Ruland nodded and acknowledged. The crew chief then pointed north along the highway. Between the two robot heads of the pilots Ruland could see a village. A yellow building stood higher than the small houses and shops of the village. It was the headquarters for the District of Phong Dien.

"That's your new home," the crew chief yelled again.

The military compound at Phong Dien was on the southern edge of the village. This meant that the farm girls who lived south of the village had to pass by the front wall of the compound to go to market. The village girls had to endure the catcalls and comments of the Ruff Puffs who spent most of the day sitting on the sandbag wall surrounding the yellow headquarters building.

The two-story stucco building had two false towers at each end. This was a popular style of the French occupation architecture of the early 1950s. Ruland had seen it on other government buildings around Vietnam. A banner was hanging between the two towers on the day Ruland arrived. Two clasped hands were painted in gaudy colors on the banner. One white hand was depicted in front of the United States flag, and one brown hand was in front of a flag of the Republic of South Vietnam. The building was the headquarters of the District Chief, Major Nguyen Vien.

Two plywood structures used by the American advisors were behind the yellow headquarters building. They were simple, rectangular buildings called SEA Huts, for Southeast Asia Huts. The buildings were designed to be temporary quarters for the Americans, intended to last just for the duration of the war, or about three years according to Pentagon strategists. Although the official designation for the buildings was SEA Huts, all the Americans called them hooches, which became the name for any small building in Vietnam.

The compound also contained two artillery parapets in the corners farthest from the highway. They were manned by a small detachment of Vietnamese Regular Army soldiers who had little to do with the local Popular Forces. The Popular Forces despised the regular army soldiers because they came from the big cities of Saigon and Danang. This impressed the local girls and made the local Popular Forces soldiers mad.

The village bordering the district headquarters was typical of the many small villages along Highway One. Small family-owned shops and cafes lined the street. The houses of the shop owners and other villagers extended back from the highway on both sides for about one hundred yards, just up to the edge of the rice paddies which bordered the village. In this particular village there was a small Buddhist pagoda and small Catholic chapel. The chapel was part of an orphanage run by an Irish priest who was there during the French war and stayed on. The priest didn't get involved in local politics. He taught French to a few of the more well-to-do shopkeepers' children and cared for the orphans of the region. His students included the orphaned children of the Viet Cong. Unlike the American advisors who had come and gone during the past few years, the priest served a purpose so no one really bothered him.

This particular section of Highway One passing through Phong Dien was a crucial link in the convoy route between Hue and Quang Tri. The most critical spot in this supply link was the bridge at the Song O Lau River. If the bridge were lost, it would be a major delay in the convoy system between the two cities. The truck drivers knew the importance of the bridge, and wondered if a rocket was aimed at them every time they crossed it.

Despite the value placed on the bridge by the generals, the bridge was not the most important spot for the truck-driving soldiers in the convoys that ran this dangerous road. The most important spot was the massage parlor on the northern edge of the village, just south of the bridge. This establishment, called The Majestic Steam Bath and Massage Parlor, was an abandoned bunker once used by French troops when it was their turn to guard the bridge. The bunker was reinforced concrete, so it stayed cool on even the hottest days. It made for a nice cool rest stop for the American soldiers heading either north or south on Highway One. They could get a cold beer, a warm massage, and a hot body for less that ten dollars if they bargained for it.

There were no buildings once you crossed the bridge heading north, just some clearings where they once stood. The northern border of the village ended at the river. It was generally accepted in the village that the

Viet Cong controlled everything north of the bridge along Highway One until you reached the Marines at the edge of Quang Tri.

A squad of Ruff Puffs was assigned to guard the bridge. During the day it was their assignment to walk along the catwalk of the bridge and shoot at anything floating toward the concrete pilings. This was supposed to stop the Viet Cong from floating satchel charges down the river in an attempt to blow up the bridge. The Viet Cong had no intention of doing this in the daytime, but it was the mission of the Ruff Puffs to prevent it just in case it should ever happen. Anyway, it was great fun for the soldiers. It also impressed the girls at The Majestic Steam Bath and Massage Parlor and their American customers who watched all this on the shaded veranda on top of the bunker. The diminutive Vietnamese soldiers seldom hit anything floating downstream with their oversized M-1 rifles, but if provided some entertainment for the Americans. It was also a way to break up the boredom of guard duty for the Ruff Puffs.

At night it was a different story. Things almost got serious. The Viet Cong would make their way along the north side of the river until they had a clear line of fire on the bridge. From this position they would fire a rocket from an RPG-7 rocket launcher in the general direction of the bridge. The 85 mm rockets were small, yet powerful enough to make small dings in the steel structure, but not large enough to do any real damage. And most of the time the rockets flew over the top of the bridge and exploded in the river. However it didn't matter if the RPG-7 rocket hit the bridge of not, the squad of Ruff Puffs guarding the bridge would retaliate by firing their day's ration of ammunition in the general direction of the attackers.

Once this was done the adversaries went back to their homes, which were often next door to each other. The Ruff Puffs figured their job was done since they were out of ammunition and their Viet Cong neighbors never made a follow-up attack because they had also used up their daily rocket allocation supplied by the North Vietnamese.

So for the rest of the night the bridge was up for grabs. The girls from the Majestic would stroll with their clients along the catwalk and enjoy the night air, and the village would go back to sleep, relatively secure in the knowledge it would be peaceful and quiet for the rest of the night. For both the Popular Forces and the Viet Cong, it was a reasonable way to fight a war. Needless-to-say, it pissed off the American advisors to no end.

When they weren't guarding the bridge, the Popular Forces soldiers were usually at the other end of the village sitting on the sandbag wall surrounding the compound. They would flirt with the farm girls as they walked along Highway One to and from the village. Once in a while, the soldiers would pass out bags of rice to the girls, which was given to the soldiers by the CIA. The CIA would get the rice from American troops who discovered Viet Cong rice caches on patrol. The American public information officers at the Rex Hotel in Saigon at the five o'clock follies were always eager to report to the American press about the amount of captured rice taken from the Viet Cong and given back to the peasants.

The whole thing was promoted as a demonstration of how the United States military was stabilizing a hamlet. The farmers, of course, would give the rice back to the Viet Cong, who in turn would hide it from the Americans. Then the American generals would base their patrols on reports the intelligence officers obtained from the prostitutes. The American troops would capture the rice again on the next patrol, and the cycle would go on.

But during this supply cycle, the farmers, the Viet Cong, and the Ruff Puffs could siphon off enough rice for their families. This gave everyone what they wanted: rice for the villagers, press releases for the American public information officers, operational success for the generals, and cash for the hookers that supplied the CIA with information.

The Air America helo with Ruland on board landed on the large asphalt-landing pad located across the highway from the compound. Almost immediately children began running up to the helicopter. The smaller children crawled on their hands and knees so they wouldn't be blown over by the force of the rotor blades. Ruland climbed out of the helo with his M-16 in one hand and his gray suitcase in the other hand. He hunched over to avoid the spinning blades and shuffled to the edge of the landing pad through the crowd of children. He stopped and looked at the yellow building across the road, then slung his rifle over his shoulder and walked toward the compound. He ignored the children as they begged for candy and cigarettes.

The villagers continued to move along the sides of the highway. Only a few old people bothered to look up at the American as he crossed the road. Ruland didn't bother to look back as the silver Air America helo took off. He looked to his left down the main street of the village, then straight ahead at the military compound, and wondered what was waiting for him during the last days of his tour.

A concrete arch painted the same yellow as the headquarters building was over the entrance to the compound. The words "Cam De Xe-dap" were printed on the arch. It looked very official. Ruland thought the words were some sort of political slogan. Later he learned it meant: DON'T PARK BICYCLES HERE.

A five-foot high wall of green sandbags extended to the right and left of the arch for about fifty yards each way, parallel to the highway. On top of the wall the Popular Forces soldiers sat in groups of two and three. They smoked their cigarettes and watched in silence as the American approached the entrance to the compound. The local soldiers had seen a lot of Americans visit the compound over the years.

A makeshift gate of concertina wire was stretched across the entrance to the compound. It was pulled back on one end to leave an opening. In front of the opening an old lady wailed over a green body bag as she rocked back and forth on her haunches. Ruland stopped within a few feet of the woman. He looked at the old lady's face and noticed her black teeth and the saliva running from the corner of her mouth. The villagers continued to move along the highway, paying little attention to either the woman or the American. Ruland walked up to the body bag, lifted his gray suitcase a little higher and stepped over the body, lightly brushing the shoulder of the old woman.

"Excuse me, mama-san," Ruland said quietly. "I'm here to save you from the scourge of communism. Sorry about the person in the bag."

Ruland entered the compound and put his suitcase down. Directly in front of the headquarters building was a flagpole surrounded by a low wall of concrete blocks. He saw a jeep parked near the plywood buildings behind the headquarters building, so he walked around the flagpole to the hooches in back of the yellow building.

Ruland heard some voices in the first hooch, so he opened the screen door and walked in. When Ruland entered the room, everyone in the room stopped speaking. The room was almost bare except for two card tables and some folding chairs near the door, and a long table facing the door. A red Coca-Cola cooler was to the right of the table. Four men sat at the long table. A heavy-set American major sat next to a small Vietnamese major. Each of the majors had an assistant at his side.

The affair appeared to be some sort of business meeting. The people in the room remained silent until the overweight American major grunted on his cigar. It was the signal for all eyes to return to him. The Major got everyone's attention and grunted again for emphasis. Ruland knew it was a signal for him to approach the senior officer.

The overweight man was Major Rod Hannah, the senior American advisor in the district. Major Hannah was a reservist from Dayton, Ohio, who until his Vietnam tour had spent a total of three days on active duty. He had waited a long time for something like Vietnam to come along. He was in ROTC in college during the Korean War, but that war ended before Major Hannah graduated, leaving the Army with a surplus of ROTC second lieutenants. In order to cut expenses they released newly commissioned second lieutenants like Major Hannah and others labeled as "marginal performers" because of their low ROTC grades.

At that time, most of the second lieutenants were glad just to get out of the Army without having to go to Korea, but a few, the more marginal of the marginal performers, joined the Army Reserve. Major Hannah graduated from Ohio State University on a Wednesday and signed on to the local reserve unit the same day. On Thursday he joined his father in the family's sand and gravel business, and worked six days a week until the war in Vietnam started. Then the Army ran out of officers and dipped low into the reserves and National Guard for volunteers. Major Hannah volunteered at the first opportunity.

Ruland walked up to the table and saluted. It was the required ritual for reporting to a new assignment.

"Sir, Lieutenant Ruland reports."

Major Hannah looked puzzled. He put his cigar back in his mouth.

"Reports for what?" Major Hannah asked.

Ruland still held his salute.

"Sir. I have orders to report to the Mobile Advisory Team located here. I'm the new MAT Team leader."

"You're what?" Major Hannah blurted out.

"You're supposed to have a MAT Team here," Ruland continued. "I'm the new team leader."

Major Hannah took his cigar out of his mouth and returned Ruland's salute with his cigar still in his hand.

"I'll be god-damned, Lieutenant. Relax...Stand at ease, Rutland."

"Ruland, sir. David Ruland."

"Well fuck me, Ruland. Somebody get him a beer...Get me one too. Charge it to me, Fujita."

The lieutenant sitting next to Major Hannah jumped out of his chair and hurried over to the red Coca-Cola cooler. He brought two beers to Major Hannah and placed them in front of him on the long table. The Major took out his dog tag chain and searched for a bottle opener among the keys and other gadgets hooked on the chain. He found the opener next to a small screwdriver and opened the beers. He handed one of the beers to Ruland.

"You don't mind Vietnamese beer, do you Lieutenant? That's about all we get this far north in the supply chain. God-damned Special Forces pukes sell it all on the black market back in Danang."

The other people in the room nodded their heads in agreement with Major Hannah's proclamation.

"How about that." Major Hannah continued. "I didn't even know you were coming." He turned to Lieutenant Fujita. "Somebody go get the MAT Team. Tell them their new boss is here."

Lieutenant Fujita walked quickly from the room. Major Hannah focused his attention on Ruland.

"Where'd you come from, Lieutenant?"

"I was with the Fourth Infantry...down in the Central Highlands."

"How'd you get sent up here?" Major Hannah asked.

"I don't know. Somebody pulled my name out of a hat, I guess."

"Have any field experience?"

"Yes sir," Ruland answered. "I was an infantry platoon leader for my first six months in country. Then I was the executive officer of my company."

Major Hannah started to laugh.

"They made you XO and you thought you had it made. Just putting in your time before going home. The Army got you, didn't it?"

"Yes sir. They tricked me again," Ruland replied without smiling.

"You Regular Army?" Major Hannah continued the interrogation.

"No sir. I was drafted. They offered me OCS."

Major Hannah squinted and looked Ruland over carefully.

"So, a college grad I suppose. You'd be out of the Army by now if you'd have stayed enlisted."

"I fell for the bit about getting management experience as an officer, Major."

Major Hannah ignored Ruland's answer.

"This is what we have to put up with around here, Lieutenant. We spend most of the day doing these meetings and bureaucratic shit with our counterparts, then Fujita spends all night writing up reports about what happened for headquarters."

Ruland clucked his tongue in sympathy, and said: "Hard work."

"What's that?" Major Hannah asked.

Ruland took a long drink on his beer and wiped his mouth and shook his head as if he was agreeing with the Major.

"I said, that's hard work, Major." Ruland responded.

"Well, anyway," Major Hannah continued, choosing to ignore Ruland's comment. "It's a job, I suppose."

Major Hannah smiled but Ruland remained expressionless. The moment of silence was broken when the door to the room swung open and Lieutenant Fujita scurried back in.

"The MAT Team's not here, Sir," Lieutenant Fujita reported. "They must be down in the village."

Major Hannah raised his eyebrows and put his cigar back in his mouth.

"That's one thing I expect you to take care of, Lieutenant. You got a First Lieutenant and two Staff Sergeants on that damn MAT Team of yours, and they spend most of their day in the village drinking beer with the gooks. I don't care what they told you before you got here. I'm the senior goddamned advisor around here and I want you to put a stop to this shit. Am I clear on that point, Lieutenant?"

Ruland remained unmoved by Major Hannah's speech. He was more interested in the fact that the Major's face had turned a deep, purple red in just a few seconds.

"Yes sir," Ruland dutifully answered.

"You and that fucking MAT Team are supposed to be training these god-damned gooks so they can use the weapons given to them by the good people of the United States of America. You're here because we're going to Vietnamize this god damned war, and we can't Vietnamize shit if you and that group of part-time shithead soldiers spend all god-damned day in that village drinking beer and screwing gook women. You understand me, Lieutenant?"

"Yes sir," Ruland answered, still unmoved and staring straight ahead, a technique used by everyone in the military when being yelled at. He had no idea what the major was talking about.

Major Hannah put his cigar back in his mouth and looked at Ruland. He noticed that Ruland was standing at attention with the can of beer held straight out in front of him.

"At ease, Lieutenant," Major Hannah ordered, letting a little blood drain from his face. "How long you got left in-country?"

Ruland smiled.

"My DEROS is in fourteen days. I got two weeks left in the Army, sir."

The blood immediately rushed back to Major Hannah's face.

"Fourteen days in the fucking Army?" he shouted, throwing his cigar across the room. "Well that's just fucking great. What the hell you going to do in two weeks? I suppose the god-damned Army sent you here to sit on your ass and drink beer with the rest of those MAT Team shit heads."

"It wasn't my idea to come here, Major. I'm getting discharged as soon as I touch down in Oakland. The Army could have released me early if they wanted to. I guess that would have been too easy."

Major Hannah shook his head.

"I should have stayed in the fucking Reserves. The Regular Army is getting all screwed up. It's those goddamned civilians who run the fucking Army in Washington. They should fire all their asses and put the military in charge."

"What I was told," Ruland offered, "you're supposed to be getting new M-16s here in a week or two. I was sent here to build a rifle range. We were told back in Saigon at Advisor School that there's some regulation out of MACV that says the Popular Forces have to qualify on their M-16s within ten days after receiving them."

Major Hannah pulled out a new cigar and began to unwrap it.

"M-16s, eh? So we're finally getting some real weapons for these slopes. You think you can build a rifle range in two weeks, Lieutenant? I don't fucking think so. Not the way these gooks work around here."

The Vietnamese major and his sergeant straightened up in their chairs and looked at Major Hannah. Ruland could see they were annoyed at Major Hannah's racial slurs, but they remained quiet.

"If you want to do one good thing before you leave this stinking country, Lieutenant, you can just get your men out of that village and working for me before you leave. How the hell we going to show these slopeheads how to win this god-damned war by hanging around that damn whorehouse down by the bridge all day?"

The Major paused and tried to light his cigar, but only succeeded in inhaling wrong and going into a coughing fit. When he recovered, his eyes watered and his face looked like a beet. He squinted at Ruland.

"Jesus H. Christ. Two fucking weeks to go in the goddamned Army and they sent you here. They should have kept you in Saigon guarding Donut Dollies."

"I can build the range for you, Major. I just need a bulldozer from the engineers for a day or two."

"No wonder this war's so screwed up," Major Hannah continued, ignoring Ruland as he once again tried to light his cigar. This time he managed to burn only a few shreds of tobacco hanging off the end so he gave up and stuffed the cigar back in his pocket.

"Just so you'll get to know the kind of people you'll be working with, Lieutenant, I want you to join in on some of our operations in the next couple of days. You can start by taking one of the Ruff Puff platoons out on an ambush tomorrow night."

The smile dropped from Ruland's face.

"But Major, they said back in Saigon I wouldn't go on any patrols with so little time left. They said all I had to do was build the rifle range. I got fourteen days...That doesn't seem fair, sir."

"I can't help it," Major Hannah said. "My job is to protect this village and Major Vien's ass. Besides, we're a little short of people. I can't help what Saigon said. If they would take some of those goddamned staff pukes out of Saigon and put them in the field, you wouldn't have to go. But we're short of officers, and an officer has to accompany each operation, and that's SOP, Lieutenant."

"Yes sir," Ruland said without thinking. He never expected anything like this.

"And take Sergeant Montague with you…If you can find him," Major Hannah shouted. "Fourteen days…If Saigon keeps making stupid-ass moves like this, it will take another two years to win this god-damn war. Christ, it'll be 1970 before we can wrap this damn thing up."

Major Hannah got up and knocked his folding chair over and kicked it.

"Stupid, fucking, god-damned chair!" he yelled. Then he stomped out of the room.

Lieutenant Fujita followed Major Hannah out before the door could slam shut. Ruland stood looking straight ahead, thinking about the night ambush assignment and what they told him back at the Advisor School about no more combat operations. He didn't notice Major Vien getting up to approach him.

"You new co-van, Lieutenant?"

"Pardon me?" Ruland said, realizing the Vietnamese officer had spoken to him.

Major Vien smiled and repeated his question slowly.

"You new co-van?"

Sergeant Tin, the interpreter, came forward and smiled.

"Major Vien ask if you new advisor. Co-van mean advisor in Vietnam. Major Vien is District Chief. I am interpreter. My name Sergeant Tin."

Ruland saluted Major Vien and shook hands with him and Sergeant Tin.

"How you doing?" Ruland said. "I'm Lieutenant Ruland.

Major Vien looked at the floor, then into Ruland's eyes.

"You say…We get new American black rifles, Co-van?"

"Yes sir, Ruland answered. "I heard they will be here in a couple of weeks. I think they're down in Danang now in a warehouse, just waiting on a convoy to bring them up here."

Major Vien turned to Sergeant Tin and smiled.

"Very good," he said as he turned back to Ruland. "You please have dinner with my officers and sergeants tonight? You bring us good news, Co-van."

"Sure, I'll be there." Ruland said smiling. "Thank you." He liked Major Vien.

"You follow Sergeant Tin. He show you room."

Sergeant Tin took Ruland to a room in the yellow building where the MAT team stayed. It was in the southern wing of the building, apart from Major Hannah's team, and the way Ruland figured, it was the easiest target for a rocket attack from the open spaces to the south of the compound. Ruland learned to think like that during his year in Vietnam. He was always aware of his vulnerability to attack. Sergeant Tin told Ruland that Major Hannah and the other district advisors bunked in the second hooch next to the building where the meeting took place.

Ruland put his gray suitcase on an empty bunk and unpacked his clothes. He hung his jungle fatigues in an empty olive drab wall locker at the end of the bunk. The locker next to Ruland's had a piece of white tape across the top with the name STAFF SERGEANT C.C. MONTAGUE, U.S. ARMY neatly printed on it.

When Ruland finished unpacking, he wrapped a towel around the tubular metal frame at the head of the bunk for a pillow and laid down. He was too tired to fall asleep just yet so he lit a cigarette and watched the smoke rise to the ceiling. The constant thud-thud of artillery firing at nearby Camp Evans didn't bother him.

Ruland lay there reflecting on how he came to be there. He didn't have any particular feelings about the war in Vietnam, one way or the other. It was just some place to be after college. He was, as he had always been, non-committal when asked about the war. When his friends in college began to take sides, Ruland just remained uncommitted, doing what he had always done on campus, which was not a whole lot. He spent four years at a small Midwestern college drinking beer and putting in just enough effort to pass the courses.

When he returned home after graduation a draft notice was waiting for him. Ruland half-heartedly attempted to enlist in a Reserve unit, and even went to the Coast Guard to see if he could get in. But all these organizations were already fully manned with the sons of the rich and a few professional athletes.

Ruland's older brother had been drafted and spent two years as an enlisted man, so he persuaded Ruland to sign up for OCS and then get in some non-combat branch like the supply corps. But when Ruland showed up at the recruiting station with his draft notice in hand, the recruiters needed to meet their quota for infantry officers. They lied to Ruland about no openings in the non-combat branches and signed him up for Infantry Officer Candidate School, telling him he could transfer to the supply corps after being commissioned. Ruland didn't exactly know how that would happen, but he went along with it.

Now, almost three years later, he lay on a bunk in South Vietnam with just fourteen days left in the Army before being discharged. His thoughts jumped around with flashes of his experience during the last three years. The problem was, he still had no idea of what he wanted to do when he got out. Ruland was thinking about the future when Sergeant Tin touched his arm.

"You come now, Lieutenant," Sergeant Tin said quietly. "Time for eat with Major Vien."

It had gotten dark out as Ruland lay on his bunk. Ruland followed Sergeant Tin through the halls of the yellow building, faintly lit by a string of small lights hanging from the hallway ceiling. They came to a large mahogany double door, behind which Ruland could hear people talking and the sounds of people eating. Sergeant Tin opened the door for Ruland and the two men entered. An old crystal chandelier left by the French hung from the center of the high ceiling of the room. It was jury-rigged to hold small, yellow bug lights, giving the room and its occupants a mustard tint. The table nearly filled the room, so the men nearest the door began to move their chairs toward the table so Ruland and Sergeant Tin could pass to the head of the table.

Major Vien looked up from his seat at the far end of the table and spotted Ruland.

"Chao, Trung-uy," Major Vien said. "You, Lieutenant, please to have dinner with my officers and sergeants."

Major Vien motioned for Ruland to sit in the empty chair next to his. Ruland walked slowly to his place of honor, letting his eyes get used to the eerie light of the yellow light bulbs.

The soldiers on both sides of the table ate quickly and talked loudly, but they still managed to keep an eye on Ruland as he moved along behind them. There were many bottles of beer on the table between the plates of food. Young Vietnamese privates were spaced around the table, ready to serve more food or run for more beer. Ruland thought it strange, how the dinner had a sense of urgency about it. There was a feeling of tenseness in the air, as if a bell were suddenly going to ring and the food and beer would be cut off. Ruland sat down beside Major Vien and was immediately handed a cold beer by one of the young privates. Another private served him a bowl of meat and cabbage and a bowl of rice.

"You like Vietnam, Lieutenant?" Major Vien asked.

"Pardon me, sir?" Ruland said, staring at the strange scene through the yellow haze.

"Major Vien ask, you like Vietnam?" Sergeant Tin repeated.

"Yes. I like the country," Ruland said to Sergeant Tin, then suddenly remembered who asked the question and turned to Major Vien.

"Yes sir. I like the country. It's very beautiful."

"You like Vietnam girls?" Major Vien asked as he began to smile.

"Major Vien ask...You like..." Sergeant Tin, the interpreter interpreted.

"I got it," Ruland said to Sergeant Tin, then turned to Major Vien. "Yes sir, Vietnamese girls are very beautiful.

"Maybe you find nice Vietnam girl in Phong Dien," Major Vien asked.

Major Vien laughed and all the men at the table stopped eating and laughed. The men stopped laughing just as suddenly and immediately went back to eating. A few of the men at the table had finished eating and were drinking beer and smoking cigarettes. They carefully studied Ruland. There was a small window near the ceiling for ventilation. Ruland had to blink his eyes to get used to the polluted air. The blinking made the strange yellow scene in front of him become out of focus. Ruland began to stare across the room, and then he remembered Major Vien had spoken to him.

"Yes sir," Ruland said, not really interested but trying to make conversation, "maybe you can introduce me to a nice Vietnamese girl in the village. We didn't see many girls in the Central Highlands, just Montagnards."

Major Vien turned very serious.

"I make joke, Trung-uy. No can do. I make joke with you. Viet Cong know I find you girl. They kill girl." He made a throat-cutting gesture with his chopsticks. "I am District Chief. I number one in district. I papa-san. Viet Cong no like me. I find you girl, they kill girl. Viet Cong make girl kill you first, then they kill girl."

Major Vien laughed and everyone in the room joined in.

"Better you see Mama-san by bridge at Majestic. She have girl for you short time. Mama-san has very pretty butterfly girl for you. Viet Cong no bother butterfly girl at Mama-san. That where Viet Cong go for fucky-fucky."

Major Vien made a gesture with his hands. The men around the table made the same gesture with their hands and laughed again. The young privates began to clear the table, so all the officers and NCOs were looking at Ruland at the head of the table.

Suddenly the mahogany doors opened and a tall silhouette appeared through the yellow smoke. The Vietnamese soldiers at the far end of the table stood up and greeted the shadow. A hand from out of the dark offered the tall figure a bottle of beer. The shadow took the beer and walked toward Ruland and Major Vien.

Lieutenant Ronnie Blossom appeared through the yellow smoke with a beer in his hand. He looked as if he were greeting pledges at a fraternity party as he moved along the table shaking the hands of the Vietnamese officers and sergeants. He was wearing a gray T-shirt with the Greek letters signifying Alpha Tau Omega fraternity on the front. He wore a pair of camouflage fatigue pants cut off at the knees and a pair of brown penny loafers with no socks. Lieutenant Blossom stuck out his hand at Ruland and smiled.

"I'm Ronnie Blossom, your assistant team leader."

"How are you?" Ruland said, offering his hand and noticing for the first time another American soldier standing behind Lieutenant Blossom.

"Fujita-san told us you would be here. We were in Camp Evans all day getting some things. We didn't even know you were coming, but we're glad to see you."

Blossom turned to the young, blond American standing behind him wearing a T-shirt advertising Bundy Surfboards. "This is Sergeant Delta Scroop, our heavy weapons specialist."

"How you doing, man?" Sergeant Scroop asked, bobbing his head like a chicken.

Lieutenant Blossom interrupted before Ruland could answer.

"Sergeant Montague is the team's light weapons specialist. I think he's still down in the village. He should be along a little later. Sergeant

Montague makes a lot of points for us in the village. He's friends with a lot of people there. He knows everybody."

Sergeant Scroop nodded his approval.

"That's good to know," Ruland said, for no special reason.

"Did Major Hannah tell you anything about Sergeant Montague?" Lieutenant Blossom asked Ruland.

Sergeant Scroop got the clue from Lieutenant Blossom that some officer talk was about to follow so he went to the other end of the table and sat down with the Vietnamese sergeants. Sergeant Scroop was not comfortable around officers and said very little in their presence.

"We got a little friction here," Lieutenant Blossom continued. The MAT Team and the Major don't exactly get along."

"No?" Ruland said. "Nobody told me much about anything here. Major Hannah just gave me a little speech about how he was the senior man around here, and that he didn't want the team sitting around the village drinking beer."

"Ya, that's sort of the problem. The Major takes this war a little too seriously. Hell, this isn't even a war. It's a game we play with the local chapter of the VC. The Major's just afraid to play, that's all."

"What's the problem?" Ruland asked. All of a sudden he felt things getting a little more complicated than he bargained for.

"Well," Lieutenant Blossom continued, lowering his voice and leaning toward Ruland, "you see we got a pretty good set-up in the village. There's this mama-san who runs a little café and massage parlor, sort of, at the other end of the village. It's called The Majestic Steam Bath and Massage Parlor. It's kind of like a rest stop for the convoy truckers during the day. You know what I mean?"

"I think I do," Ruland answered hesitatingly, knowing he was getting in deeper.

"But it's been a little too dicey for the trucks to make their runs at night since the Tet Offensive, so business is kind of slow. The convoys only come through here two or three times a week, mostly during the day, so Mama-san gives the MAT Team kind of a discount with the beer and things at night. The girls treat us pretty good, you know? And we get Mama-san a few old things from Camp Evans every time we get a chance, and help her out with supplies and things."

"The Major doesn't like it? Is that it?" asked Ruland.

Lieutenant Blossom stood up straight.

"We've been doing our jobs and all that."

"What's the matter then?" Ruland continued the questioning.

"Well, the problem is…the Major thinks Mama-san supports the VC and we shouldn't be going there giving her business and all that."

"Does she?" Ruland asked.

"Does she what?" Blossom countered.

"Does she give money to the VC?"

Lieutenant Blossom looked surprised.

"Of course she does! She pays the VC a little money and they don't bother her. Hell, I see'em in there all the time. They're good people. I got no problem with them. They just get a little protection money from Mama-san. How else they gonna finance this war? It's the American way. It's no big-time war here in this village. There ain't no North Vietnamese Regulars here, just some irate farmers who don't like being shoved around by some government in Saigon. The way I see it, it's that state's rights thing and all that. Hell, I got no problem with that."

"But it bothers Major Hannah. Is that it?"

"Man, you ain't shittin' it bothers him. Sergeant Montague's been down in that village about a week now and the Major thinks he's out running ambushes with Mama-san's VC girls against the 1st Cavalry outside of Camp Evans." Lieutenant Blossom paused and leaned closer to Ruland.

"I don't know how you feel about the whole thing, but I thought I'd better tell you before the Major got to you."

Ruland leaned even closer to Blossom.

"Well. I'll tell you where I stand, just so you'll know. I got fourteen days left in the Army. There's a truckload of M-16s waiting in Danang for these Ruff Puffs and I was sent here to make sure a rifle range is up and running when those weapons arrive. And then I'll be out of here."

"Holy shit," Lieutenant Blossom said as he began to giggle. "Man, that's wild."

"If the rest of you on the MAT Team got something going on in that village, that's your business," Ruland continued. I just want to build that damn rifle range and catch the first plane back to the world and get my discharge in Oakland and forget about Vietnam, Phong Dien, and The Majestic, or whatever it's called. Just don't get me killed in the next two weeks. That's all I ask."

"Fourteen days," Lieutenant Blossom repeated the words through closed teeth. "Can you believe that? That's fucking amazing." He shook his head and laughed. "But don't worry. We'll take care of you."

Major Vien was eager to speak to Lieutenant Blossom, so he interrupted and spoke to Lieutenant Blossom.

"Sit down, Trung-uy. Sit down. Eat food and drink beer. I have favor to ask of you. You maybe buy me a small television at PX? Now we have generator working good, I would like television. Maybe I can get American TV station. I give you little extra money for job."

Ruland knew it was time to leave. He didn't want to hear what sounded like black market business. He didn't want to get involved.

"You two talk business. I've had enough beer. I'm going to turn in now. I haven't had a chance to sleep much the last two days. Just naps whenever I could catch them. I'm still a little tired."

"OK, boss," Lieutenant Blossom said, slapping Ruland on the back. "We'll see you later. I think Sergeant Scroop and me will have a few beers. Old Major Vien here throws some pretty good parties. Hell, he can afford to. He sells most of his supplies he gets to the Viet Cong."

Lieutenant Blossom laughed and slapped Major Vien on the back. The Vietnamese officer laughed politely and motioned for Lieutenant

Blossom to take Ruland's chair. Ruland shook hands with Major Vien and thanked him. He headed for the door through the yellow haze. The men at the table all stood up and shook hands with Ruland as he passed by. Sergeant Scroop stood up at his best Southern California version of attention and bobbed his head at the new team leader.

Ruland walked outside in the cool night air and went to the flagpole in front of the building. He looked off at the lights of Camp Evans to the south as the compound's new generator powered the flickering lights of the yellow headquarters building.

October 9, 1968

Ruland always found it difficult to sleep late in Vietnam. By six o'clock in the morning the sweat would settle in a damp pool between his shoulder blades so that when he first moved, in the half-sleep of waking up, the warm damp spot would became soggy and unbearable. He found it was impossible to sleep past seven o'clock in Vietnam unless he was drunk.

The other bunks in the MAT Team's room were empty when Ruland awoke. He didn't know if anyone had slept in the room the past night. The bunks were all neatly made with the standard military 45-degree folds in the corners. Everything in the room was in its place.

"Everything is neat and tidy," Ruland thought to himself.

A small orange dog was sitting in the middle of the room looking up at Ruland, apparently waiting for him to wake up. When the dog saw Ruland moving he approached the man on the bunk and waited for his head to be scratched. The dog had a collar on with GI dog tags. Ruland thought that was appropriate as he leaned down, scratched the orange dog's head, and read the name on the dog tags.

"Hello, Stanley," Ruland muttered to the dog. "This must be your hiding place."

Ruland learned about the Vietnamese peasant's taste for boiled or roasted dog in the Vietnamese culture classes at the advisor school in Saigon. He figured the Americans' bunkroom was a sanctuary for the small dog. Either that or Stanley wasn't big enough for a meal yet.

The only person in the room was the cleaning mama-san, shuffling around in her rubber slippers and black pajamas. Ruland was not surprised to wake up with a cleaning woman in the room. They were always around the American barracks. Americans called all of the cleaning women in Vietnam Mama-san, regardless of their age.

This mama-san was still in her twenties, but she looked much older. Her front teeth were already black from chewing betel nuts. Ruland understood that in Vietnam, a mama-san always came with the building. This one was probably hired on as a teenager when the first American advisors came to the compound, and just stayed on. It was a good paying job for the women. It provided money not only for the woman's immediate family of a husband and two children, but her aging parents and several uncles, aunts, and cousins. MACV put out a directive that the advisors were to pay domestic help at a comparable local wage for the same service. But Americans always over-paid, because the two dollars-a-week recommended wage always seemed unfair.

Ruland took a pair of green jockey shorts, a green T-shirt, and his last set of clean fatigues from his gray suitcase. He never liked to carry a standard issue duffel bag because his fatigues got too wrinkled. He dressed with the cleaning woman watching closely out of the corner of her eye as she cleaned the room. The woman giggled when Ruland took off his underwear. Back in the base camps the cleaning mama-sans seemed to always be around when it was time to get dressed, so Ruland was used to undressing in front of them. The cleaning women would shake their heads and mumble something. The massage parlor girls said that all the mama-sans got together at the mid-day meal and compared the Americans soldiers with their Vietnamese husbands.

Ruland took a can of chopped ham and eggs from a stack of C-ration cartons in the corner of the room. There were always plenty of chopped ham and eggs available because most GIs wouldn't eat them. Ruland figured he was one of the few people who liked them. When he was in the field with the infantry he would heat the small green can with a piece of plastic explosive the size of a golf ball. You could pull a piece of the putty-like material from the ball for a fuze and light it. The plastic explosive would burn intensely for about a minute to heat the food. Ruland would usually trade the package of dried up cigarettes in his c-rations for a small can of cheddar cheese and melt the cheese over the top of his chopped ham and eggs.

"Now for the cheese topping," Ruland said to the woman, looking around the room.

The woman shook her head and exhausted her English vocabulary.

"Beaucoup crazy GI."

Ruland found a can of cheddar cheese in a corner shelf of excess C-rations and carefully spooned it on top of the chopped ham and eggs. He didn't see any C-4 plastic explosives around, so Ruland heated the can over a candle stuck in a glass ashtray that advertised a French restaurant in Saigon. When the cheese began to bubble on top of the eggs, it was done.

Ruland took the can and a plastic spoon from the carton and walked out of the yellow building and into the courtyard of the compound. He took a couple of deep breaths to clear his head from the smoke of last night's party. The Ruff Puffs were sitting on top of the sandbag wall smoking cigarettes and watching the new co-van carefully.

An Army Captain who was squatting, Vietnamese-style, at the base of the flagpole studied Ruland carefully. He had a carefully waxed handle-bar mustache that he groomed with his thumb and index finger as he watched Ruland walk across the open courtyard. He didn't nod his head or appear to expect a greeting from Ruland. The man was Captain Moss, an Army intelligence officer assigned to the district for the Phoenix Program, a special program Ruland would learn about later. Captain Moss was the type of person that made people feel uncomfortable just by his presence.

Ruland walked past the flagpole, saluted the seated captain with his free hand, and walked out to the concrete archway at the entrance of the compound. The concertina wire gate was pulled across the entrance. He stopped at the entrance and slowly ate his can of chopped ham and eggs with cheddar cheese.

Ruland studied the small shacks of the village across Highway One beyond the helo pad. The shacks looked out of place compared with the neat stucco houses in the middle of the village. The shacks were the homes of the farmers who used to live outside of the village near their rice paddies, but were moved to the village as a resettlement project to protect them from the Viet Cong. It was a temporary move done in 1965. The plan was to keep the farmers in this temporary housing settlement outside the village until the American advisors declared it safe for the farmers to return to their farms. But the CIA began to give free rice to the displaced farmers, so they were in no hurry to get back to their farms.

The shacks were originally surplus Army tents, but over the years additions were built on the tents, mostly from packing crates retrieved from the Camp Evans dump. The canvas from the original tents had rotted or been cut up and used for more practical things like bags or sandal straps.

There were only a few people on the highway at this time of morning. It was late in the day for these village people. The farmers had already been to the market in the village.

From a shadowy opening in one of the bunkers built into the sandbag wall, Ruland noticed an old Popular Forces soldier emerging after his night of guard duty. The old man noticed Ruland and walked up to him. The old soldier was dressed in faded tiger fatigues and wore a Chicago Cub's baseball cap of blue felt. The old man smiled at Ruland and made a smoking motion with his hand.

"Ban cho toi thuoc la?" The old man asked.

Ruland nodded, understanding what the man wanted. He offered the old man a cigarette and a pack of matches. The old man tore off the filter of the cigarette, lit the ragged end of the cigarette, and put the matches in his pocket. He stared across the highway, the cigarette dangling from his lower lip. He then took the cigarette from his mouth and tugged at Ruland's sleeve.

"Parlez-vous francais, Lieutenant?"

"No, I'm afraid not," Ruland answered and shook his head.

The old man smiled and shook his head.

"American co-van no speak francais."

The old man sighed and spoke very slowly to Ruland.

"American…French…Japan…Many people come Vietnam. Nobody stay long time. No learn speak Vietnam. Many people…"

The old man laughed to himself.

"You speak all these languages?" Ruland asked.

"Oui," said the old man.

"How did you learn them," asked Ruland.

"I soldier with them. Sometimes fight with…Sometime fight…How you say…?"

"Against," Ruland offered.

"Oui," the old man chuckled.

Ruland looked at the old man.

"You fought with the French?"

"Non, Lieutenant. Me Viet Minh," the old man said proudly.

"Then how come you fight against Viet Cong today?"

The old soldier shrugged his shoulders.

"Too old. Viet Cong live in ground. Ground too wet. Give leg pain."

"Do you like the Americans?" Ruland asked.

The old man shrugged his shoulders again.

"Francais…American…Does not matter. Young man…maybe fight American soldier. What does matter? Too old fight American. Too wet in ground. Make pain in leg. What does matter? Another people, my country. No matter. My country. No American. No Francais. No Japan."

The old man paused and sucked his cigarette. He smiled at Ruland.

"You leave soon like Francais," the old man continued. "Viet Cong return village. Then Viet Cong number one. American number ten.

The old man laughed, then looked at Ruland seriously.

"Why you here, Lieutenant?"

"I don't know," Ruland answered honestly.

The old man laughed again.

"Viet Cong fight for...how you say...purpose. Francais and American soldier, no purpose. Comprendez-vouz, Co-van?"

Ruland looked down at the ground and made a small circle in the sand with the toe of his boot.

"This is a funny war. No one ever gave me much of a reason, let alone a purpose. Anyway, I wasn't doing much at the time. I might as well do this."

Suddenly there was shouting and laughing coming from the far end of the sandbag wall nearest the village. Two Ruff Puffs ran up to the concertina gate and pulled it back to make the opening a little wider. A tall, black American soldier wearing tailored, black Viet Cong pajamas and a black beret appeared under the concrete archway. He was carrying a World War II grease gun and a small knapsack. The man approached Ruland and saluted.

"Lieutenant Ruland, I am Staff Sergeant C.C. Montague, reporting for duty. I am a Korean War combat veteran and have spent more time in the chow line than you have in the Army. I have just been in the village winning the hearts and minds of the people."

The black man's teeth flashed a smile. His four front teeth had gold inlays of a heart, diamond, club, and spade.

"I knew you were here," Sergeant Montague continued, "because all the village girls are talking about the new Co-van. Very pretty, they're saying. They're probably figuring a price for your head right now."

Sergeant Montague laughed and pulled a beer out of the small knapsack he was carrying. He opened the can with a can opener attached to his dog tags. He took a long drink and handed the beer to the old Vietnamese soldier without looking at him. The old man smiled and tipped the beer up and finished it without stopping.

"Lieutenant," Sergeant Montague said as he inhaled to hold back a belch, "I think you ought to get together with the Major tomorrow and get things straight right from the start. Now don't let him pressure you, just 'cause he's a major and you're only a piss-ass lieutenant, no disrespect intended, Lieutenant. It's just that, hell, Lieutenant, he don't even write your fitness report. It come out of MACV or someplace."

Sergeant Montague reached back into the knapsack and pulled out another can of beer and opened it. He took another long drink, spilling some beer out of the corner of his mouth. The old man's eyes lit up. Ruland knew he should say something, so he seized the moment.

"What seems to be the problem, Sergeant Montague?"

The tall, black man stared at Ruland in disbelief.

"Begging the Lieutenant's pardon, the Major is about to put this village off limits. Hell, if I don't come out of this war dead, I at least want to come out of it rich. This little village is the best damn thing ever happened to me, Lieutenant. Back in the world I'm just another field-hand nigger when I leave the base at night. Why do you think they put all those Army bases in the South, Lieutenant? It's to make all us niggers transfer overseas to do all the dirty work white folk don't feel comfortable doing. Like this war here. But this old nigger knows it's better duty over here. And when it's a war like this one, where nobody knows what the fuck is going on, I stand to make a few dollars in the deal. Hell shit, man, I'd stay here forever if I could. I'm a white man here, Lieutenant."

Ruland started to laugh.

"Sergeant Montague, let me give it too you straight. I got fourteen days left in the Army. You can run for village council for all I care. I'll talk to the Major, if you think it will keep a good thing going for you. But just don't get me killed before I can get out of here in one piece. That's all I ask of you."

A smile grew on Sergeant Montague's face, displaying the four suits of the card deck in gold.

"I understand what you're saying, Lieutenant. I know where you're coming from."

Sergeant Montague laughed loudly. He handed his beer to the old man and pulled a third beer out of his knapsack, opened it and handed it to Ruland. Both men looked at each other and knew exactly what was expected of the other.

"Well, Lieutenant," Sergeant Montague said as he reached for Ruland's hand to shake it, "I got to go to Camp Evans now on some business for an hour or so, but we'll talk more about your assignment when I get back." Then he added in an afterthought, "With the Lieutenant's permission, of course."

"Of course," Ruland said, playing the game. "I'll be right here. I don't intend on leaving this compound during the next two weeks any more than I have to."

The two men exchanged salutes and Sergeant Montague performed a precise, drill sergeant's about face and started walking down Highway One toward Camp Evans. A crowd of children seemed to come out of the roadbed to follow him. The children had to run to keep up with the tall man's long stride. Ruland took a sip of the beer and handed it to the old man still standing there. The old man nodded, accepting the beer with a smile. Ruland turned and walked back to his room. Major Hannah was there waiting for him.

"How you doing, Ruland?" The Major asked as Ruland entered the room. "This room all right with you?"

Ruland stopped when he saw Major Hannah sitting at the table. There was sort of an unwritten rule about senior officers not entering junior officers' rooms uninvited.

"I'm doing fine, sir," Ruland answered.

The Major was puffing on one of his cigars.

"I wanted to tell you what we have planned for you tonight," Major Hannah said with a smile.

"Planned for tonight, sir?"

"Well, Lieutenant, I told you it was SOP to have all my new arrivals get to know these Popular Forces troops as soon as they can. Now I know you already had a few beers with Major Vien and the rest of the gooks last night. That's all right, but that don't count. I want you to get to know the real Ruff Puffs, not just the officers and non-coms. You know what I mean?"

"What do you want me to do, Major? You know I don't think this is right with me having just a couple of weeks left."

"Noted, Lieutenant." Major Hannah grinned as he took a long drag on his cigar, then paused to study the young lieutenant. "I want you to go out on an ambush. The sooner the better, I say. So tonight is a good time to do it. I want you and Sergeant Montague, providing he's not lost in the village again, to take one of the PF platoons out and set up about seven or eight clicks from town. I'll let you know where I want you to go after I coordinate this with the operations folks at Camp Evans. I don't want the American grunts crossing paths with you and the gooks. They'd kick your ass. Any gook in the bush is VC to an American grunt. He don't know the difference between a Ruff Puff and a VC."

"What is the difference?" Ruland wisecracked.

"The Viet Cong have the latest U.S. equipment," Major Hannah answered seriously.

"All right," Ruland said as he let out a deep breath, "if that's what you want me to do. But remember I wasn't planning on going on any operations. I thought the rule was, you don't go on patrol your last month in country."

"Maybe that's the rule in the god-damn Fourth Infantry, but it's not the rule here, Lieutenant."

"They told me back in Saigon I was supposed to come here and build a rifle range and that was it. Nobody said anything about going on any operations or ambushes."

"Well that's tough shit, Lieutenant. You're in this man's Army until Uncle Sam says you're out and not before. And as long as you're in the

Army, you'll take orders from me. I'm the senior goddamned advisor around here. I don't care who told you what back in Saigon. You're taking these slopes out tonight on an ambush. Do I make myself clear, Lieutenant?"

The Major got up from the table and walked toward the door, kicking Stanley out of the way.

"God damn dog," he said, then stopping when he remembered something.

"Oh yeah, one more thing, Lieutenant. The ARVN artillery here is going to cover you. The cannon-cockers at Camp Evans won't provide fire support for the Ruff Puffs, unless you've made contact and there is an American with the unit."

Major Hannah walked past the cleaning mama-san and slapped her on the rear as he walked by. The woman sputtered something at the Major. He laughed and shook his head, apparently amused by the little people who worked around the compound.

Ruland sat down at the table to think a while until he remembered the red Coca-Cola cooler in the other plywood hooch that served as mess hall, meeting room, and office for the American advisors. He went around back of the yellow building and into the building. He got a can of Ballantine's beer from the cooler and returned to his room. After opening the beer, he took his portable radio out of the gray suitcase and tuned it to some Vietnamese music. When he finished the beer, he went back to the cooler and got two more. He was able to finish one of the beers but the heat and his lack of sleep caught up with him. Ruland placed a green towel on his bunk to absorb the sweat, then stretched out and went to sleep.

Ruland woke up around three o'clock. The cleaning mama-san and the empty beer cans were gone. Ruland took a box of C-rations out of a new case and selected tuna and a can of crackers. He thought that would be nice and light. Ruland took the can of tuna out to the sandbag wall near the concrete arch and climbed on top of the wall. The Ruff

Puffs on the wall nodded at Ruland. He waved his hand and jerked his head back to acknowledge them, then found a comfortable looking spot and sat down cross-legged and ate the tuna fish and crackers.

After he finished his meal, Ruland leaned back on his elbows and watched the people pass by on Highway One. They were mostly young girls on the road at this time of day. They shuffled by with carrying sticks on their shoulders dangling five-gallon cans of water on each end. After a while a Vietnamese civilian wearing a tan business suit passed by on an old British motorcycle. The man disappeared to the south after a skillful slalom through the village around the young girls and an overloaded bus. The girls giggled at the mystery man in city clothes.

A few minutes later, a convoy of American trucks sped past the compound in the opposite direction toward Camp Evans on a return trip from Quang Tri. The American truck drivers looked menacingly at Ruland as the oversized deuce-and-a-half trucks forced the local villagers into the ditches. The Americans whistled and yelled obscenities at the village girls, but the girls didn't look back.

Ruland suddenly realized he was now on the periphery of the war. The U.S. soldiers thought advisors were crazy for living with the Vietnamese, and the Vietnamese thought the advisors were crazy because they always tried to do everything so fast. However, there was one thing the Popular Forces appreciated. The American advisors took up a lot of time working with the Vietnamese officers on new ideas and projects, so the Popular Forces officers had less time to mess with the troops.

Ruland spent the rest of the afternoon watching life on Highway One. His uniform became soaked in sweat in the hot sun so he decided to take a shower before he went on the ambush. The Americans, or maybe it was the French when they lived in the yellow building, had constructed a rainwater holding tank and shower in a corner of the compound. It usually stayed empty during the dry season, but Sergeant Montague made some arrangement to have the tank filled up by an

American water truck each time it went north to re-supply the Marines at Quang Tri.

Ruland got undressed in the MAT Team's room, wondering where the other team members of the team spent the day. He walked to the shower with a towel wrapped around him. The Ruff Puffs whistled at him from their sandbag perches along the wall. Ruland waved his hand back at them. The water in the shower was warm from the sun. But it didn't make Ruland feel any cooler. He walked back to the room and discovered the cleaning mama-san had a set of his fatigues cleaned and pressed lying on the bed. Sergeant Montague walked into the room as Ruland was getting dressed.

"Lieutenant. Your troops are gathering out front. You ready to strike a blow for freedom?"

Ruland sat on the edge of the bed and tied his boots.

"I guess I'm as ready as I'll ever be."

Ruland looked out the small window at the rag-tag soldiers milling around the flagpole.

"I got the ambush site from Major Hannah," Sergeant Montague said. "The ARVN artillery here in the compound has got our position plotted, so we're all set, Lieutenant. Don't worry, I'm not going to let anything happen to you."

Sergeant Montague had some ammunition, signal flares, and web gear neatly stacked on the table. Ruland quietly finished dressing. He put a C-ration can of hot dogs and beans in one of his pant's pockets and a can of crackers in the other pocket. He put a magazine in his M-16, but kept the chamber empty. Ruland was very safe with a rifle. He learned it from hunting with his father, not from the Army. Ruland slung the pistol belt with two magazine pouches hooked on it over his shoulder and walked out to meet the troops.

Fifteen soldiers from one of the Popular Forces platoons were standing around the flagpole in front of the yellow building. Lieutenant Tram, the platoon leader, noticed Ruland and Sergeant Montague approaching so he ordered the platoon to fall in at attention. A few of the men didn't understand the order so Lieutenant Tram ran over to them and beat them on their steel helmets with his hat until they joined the formation. Their fellow soldiers laughed hysterically at this.

A crowd of villagers began to gather outside the main gate to watch their village defense force in action. They laughed and cheered as the platoon slowly formed under the guidance of Lieutenant Tram's hat. Some young boys outside the gate pointed at Ruland and said something to their sisters. The girls got embarrassed and swatted their brothers.

"I thought these ambushes were supposed to be a secret," Ruland said to Sergeant Montague as they stopped in front of the formation. "Everybody and his mother must be outside the gate."

"Hell, Lieutenant. We're bringing the war to the people just like MACV says we're supposed to do. This village is mostly Viet Cong anyway. They just want to know where we're going so they can stay out of the way."

The two Americans exchanged salutes with Lieutenant Tram. About half the PF soldiers, unsure about the rules of saluting, managed to salute without dropping their rifles. The crowd outside the gate loved it.

"This here is Lieutenant Tram," Sergeant Montague said to Ruland.

"How do you do," Lieutenant Tram said. "I very happy meet you."

"Chao, Thieu-uy," Ruland greeted the Second Lieutenant platoon leader in his best Vietnamese. "Ong manh khong?"

"I very fine, thank you," Lieutenant Tram answered, obviously pleased with Ruland's attempt.

Sergeant Montague interrupted. "Lieutenant Tram here knows the spot the Major picked out for the ambush. It's down by the river past the bridge. And I talked to the artillery, so we got some targets on call if we need them."

"Does the US artillery at Camp Evans know where we are in case they decide to fire some H and I in our direction?"

"Sort of, Lieutenant. They got our grid square. So we should be OK."

"How 'bout the ARVN guns here. Are they any good?"

"Sometimes," Sergeant Montague said with a smile.

"What do you mean 'Sometimes'?"

"Sometimes they hit the target, sometimes they hit you. You just gots to be on your toes. You know what I mean, Lieutenant?"

Ruland looked at the soldiers in formation and smiled.

"Ya, I know. But I still think it's pretty low of Major Hannah to send me out on this with as little time as I got left. There should be some rule about this in MACV. What do they want out of me, anyway. Hell, I was drafted. I just went to OCS because I figured I'd get a desk job or something safe."

"There is this rule, Lieutenant. The rule is: The Army gets their money's worth out of you until the last day. You lieutenants get almost five hundred dollars a month for this, counting combat pay. They pay us po' folk like me just enough to shuffle along. If you don't want to play officer no mo', then you better start shufflin'."

Sergeant Montague smiled at Ruland with his gold-inlayed front teeth and handed him a map with the ambush site and the artillery targets marked in grease pencil.

"You ready to go, Lieutenant."

Ruland slung his M-16 over his shoulder and stuffed the map in his pant's pocket.

"Let's get this thing over with," Ruland said with a sigh.

Lieutenant Tram yelled at the platoon and they started to walk out of the compound through the barbed wire gate in single file. Ruland took his place near the middle of the file next to Lieutenant Tram and the radioman. Sergeant Montague and Stanley the dog fell in at the end of the line. The men moved out past the crowd of people by the archway and on to Highway One, moving toward the village. Several villagers and children trailed along behind as if in a parade.

The platoon moved into the village and the soldiers waved to their friends, yelling and laughing. Their friends would laugh and yell back at the soldiers and make believe they were firing imaginary rifles. The PF soldiers would point their weapons back at the villagers and laugh. The children would fall down on the edge of the highway and play dead. As the file passed down the main street of the village, interest in the parade wore off. The villagers in the procession began to drop off in groups of two and three.

At the end of the village, just before the bridge, the platoon passed by The Majestic Steam Bath and Massage Parlor. Three of the girls were lined up along the white picket fence surrounding the old French bunker. The building had become a landmark on Highway One, and was the leading business establishment in the village. The men in the platoon yelled at the girls and the girls yelled back at their countrymen in bar-girl English.

"You number fucking ten!" one girl yelled back at the PF soldiers.

"Vietnam soldier have ti-ti cock", another girl yelled.

The Popular Forces soldiers laughed and said something back at the last girl and made a gesture with his two hands between his legs. The girls giggled hysterically and gave the soldier the finger. All three girls watched Ruland as he walked in front of the picket fence surrounding the old French bunker that was now a brothel. When Ruland was directly in front of The Majestic, the girls spoke to him.

"Hey, Lootenant Ruland. When you come visit us? You drink beer and lay in bed all day in compound. Why you no drink beer at Majestic?"

"I not let you sleep," another girl interrupted. "I give you nice massage."

Ruland didn't know how many of the soldiers understood English, but they all laughed at the girls' jokes. A few of the Ruff Puffs turned to Ruland and made an international gesture with their index finger of their right hand and a circle formed by their left hand, then pointed to the last girl who spoke at the fence.

The platoon came as close as it ever would to a marching unit when it passed in front of The Majestic and marched onto the bridge over the

Song O Lau River. The soldiers liked the sound of their stomping feet as they crossed the bridge. Sets of eyes looked out from the slits in the sandbagged bunker at the end of the bridge. The eyes belonged to the ambush platoon's fellow Ruff Puffs settling in for guard duty for the night. The noise of the men stomping their feet on the planking of the bridge apparently woke them up. Ruland looked back to see one of the girls from The Majestic run out to Sergeant Montague at the end of the file and hand him a few cans of beer, which he immediately stuffed in his knapsack.

The sun began to set as soon as Ruland walked on the wooden planks of the bridge. Up ahead, the point man just left the bridge and turned right to follow the trail along the north side of the riverbank. The platoon was in Viet Cong territory now and the PF soldiers appeared to become a little more serious. A few of them put ammo clips in their out-of-date M-1 rifles and locked a round in the chamber. The file of men became silhouetted against the red horizon.

Ruland and Sergeant Montague were both a head taller than the other men, and seemed out of place in the formation. When Ruland turned back again to check on the rear echelon, he realized how easy a target he would be for a sniper. He started to hunch over a bit to blend in with the file. The Ruff Puffs thought this was some sort of American marching tactic so they all hunched over too. When it became too uncomfortable Ruland stood up straight and the allies followed his lead. The group finally reached some tall bushes farther down the river that were above Ruland's head. That made him more comfortable. All he had to worry about now was stepping on a land mine.

Ruland figured the platoon walked for about five kilometers before the point man stopped and looked back at Lieutenant Tram. The lieutenant looked back at Sergeant Montague, who gave the thumbs up sign back to Lieutenant Tram. The platoon leader waved his hand to the soldiers and the Ruff Puffs moved off to the left side of the trail. It was getting dark fast. Sergeant Montague quickly set up two claymore anti-personnel mines facing down the trail. Ruland could tell Sergeant Montague was a professional by the way he moved around the explosives. Sergeant Montague strung the wires back to the spot Ruland and Lieutenant Tram had selected to control the ambush.

"Here you go, Lieutenant," Sergeant Montague said in a half-whisper as he handed the claymore detonators to Ruland. "You can kick this thing off if you see a shadow or something on the trail." Sergeant Montague looked up and down the trail.

"And watch out for the water buffalo," Sergeant Montague continued. "They'll wander through here and surprise you." Sergeant Montague pointed to Ruland's M-16. "And whatever you do, don't use that little pea shooter on the water bulls. It only makes them made as hell and then we're in real trouble. If you see a water bull on the trail, just let him pass by and hope he doesn't smell you. They hate the smell of Americans, especially you white boys. Drives them crazy."

Ruland took the claymore detonators and looked around at the Ruff Puffs taking their positions quietly in the dark.

"They appear to know what they're doing," Ruland whispered to Lieutenant Tram.

Ruland took a deep breath and let it out slowly as he surveyed the ambush site as Sergeant Montague settled in beside him. It was now completely dark. Satisfied with the positions the men had taken, Ruland leaned over and whispered to Lieutenant Tram.

"How do we call in the ARVN artillery from back in the compound if we need them?"

Lieutenant Tram jumped to his feet with a big smile on his face. "Yessir, Roo-tenant. Number one ah-til-ly."

Lieutenant Tram yelled at the radioman. The radioman then yelled in his hand mike.

"OK, Roo-tenant," Lieutenant Tram said proudly. "Ah-til-ly on way."

Ruland looked at Sergeant Montague in disbelief.

"He didn't do what I think he did, did he?"

"Lieutenant," Sergeant Montague said as he closed his eyes and smiled, "sometimes these Ruff Puffs don't understand English as well as we think they do. I got a soul feeling that ol' Lieutenant Tram here is about to demonstrate the accuracy of his countrymen's big guns."

The sounds of two artillery guns were heard in the direction of the village. Lieutenant Tram smiled and pointed to the sky overhead. Ruland turned to Sergeant Montague.

"Tell me that's not for us."

Before Sergeant Montague could answer, Ruland heard the whine of incoming artillery shells. The two Americans hit the ground and pulled their cloth jungle hats down over their heads and gritted their teeth. Ruland closed his eyes and waited. He heard a POP...POP...overhead. The sky immediately lit up as two parachute flares began to float gently to earth. The Ruff Puffs were on their feet. They whistled and cheered at the fireworks, and commented on the accuracy of their fellow civil defenders. Ruland shook his head and turned to look at Sergeant Montague, who was on his back, holding his belly in laughter.

"What the hell do we do now?" Ruland yelled at Sergeant Montague. "First we form a parade through the middle of town, then we pinpoint our position for every frigging Viet Cong in the district. And these assholes are cheering."

"Lieutenant, they're cheering because they're safe. There's no VC going to come through here tonight. Ol' Charlie will work on the other side of town now...Plenty of good spots to launch a rocket at the compound south of town. We just told the Viet Cong where not to go, if he don't know already. This is part of the game, Lieutenant. The Viet Cong gots to know where we are so they don't run into us."

Ruland shook his head in disbelief.

"Well, what do we do now? Why don't we go back to the compound? We can't do anything here tonight."

Sergeant Montague straightened up in mock amazement.

"And get ambushed by some gung-ho Marines? No sir, Lieutenant, not me. Just relax and settle back. Hell, it's safer here tonight than back home in East St. Louis."

The light from the flares began to flicker and fade. Ruland looked down the trail at the Ruff Puffs as they began to light their cigarettes and relax. One group lit a candle so they could play cards. Sergeant Montague pulled two beers from his ever-present knapsack and handed one to Ruland.

"Might as well have a nightcap, Lieutenant. You'll get used to the type of war we're fightin' here. It's a little looser than that uptight infantry shit you were used to in the Central Highlands."

Sergeant Montague laughed to himself as he opened his beer.

"Remember, Lieutenant, when you're gone in a couple of weeks these people will still be here. They been at war with some American or Frenchman or Japman or whoever ever since they can remember so they don't get excited about shit like this. American officers the only ones get upset by this. You people got your one-year tour to prove you can screw things up and still get that promotion and a Bronze Star. So things like this make officers nervous. These people live here, Lieutenant, and they going to stay here when you're long gone. Sit down and have a beer. I ain't going to let nothing happen to you 'til it's your time to go home. I'd have to do all that damned paperwork if I did."

Ruland opened his beer and sat down on the ground facing Sergeant Montague.

"So this is what they're talking about. We're turning the war over to the people. This is the Vietnamization the Pentagon's so proud of."

"That's right, Lieutenant, that's right. This here's the light at the end of the tunnel."

The two men sipped on their beer and watched the Ruff Puffs set up camp for the night. This quiet time with an officer was always uncomfortable for a professional NCO like Sergeant Montague, so he didn't attempt to make small talk with Ruland. Sergeant Montague finished his beer, took a poncho liner out of his knapsack and made a pillow out of it. Then he laid down and quickly fell asleep. Ruland was a little nervous about sleeping on an ambush so he decided to stay awake all night. But after a while Lieutenant Tram motioned for Ruland to go to sleep, and Ruland decided he would try it. He figured Sergeant Montague was right. They were safe for the night.

The Viet Cong did fire three mortar rounds at the bridge that night from the flat, sandy area south of the compound. One of the rounds landed in the soft mud of the riverbank and didn't detonate. It would be recovered by some children the next morning, who would sell the dud shell to the CIA. The other two mortar rounds landed just north of the bridge on Highway One and made two small pockmarks in the asphalt. They were small 60mm mortar rounds, so they did little damage.

After the nightly attack on the bridge, most of the villagers soon went back to sleep, knowing that the nightly attack on the bridge was over. They were safe for another night.

October 10, 1968

When Ruland woke up the next morning Sergeant Montague was eating a can of C-ration peaches. The Ruff Puffs were sleeping along the side of the trail. They followed the rules of a good ambush and remained in their positions. At least they didn't move after they fell asleep. A few of the soldiers were arm-in-arm, comrades for the night. Some of the villagers were already walking down the trail on their daily journey to the village market. Children jumped over the two claymore mines to play with Stanley, who was running around from soldier to soldier in search of a morning snack. An old man stopped and looked at the group, picked up the anti-personnel mines and threw them off to the side of the trail. Ruland looked at the scene while he fumbled for a cigarette.

"Let's get back to the compound," Ruland said to Sergeant Montague. "We've held off the red tide of communism for another night."

"Yessir, Lieutenant," Sergeant Montague quickly responded.

The tall black man jumped up and moved among the soldiers, kicking them on the bottoms of their sandals to wake them up.

"All right, damn it! Let's get this show on the road! Old Uncle Sugar's paying me ten dollars and three squares a day to look after you freedom fighters. The least you can do is get your ass in gear in the morning."

The soldiers woke up and casually began to stroll back to the village along the river trail. About half of the men dragged their oversized M-1 rifles behind them like rakes, leaving a pattern of parallel lines in the sandy trail. The rest of the soldiers carried their rifles on their shoulders like farmers returning from the fields with their pitchforks. The soldiers walked down the trail at their own pace, yawning and half awake. Ruland, Sergeant Montague, and Lieutenant Tram followed along behind. Stanley ran ahead of the group, eager to return to the relative security of the compound.

By the time Ruland reached the bridge, the PF soldiers in the lead had broken off from the haphazard formation and returned to their homes in the village. Two farmers who had already been to the market passed Ruland and the others on the bridge, returning to their hamlets. Neither farmer looked up at the two Americans. A small boy who was fishing on the bridge shouted at Sergeant Montague.

"Hey Sergeant Montague! You make pretty lights last night. Number fucking one lights."

On the other side of the bridge, the business day at The Majestic Steam Bath and Massage Parlor had begun. One of the girls was outside the old French bunker dressed in a cotton mini-skirt she had fashioned after an outfit she saw in a movie magazine. She stood behind the picket fence discussing terms with two American soldiers sitting in a five-ton truck. The girl noticed Sergeant Montague and yelled.

"Hey, Sergeant Montague! Bring new Co-van here and have beer!"

Another girl was standing just barely out of sight in the front door. She was wearing a transparent pink nightgown.

"Sergeant Montague," she yelled. "You bring Rootenant Rurand to Majestic. Don't go Thuy Van's! I give Rootenant Rurand number one deal! Have beer, nice massage, fucky-fucky, have sleep! Be good for you, Rootenant Rurand!"

Ruland turned to Sergeant Montague.

"How'd they know my name?"

"The Viet Cong probably told them," Sergeant Montague answered.

Sergeant Montague smiled and waved at the girls. Ruland looked back at the girls, then turned to Sergeant Montague.

"Want to stop for some coffee or something?"

"You don't want to mess around The Majestic in the morning, Lieutenant. That's when Captain Phoenix makes his Intel rounds. He'll turn you in to Major Hannah, who'll send you back to the world with an Article Fifteen in your back pocket. That's not going to help you get a job when you get out. And for a bonus, there's always a chance one of those girls picked up a case of the clap from some truck driver, and she'll send you back with a surprise in your front pocket. I'll take you to a cafe in the village I think you'll like. We can get a cold beer there. Nothing like a cold beer first thing in the morning before the temperature hits ninety."

Sergeant Montague and Ruland walked past The Majestic and into the village. Ruland looked back occasionally at the girls just coming out to take their positions along the picket fence before the convoys began their run from Hue to Quang Tri and back.

"Don't worry, Lieutenant," Sergeant Montague continued, "I'll take care of you. That's what I get paid for...Somebody's got to watch out for you young college grad officers, or you would really screw this war up."

Sergeant Montague laughed and Ruland nodded his head, smiling. Ruland had seen plenty of the college grad officers Sergeant Montague was talking about, so he couldn't disagree.

Ruland had to walk quickly to keep up with the tall black man. He studied Sergeant Montague as they walked together into the village. The children followed along behind the two men, skipping and singing a French song.

This was the third tour in Vietnam for Staff Sergeant C.C. Montague. He was one of those career Army soldiers who dreamed of a war like Vietnam. Sergeant Montague's first assignment in Vietnam was in 1963 with a Special Forces team in the Central Highlands. He lived with the Montagnard tribes in a little settlement near the intersection of Cambodia, Laos, and South Vietnam. The Special Forces Team would try to intercept the early North Vietnamese advisors to the Viet Cong as they crossed the borders into South Vietnam. Sergeant Montague enjoyed working with the Montagnards. These native tribesmen were tough fighters. They saw the North Vietnamese intruders into their mountain territory as a threat to their way of life. So they were perfect allies for the American advisors.

The second tour for Sergeant Montague was as a platoon sergeant with the First Infantry Division, the Big Red One. He volunteered to return to Vietnam following a one-year assignment back in the States. He wanted to go to a straight-leg infantry unit because the Special Forces operations were getting too involved with the CIA and their psychological warfare games, so he wasn't interested in another tour with them. Sergeant Montague served his year in the field with the Big Red One as a platoon sergeant, went back to the states for a year, then volunteered for Vietnam again.

For his third tour, Sergeant Montague didn't want to go back to a regular infantry unit. They were getting too many eighteen-year old soldiers and twenty-year old officers. He felt these new kids were too unprofessional and dangerous to be around, so he put in a request to be assigned to one of the new Mobile Advisory Teams. He liked the idea of working independently in one of the small villages of Vietnam. He wasn't really interested in fighting the war, but in making some money this time. "Mercenary gold", he called it.

This was Sergeant Montague's nineteenth year in the Army, and he wanted to retire after twenty years with some ready cash when he got out. He had managed to build up a considerable savings account back in East St. Louis from the marathon poker games that went on at Camp Evans. He sent most of his winnings home at the end of each week by money order. And to boost his earnings, he would not be adverse to taking some of his winnings and buying a few hard-to-get items like televisions and tape recorders from the PX and sell them at a profit to Vietnamese officers.

The assignment at Phong Dien was perfect for Sergeant Montague. It was just up the road from Camp Evans, where there were round-the-clock poker games for steady income. It was also on the commercial route of Highway One, which was ideal for Sergeant Montague's television and tape recorder resale business. He was making a lot of money in the war.

This was also the third time Sergeant Montague had been a staff sergeant. Every soldier returning from Vietnam had thirty days leave on the books before reporting to his next unit. Sergeant Montague always stretched his thirty days to fifty-five days, just short of the sixty-day point when AWOL legally becomes desertion. So when Sergeant Montague reported to his next unit after his extended leave he was immediately busted to buck sergeant. But that was all part of his plan. Sergeant Montague didn't want the responsibility and paperwork of a senior stateside NCO. He preferred the rank of buck sergeant, and enjoyed emphasizing the "buck" in his rank when he introduced himself to white officers.

Before returning to Vietnam, "Buck" Sergeant Montague would quickly get promoted to Staff Sergeant because of the shortage of noncommissioned officers in the war. He was a professional soldier and he knew what he was doing in the field, no matter what the assignment.

But there was no next assignment this time for Staff Sergeant C.C. Montague. After this "twilight tour", Sergeant Montague intended to return to East St. Louis for good and become a partner in his cousin's liquor store. But he did want to retire as a Staff Sergeant, so he kept out of trouble as best he could, while still keeping his hand in the poker circuit. There were some big money games at Camp Evans, and some interesting easy money opportunities with the Vietnamese officers who traveled Highway One.

Sergeant Montague had an efficient system going. He would take his extracurricular earnings and exchange the wartime military pay currency, or MPC, for Vietnamese piastres in the local village at a healthy profit. Then he would exchange the Vietnamese piastres with the CIA for MPC at another profit, claiming he collected it from "recently deceased" Viet Cong. He would send the money to his cousin in East St. Louis in increments of one hundred-dollar money orders.

If he had any unexpected big winnings, Sergeant Montague would use the cash to buy an interest in one of the shops in the village. Sergeant Montague figured it was only a matter of time before the United States would leave Vietnam and the North Vietnamese would take over the village. Then Sergeant Montague could write off the loss of foreign investments for a substantial tax break. That is, if he ever decided to pay taxes.

Sergeant Montague and Lieutenant Ruland walked through the village until they arrived at a plain, whitewashed building with a tin roof. There was a dusty blue and white striped awning on the front of the building that provided shade for five small tables. The only thing that identified the building as a cafe beside the tables was another one of the old red Coca-Cola ice coolers near the door that led to the interior of the building.

Sergeant Montague pointed to one of the tables and made a drinking motion with his other hand. Lieutenant Tram had walked on down the street ahead of the two Americans, so Sergeant Montague whistled at the Vietnamese officer and made the same drinking motion with his hand. Lieutenant Tram turned around and walked back to the small cafe to join the two Americans.

Ruland, Sergeant Montague, and Lieutenant Tram sat down at a table in the shade of the awning. A Vietnamese woman came out of the shadow of the doorway and stood beside the table, smiling at Sergeant Montague. She was an attractive woman in her early forties. Ruland noticed her front teeth were not black from chewing betel nuts like the other women in the village. She looked at Sergeant Montague and smiled. Sergeant Montague winked back at her.

"Three beers, Madame…with ice, s'il vous plait," Sergeant Montague said, then turned back to Ruland. "She used to live with a French officer back when they were doing their thing here. Old

Frenchy left something behind a white boy like you might be interested in. I'll tell you about it later."

Ruland raised his eyebrows and tilted his head. He didn't know what Sergeant Montague was talking about, but was too tired to ask anymore about it.

The woman walked over to the red cooler and took an ice pick off a hook above the cooler. She lifted the lid, then leaned over and chipped off three pieces of ice from a large block inside the cooler. Sergeant Montague looked at the woman's bottom when she leaned over, then winked at Ruland. The woman wiped the sawdust off the ice and put it into three tall glasses, then took three bottles of warm Vietnamese beer from a wooden case beside the cooler.

"Ya know, Lieutenant," Sergeant Montague mused. "Beer's the best thing in the world for you. Beer got lots of carbohydrates. To my way of thinking, it's liquid bread. Only way to beat this damn heat. Just have a cold beer in the morning instead of coffee and toast. Best thing in the world for you."

Sergeant Montague stood up and growled at the children who were gathering just at the edge of the awning, doing his cowardly lion imitation from the Wizard of Oz. The children jumped back, laughed when they saw Sergeant Montague smiling, and returned to their spots after he sat down again.

The woman returned to the table with the three beers and the three glasses filled with the large chunks of ice. The ice was still covered with flecks of sawdust. The woman yelled at the children and they scampered to the edge of the cafe and took up their predetermined positions to watch the three men drink their breakfast beer. After she was sure the children were settled, the woman opened the bottles with an opener she had in her pocket. She wiped each bottle top with the palm of her hand before pouring the beer in a glass. She smiled at Sergeant Montague the entire time.

"I think you've been here before, Sergeant Montague," Ruland commented.

"What do you mean by that, Lieutenant?"

"You know what I mean," Ruland said, looking up at the woman waiting to be paid.

"Now, Lieutenant, I just got a little business investment in this place, that's all."

Sergeant Montague began to reach for his money, but Lieutenant Tram stopped him by grabbing his arm.

"I buy, Trung-si," Lieutenant Tram said.

"Merci, Thieu-uy," Sergeant Montague said, not wanting to insist on buying the beer and make the Vietnamese officer lose face.

"I'll get the second round, Sergeant Montague," Ruland announced.

Sergeant Montague sat up straight.

"I said 'a' beer was good for you in the morning, not two beers. I got to keep a clear head. I got things to do at Camp Evans, Lieutenant...business things."

"You can go on ahead," Ruland said. "I think I'll have a couple of beers then go get some sleep. I can't be expected to work on that rifle range during the day if the Major sends me out all night. Besides, we can throw together a range in a couple of days."

"You know, Lieutenant, that's the trouble with this damn war."

"What's that, Sergeant Montague?"

"Everybody's in such a god damn hurry. You don't have to be in such a hurry to build that rifle range. They'll make you work round the clock if you let them. Hell, we could get just as much done in this war if they'd put us on a forty-hour week...probably get more done. We don't need all this overtime shit."

"You think so," Ruland commented, anticipating a speech from Sergeant Montague.

"Hell, I know so, Lieutenant. It's been the same since the Americans got here. No sooner we get back from some night operation, and then the man got some day patrol scheduled for you. The Viet Cong's smarter than that. They just pull off some ambush or rocket attack that lasts two…three minutes at most. Then they go home. Even these Ruff Puffs take a two-hour nap during the day, Lieutenant. It's only us damn fool Americans who are taking this war so seriously."

Sergeant Montague paused to reflect.

"We was just advisin' these people the first time I was here. Second time I was here we was doing full-scale operations to help them out. Now we are fighting the whole goddamn war for the South Vietnamese. We're taking over their Army…god damn American generals and those CIA pukes intimidate the Vietnamese generals so that they don't do nothing anymore. Can't blame 'em. We got all the damn Americans out in the field doing the dirty work and the damn Vietnamese back in base camp dressed up in tiger fatigues posing for the New York Times. No wonder the folks back home getting upset with this war. We ain't lettin' the Vietnamese do shit."

"Ya, it's getting to be a touchy subject back home," Ruland commented, allowing Sergeant Montague time to catch his breath and take a drink of beer.

"God damn Viet Cong got us just where they want us. They know Americans try to do everything too fast. All Charlie got to do is take a few shots at us once or twice a day and a whole bunch of Pentagon assholes get nervous and send out two or three battalions of draftees to chase Charlie down. Then it becomes a two-week operation after a four-man squad of VC. The draftees get pissed off and write their mothers 'cause they're tired of C-rations and leeches in their shorts. And the draftees can't find nothing 'cause they weren't trained for this type of shit so the staff officers back in base camp keep them out another week or two, just long enough for these kids to get tired and careless, and a few of them manage to blow their legs off stepping on a land mine."

Sergeant Montague stopped and looked down, briefly remembering the scene he had just described. He shook his head to clear the memory, then continued.

"Then the Pentagon pukes tell the public information officer assholes to make a big deal out of the whole operation, so they give it a name like PASSIVE THUNDER or FREQUENT DOUCHEBAG or something stupid like that and all of a sudden you got fifteen reporters and cameras following this whole mess around."

Sergeant Montague paused for another drink of beer. He was working up a sweat preaching about his favorite subject. Ruland knew Sergeant Montague was on a roll so he didn't interrupt.

"Then," Sergeant Montague continued, "these asshole reporters find some draftees smoking pot and lying about how they frag officers. And they get a nice messy picture of some All-American, blue-eyed, white farm boy from Indiana or Kansas with a leg blown off cause he got too tired and decided to walk on the trail instead of beside it. Meanwhile, ol' Charlie's sittin' back in his hooch laughing at us and watching the TV he bought from the PX with the money he got by selling dope to those same draftees we send out in the field. I'm telling you, Lieutenant, this war's getting all fucked up. We got so many goddamned people running it and trying to do things that nobody knows who's in charge. This is my last tour, Lieutenant. Too many unprofessional people involved in this war. It used to be fun."

Sergeant Montague took a sip of beer and closed his eyes to think about what he last said. He smiled to himself as the cool liquid slowly slid down his throat.

"How would you run this war, Sergeant Montague?" Ruland asked, then realized he would probably set Sergeant Montague off again.

"I don't know for sure, but I know what I wouldn't do, Lieutenant. I wouldn't send no draftees over here. No offense, Lieutenant, but you and the other draftees don't want to be here, your momma don't want you to be here, your girl don't want you to be here, and your friends who were smart enough to get out of the draft think you're stupid for gettin' drafted in the first place and comin' here. I'd make it like the old days with the advisors just advisin', and lettin' the Vietnamese do the fighting. We could send over a couple of Ranger battalions made up of lifers to clean up the rough spots. And I'd let 'em do what they's trained to do. And, there would be no communication lines to Washington Dee Cee, that's for damn sure."

Sergeant Montague stopped and shook his head. "As soon as those draftees showed up in-country, I knew we'd had it." He paused again. "And then the experts from the CIA and the Pentagon showed up in force to tell us how to fight. It's all downhill from here, Lieutenant. We're gonna lose this one. I'd bet my ass on it."

Lieutenant Tram smiled and nodded his head. He only knew a few words of English, so he didn't have the slightest idea of what the two Americans were talking about. But he liked Sergeant Montague because he was a good man to have with you in the field, and he offered the best money exchange in the district for military pay currency.

Suddenly the children who had been watching the three men at the table jumped up and ran to the middle of the highway. They looked down the highway in the direction of Camp Evans, then ran to the side of the road and stood, as if they were waiting for a parade. Soon an armored cavalry assault vehicle churned past the children, creating a roostertail of dirt with one track off the shoulder of the blacktop road. The M-113 armored vehicle was followed by second ACAV and an M-48 Patton tank. All the armored vehicles had a red and white cavalry flag on their antennas. A deuce-and-a-half truck followed, leading the convoy of trucks. The convoy of trucks began passing in front of the cafe, all going very fast, and all with apparent disregard for the villagers along the edge of the highway.

American soldiers in the trucks riding shotgun threw chocolate from their C-rations at the children, cheering whenever they hit one. After five of the convoy trucks had passed, the pace slowed down. The vehicles began to spread out in the convoy. Suddenly one of the trucks pulled up in front of the cafe, scattering the children.

A fat American sergeant with short gray hair jumped from the driver's side of the truck and waddled to the cargo area in the rear. The fat sergeant turned and carefully appraised Ruland and Sergeant Montague. The man quickly identified the two Americans as advisors, figured they were harmless, and continued on with his business. He lifted the canvas flap to the cargo section and was handed a case of American beer by two black arms hidden behind the canvas. The pair of arms continued to pass the cases of Budweiser to the fat sergeant until ten cases were stacked neatly by the side of the highway. The sergeant looked around nervously as another truck passed by.

Then, from the dark doorway of the café, a young Eurasian woman appeared and ran past Ruland's table out to the stack of beer. The woman stopped in front of the fat sergeant and handed him a stack of American military pay currency, then yelled to the children in Vietnamese. The children quickly picked up the cases of beer and carried them under the awning and stacked them beside the red Coca-Cola cooler. The tallest of the children covered the beer cases with a green tarp.

When the children finished their work, the young woman gave the tallest boy some of the MPC. The boy ran down the street with his helpers following and yelling for their share of the wages. The fat sergeant jumped back in the truck and it rejoined the line of vehicles. A final armored assault vehicle signaled the end of the convoy.

The young woman watched the convoy speed off out of town, then walked back toward the door of the cafe with her head held high in the air. When she was beside Ruland's table, she stopped suddenly bowed formally in front of Ruland. She spoke with her head still bowed.

"Chao, Trung-uy. Trung-uy manh khong?"

The young woman raised her head slowly and looked Ruland squarely in the eyes. She had the classic beauty of the mix of East and

West. Ruland was startled, and immediately entranced with the young woman's intense eyes.

"Uh…Good Morning," Ruland said as he stood up and knocked his beer over. Then he turned to Sergeant Montague. "What's she doing here?"

"She lives here, Lieutenant," Sergeant Montague said, obviously enjoying this. "She's half-Vietnamese and half-French. Remember our waitress here and that French officer I told you about. This here's their daughter."

The beautiful young Eurasian continued to stare at Ruland and did not speak. She seemed to be asking Ruland the same question in her eyes: "What was he doing here?"

The woman was taller than her mother and the rest of the women in the village. Her high cheekbones and long black hair framed her green eyes. She was the most beautiful woman Ruland had ever seen. Ruland was obviously flustered and didn't know what to do. He bowed to the young woman and managed to mumble the few words he learned at the Advisor's School in Saigon.

"Toi la nguoi My…co-van!" Ruland shouted. Then he followed with the translation, slower and much louder than necessary. "I…am…American…advisor!"

In a flash, the oriental beauty of the young woman's eyes dissolved into the smile of a French schoolgirl. She cupped her hands over her mouth and started to giggle. Then she leaned forward and grabbed Ruland's hand and started shaking it.

"You hear that, Sergeant Montague," she shouted. "He co-van My. I…American…advisor!" The young woman began to giggle again so she covered her mouth with her hands again. "You OK, Lieutenant Ruland. You number one GI."

The young woman dropped her hands and ran over to the cooler and got another chunk of ice and a bottle of Vietnamese beer. She ran back to the table, wiped the sawdust off the ice, dropped the ice in Ruland's glass, and set the beer in front of Ruland.

"Here you go, Lieutenant David Ruland. Welcome to Phong Dien. My name is Thuy Van. This is my café. You come drink beer here anytime. I give you good deal. You protect Phong Dien, right? Like last night when you make fireworks and sleep down by river."

The young woman laughed again and looked at Sergeant Montague. He was laughing so hard he had tears in his eyes. Ruland was embarrassed so he turned to Sergeant Montague.

"What the hell's so funny, Sergeant?"

Sergeant Montague managed to catch his breath. "She didn't think you was no Viet Cong advisor, Lieutenant. She figured out real early you was an American advisor. Hell, she knows who you are, where you're from, and probably the size of your scivvy shorts. Christ, Lieutenant, Thuy Van knows everything that goes on in this district."

"I sorry, Trung-uy," Thuy Van said, realizing she had embarrassed Ruland. "No be mad at me. I just make fun. We will be friends."

Ruland didn't notice the jeep that suddenly pulled in front of the café. Three Korean soldiers sat stiffly in the jeep and looked straight ahead.

"You sit down, Trung-uy," Thuy Van said, nodding to the Korean soldiers. I give you free beer."

"OK." Ruland said, feeling a little foolish. "As long as it's one of those American beers, it's a deal."

Thuy Van walked quickly to the Korean solders' jeep and smiled back at Ruland. She took a handful of MPC from one of the Korean soldiers. The children suddenly appeared again out of the shadows and shuffled the ten cases of Budweiser that had just been delivered to the edge of the road and loaded them into the back of the Koreans' jeep. Thuy Van turned and yelled back at Ruland as she counted the money.

"No can do, Trung-uy. American beer already sold to Korean sergeant. Now he drive up Highway One and sell to American Marines at

Quang Tri. Marines get American beer. Koreans make money. I make money. Everybody happy."

"But that's where the beer was going anyway, up to the Marines at Quang Tri," Ruland yelled back at Thuy Van.

"That's right, Trung-uy. But I am what you call...middleman. Good business, huh, Ruland."

"I guess so, Thuy Van," Ruland said as he smiled at the mysterious young woman.

Thuy Van turned her head when she heard Ruland say her name. She looked at Ruland again squarely in the eyes. Her smile slowly faded as her mood moved from the openness of the West to the closely held thoughts of the East. She studied the young American officer carefully. Ruland was obviously affected and had to look away from the young Eurasian's intense green eyes.

She turned again quickly to the business at hand and shook the hand of the Korean sergeant. The jeep spun its wheels on the gravel and squealed its tires when it reached the blacktop. Thuy Van walked quickly past the tables counting her money. She disappeared into the dark doorway without looking at Ruland.

Ruland and Sergeant Montague remained at Thuy Van's café to finish their beer. Ruland didn't want to appear too eager to know more about the young woman, so he asked Sergeant Montague some questions about her only in passing conversation. Sergeant Montague knew that Ruland was interested in Thuy Van but he also knew it was hard for an officer to confide with an enlisted man in this type of thing, so after he fended off a few questions. Ruland stopped asking them. When the men finished their beer around mid-morning, they returned to the compound in silence.

Sergeant Montague stopped at the compound just long enough to shower and change clothes before going on to Camp Evans for a poker game. Ruland took a shower and laid down in his bunk for a short nap. He slept most of the day.

Ruland was awakened by Sergeant Scroop around five o'clock. Sergeant Scroop was banging on his wall locker trying to get the door to close. Sergeant Scroop apologized, and offered to make up for it by giving Ruland one of his prized meals of hot dogs and beans for dinner. Sergeant Scroop sat quietly nodding his head while Ruland ate the cold hot dogs and beans. When Ruland finished the can, he thanked Sergeant Scroop and got dressed. The cleaning mama-san had washed and pressed Ruland's fatigues while he slept.

Ruland got a couple of beers from the plywood building and went out to the sandbag wall. He sat on the wall, watched the people move back and forth on Highway One, and listened to the sounds of Vietnamese music coming from the radios of the Ruff Puffs on guard duty as it slowly got dark.

Around ten o'clock Major Vien made his inspection rounds and told the guards to turn their radios off. When Major Vien returned to the yellow building all the radios were turned on again. Ruland sat on the wall in the dark a little while longer, listening to the melancholy Vietnamese music. When all movement stopped on Highway One, he returned to the MAT Team's room and read a ragged issue of Playboy until midnight.

October 11, 1968

The next day Ruland stayed in his bunk until the other MAT Team members had dressed and left. He got up once early in the morning to put a towel on the bunk to absorb the perspiration. He stayed in bed and thought about Thuy Van, then decided to walk down to the village after he got something to eat. But before he could get out of bed, Lieutenant Blossom returned to the room to tell him that Major Hannah had called all the American advisors to the mess hall for some sort of meeting.

Ruland got dressed and found a can of C-ration pound cake and went around the back of the yellow building to the mess hall. He entered the plywood building, poured a cup of coffee, and sat down in a folding chair in front of the long table.

Lieutenant Fujita, Sergeant Montague, Sergeant Scroop, Major Vien, and Sergeant Tin were already lined up in chairs facing the long table as if in a classroom waiting for the teacher. The table had the green Army blanket draped over it so Ruland figured the meeting must be important. Captain Moss was sitting on the Coca-Cola cooler. Major Hannah was standing behind the table trying to light his cigar. To Major Hannah's right was a civilian named Mr. Dryman.

Mr. Dryman was dressed in a blue, buttoned down Oxford shirt and a pair of double-knit black pants. He had a silver revolver in a black side-holster on his right hip, which he tapped impatiently waiting for the meeting to begin. Sitting at the end of the table was another civilian named Mr. Priorto. His uniform differed from Mr. Dryman's only by the ornately embroidered Philippine shirt he was wearing. Both men had short hair. Ruland knew they were government employees from the Pentagon. Taped on the wall in back of Mr. Dryman was a map of the district. The map was covered with different colored dots.

Ruland took one of the folding chairs that was leaning against the wall and placed it next to the Coca-Cola cooler. Captain Moss got off the cooler when Ruland sat down and walked to the other side of the room, squatted Vietnamese-style on the floor, and stared at Ruland. Lieutenant Blossom entered the room half-awake, scratching his stomach. He took Captain Moss' place on the cooler.

Major Hannah stood up to officially start the meeting. He took a drag on his cigar and discovered it wasn't lit. Everyone in the room watched as he took out his Zippo and lit the cigar.

"I guess that's everyone, isn't it, Fujita? I called you here because Captain Moss wanted everyone present so Mr. Dryman here can explain some new Intel system or something. Mr. Dryman is from CORDS." Major Hannah paused and thought a second. "I forgot what the hell that is."

"Civil Operations and Revolutionary Development Support, Major," Mr. Priorto interjected. "We're from Plans and Programs division."

"OK, Plans and Programs," Major Hannah corrected himself. He then noticed Ruland leaning back in his chair while he opened his can of pound cake.

"Lieutenant Ruland, you're new in this part of the country so it might behoove you to pay attention."

"It might save your life in combat someday," Ruland muttered the favorite phrase of drill instructors under his breath.

"What was that?" Major Hannah asked.

"I said I got all day, sir," Ruland answered.

"All right, Mr. Dryman…" Major Hannah continued, "it's all yours. But don't take all day and night. Remember we got the World Series on Armed Forces Radio sometime tonight. What time is that game, Fujita?"

"I think it'll be on around 0200 in the morning."

"Is that live or delayed?"

"It'll be a live broadcast from St Louis, sir."

"We'd appreciate it you would finish before the game, Mr. Dryman."

Major Hannah laughed at his attempt at humor and Lieutenant Fujita followed suit.

"No problemo, Major," Mr. Dryman said without smiling. "It doesn't take that long to explain something that I think you all will be very excited about."

Mr. Dryman rose from his chair slowly and looked around the room, stopping briefly to stare at each man's face. He looked carefully at Ruland struggling to open his can of pound cake with his P-38 can opener. Dryman was well aware that most junior officers knew little about Washington and the Pentagon and its self-proclaimed importance, so he waited until Ruland looked up before beginning.

"Thank you, Major Hannah," Mr. Dryman continued. "Before I get into this, I'd like to take just a minute and thank you folks for the great job you're doing over here. Folks back at the Pentagon, especially in OPS-67 Delta, would give their eye teeth to be over here full-time, and right smack-dab in the middle. Yessir, I can speak for Mr. Priorto when I say that, can't I, Vern!"

"You sure can, Darrell," Mr. Priorto said and started to stand up until he realized Mr. Dryman was going to continue his speech.

Ruland leaned toward Lieutenant Blossom and whispered, "I sure hope they appreciate what we're doing. They'd be out of a job if we weren't here."

Lieutenant Blossom laughed at Ruland's comment. Captain Moss remained expressionless, squinted his eyes, and nodded his head toward Ruland. Major Hannah got up from his seat behind the long table and moved to the red Coca-Cola cooler, shoved Lieutenant Blossom off, reached in and got a coke and opened it. As soon as he opened it, Sergeant Montague went to the cooler and got a beer. Lieutenant

Blossom and Sergeant Scroop followed them. Mr. Dryman clenched his teeth and waited for the procession to stop before he would speak.

Major Hannah broke the silence. "Go ahead, Dryman, we're listening."

"Gents," Mr. Dryman began his briefing through clenched teeth. "I'd like to take just a minute of your time to talk a little about HES, the Hamlet Evaluation System."

All the men in the room with drinks in their hands took a long swig in unison and led out a deep breath. Most of them had seen many of these new programs out of the Pentagon, so they settled in for another presentation. Vietnam was a great testing place for bad ideas.

"As I was saying, gents," Mr. Dryman went on, disappointed at the obvious lack of enthusiasm for his announcement, "HES is something we are very excited about, and your district is one of the first to receive the system. First, a little background. Those of us at CORDs, and to some extent the folks at MACV G-2, and their counterparts in the CIA involved with the Phoenix Program felt we weren't getting a leg up on this problem of how to determine if a village is friendly or enemy. So the Assistant Deputy Secretary of the Army tasked a major think tank, who just between us works for the CIA, to come up with a system we could promulgate to you folks in the field to make your job just a little bit easier."

Major Hannah took another drink of his coke and belched.

"You'd make our job a damn site easier, Dryman, if you'd just get to the fucking point," Major Hannah said through exhaled gases.

"What these contractor folks have done, Major," Mr. Priorto interrupted, "is to develop an accountability program which will be used in your district. It has a lot of people in some pretty high-up places excited and watching. Isn't that right, Darrell?"

"That's right, Vern. The Hamlet Evaluation System, or HES, is a computer-based monthly report that places the hamlets in your district on a scale. The scale will tell you gents if the inhabitants of that particular hamlet are friendly to Saigon and her allies."

Mr. Dryman smiled and waited for a response. The room was silent.

"What did this little project cost the taxpayers," Sergeant Montague asked, always concerned about money.

"I'm afraid that's classified and doesn't really concern you, Sergeant," Mr. Dryman said quickly, and continued on. "What the research folks have done, gents, is taken the record of anti-American, slash, anti-Saigon incidents in each hamlet in this district since 1965, and run that data through the computer."

Mr. Dryman motioned to Mr. Priorto, who jumped to his feet and took a large poster board out of a vinyl carrying case and placed the board on the table so everyone in the room could see it.

Mr. Dryman went on. "The contractor has come up with this matrix of six distinct categories of hamlets."

Mr. Dryman leaned over the table and spoke in a low voice. "Let me remind you that what you are seeing is classified, so let's keep it within these four walls."

Mr. Priorto looked at the poster board, turned it right side up, and smiled. The board was an elaborate graph with HES spelled across the top in large letters, and CORDS printed in even larger letters across the bottom. There were six lines on the graph, each line a different color.

"What do you think of that, gents?" Mr. Dryman asked the group.

Major Hannah finished his coke with one long drink, belched, and smashed the can with one hand on top of the table. He leaned forward in his chair and studied the graph for a few seconds and nodded his head.

"What the fuck's it mean, Dryman."

"It means, Major," Mr. Dryman said, a little irritated at the Major's lack of interest, "is that the bottom line is now clear."

He pulled a collapsible pointer out of this pocket and extended it, nearly poking Mr. Priorto in the eye.

"The three major categories are as follows: Level A- A hamlet where there is adequate security and the Viet Cong Infrastructure has been eliminated, i.e., a place where an American can traverse, day or night, without any danger to his person. Level C is a hamlet that is subject to infrequent Viet Cong harassment and the Viet Cong Infrastructure is identified but still operating, i.e., a place where an American can only traverse in the daytime without danger to his person. Level VC is the last category. It is a hamlet that is under communist control, in other words, a place where an American can traverse day or night, with a high probability of being wounded. Levels B, D, and E fall into place as separate levels of security. As you can see, gents, we have color-coded the system for ease of understanding. We have your basic green, yellow, and red for the three major levels I just defined."

Mr. Dryman slapped the poster board with his collapsible pointer, striking Mr. Priorto's finger.

"Green for go; red for no-go; yellow for take your chances," Mr. Dryman concluded proudly.

Ruland finished off his last bite of pound cake and washed it down with a drink of beer.

"What's the difference between a hamlet where you could get killed and a hamlet where you could get wounded?"

"It's a statistical thing, Lieutenant. I don't have time to go into it right now." Mr. Dryman started to tap his collapsible pointer on the poster board. He noticed Ruland was smiling.

"You see, the computer folks at CORDS analyzed these villages in your district and came up with a matrix that's been approved by a lot of high-ranking folks at DOD. The Pentagon doesn't give out these three million dollar contracts to just anybody, Lieutenant."

Ruland was still smiling. It annoyed Mr. Dryman, and he began to swat the poster board with the pointer, nearly knocking it out of the hands of Mr. Priorto.

"It's based on historical data and probability, Lieutenant. We know that the friendlies have gone into some hamlets and have been killed, and the same friendlies have gone into other hamlets of the same demographics and psychographics and only been wounded. All this is extremely important information to movers and shakers of this war back in the Pentagon."

Ruland looked over at Lieutenant Blossom, who had his mouth open while reading his beer can.

"HES is your best friend, Lieutenant," Mr. Dryman wouldn't let up. "It can tell you what your chances are of getting killed or wounded. I would think that would be pretty important to you."

Mr. Dryman smacked his pointer again on the poster board, this time knocking it out of Mr. Priorto's hands.

"The trouble with you young officers today is that you don't appreciate what the Department of Defense is doing for you. We're giving you the knowledge that when you enter a hamlet you'll know if you're going to get killed or wounded. Hell, I never had that back in Korea. You don't know how lucky you got it, Lieutenant."

"If you can't see it, Lieutenant," Mr. Priorto added, "then I suggest you'd better do a little homework."

Ruland wiped off the top of his beer can with his sleeve. "If your computer says I stand a good chance of getting killed or even wounded in some hamlet, why should I go in there in the first place?"

Mr. Dryman and Mr. Priorto stood in amazement. Mr. Dryman sat down at the table and looked at Major Hannah. "You see what we're up against, Major? We're trying to make this a winnable war and nobody cares."

"Right…Right…" Major Hannah said, realizing he had been spoken to. "What about this village outside the compound, Dryman, how do you classify it?"

Mr. Priorto quickly scanned a computer printout, pulled out his own collapsible pointer, and indicated a color on the graph.

"It's graded C…safe at day, unsafe at night."

"What about at night," Lieutenant Blossom came to and asked. "Am I going to get killed, wounded, or maybe just get laid?"

Mr. Dryman stood up suddenly, ignoring the question that was vitally important to Lieutenant Blossom and his nighttime activity.

"Major Hannah," Mr. Dryman said quietly, "I've got some higher level information I'd like to cover with you and Captain Moss now, if you don't mind?"

Major Hannah belched and shrugged his shoulders. Knowing that was their cue to exit, Ruland and the rest of the men left the mess hall without a word.

Ruland walked back around the yellow building toward Highway One. He passed by the generator shack that supplied the power to the yellow building. Two Ruff-puffs were trying to start the generator with a crank. It took the strength of both men to turn the engine over.

He continued on past the barbed wire gate and out onto the highway. Ruland looked into the village past the stream of people going to the public well for their day's supply of water. Ruland turned and walked down the road, away from the village and toward the flat sandy area to the south of the compound. The sun hadn't begun to bake the white sand so it was still fairly cool. Ruland had seen this flat area when he flew in on the helo three days earlier. The spot was nice and level and was close to the compound. It was a perfect place to build the rifle range. Ruland walked out on the sand and began to pace off the boundaries of a rifle range. The villagers on the highway laughed at the American marching across the barren field.

At the corners of the would-be rifle range, Ruland stopped and formed a small pile of sand with his hands. He outlined an area of fifty paces by one hundred and fifty paces. The short distance would be the firing line. There was room in the rectangle for targets at twenty-five, fifty, and a hundred meters he figured. Since the M-16s were only good up to about fifty yards, the rectangle would be adequate for the Ruff Puffs to train and qualify on their new rifles.

When Ruland stood on the imaginary firing line and looked down the range he discovered his first problem. Beyond the target area to the northeast, farmers were working in their rice paddies. Ruland looked in the other three directions. The compound was to his left, Highway One was behind him, and a few displaced squatters lived in shacks off to his right, toward Camp Evans. Ruland decided the only solution was to build a pile of sand, or some sort of berm, along the boundary of the range to protect the farmers in the rice paddies. He didn't have any idea on how he would do this, but he wasn't worried. He figured he had done enough work for the day and that he would think about it later. The sun was almost overhead now and it was getting hot on the white sand.

Ruland walked back to the compound, got some beer out of the cooler, and went back to the entrance to the compound and jumped up on the sandbag wall. He sat on one of the sandbags used as a stool by the Ruff Puffs. He opened one of the beers and took his portable radio out of his pocket and placed it beside him.

The villagers passed by on the highway. Ruland was looking toward the village, and was surprised when Thuy Van rode by on her bicycle from the direction of Camp Evans. She pretended not to notice Ruland, then suddenly she turned her head and smiled at him. Ruland smiled and waved.

"Hey," Ruland yelled. "Where are you going?"

Thuy Van turned her bicycle around in the highway and stopped, facing Ruland.

"What you mean, 'Where you going?'" Thuy Van shouted back.

Ruland slid off the top of the sandbag wall onto Highway One and walked toward her. A few of the Ruff Puffs on guard at the other end of the wall noticed Ruland moving toward the young woman and began to talk to each other and quietly laugh. The soldiers didn't know Ruland very well and didn't want to embarrass him. But when Ruland reached Thuy Van and put his hands on the handlebars of her bicycle, one of the soldiers whistled at the couple. Thuy Van stuck her chin out, flashed a menacing glance at her countryman, and then smiled sweetly at Ruland.

"What I meant was," Ruland said, "if you're going back to your cafe, I'd like to join you."

Thuy Van's eyes opened wide in mock disbelief. "You mean you want date with me?"

"Well, not exactly. I thought maybe we could sit at one of your tables and you could tell me a little about the village."

Thuy Van squinted at Ruland suspiciously. "Why you want to talk about the village, Ruland?"

"It doesn't have to be about the village, I just thought we could talk a while."

"Why?"

Ruland didn't like to be put on the spot. He was getting to feel a little uncomfortable. "Just so I can get to know you, I suppose."

"Why?"

"I just want to talk with you."

"Then you want a date?" Thuy Van said with a laugh.

"All right then, how about a date?"

Thuy Van's green eyes sparkled. "Sorry, Ruland. Too busy. Some other time maybe. See you later, Ruland."

The young woman pulled the handlebars of her bicycle out of Ruland's hands and turned up the road toward the village. She smiled at Ruland and began to ride away, down the middle of the highway without looking back. Ruland followed her with his eyes.

Thuy Van had the pant legs of her black silk pajamas pulled up so they wouldn't get caught in the bicycle chain. Her legs were straight and strong, not like the slightly bowed legs of the other Vietnamese girls. Ruland watched her disappear into the village. He walked back to the sandbag wall and climbed on top. He took his portable radio out of his pocket and tuned in the Armed Forces Radio station. The music was just ending.

"Don't you forget now, tonight is the seventh and final game of the 1968 World Series. We got the St. Louis Cardinals and the Dee-troit

Tigers going at it. For those of you who can hang in there, Armed Forces Radio will bring the game to you live. That's right, I said live, at 0300 tomorrow morning. That's three o'clock in the morning for all you Air Force types. In the meantime, let's have a few more heavy sounds from the vacationland of the Orient. This is Armed Forces Radio…Vee-et-nam."

Ruland quickly switched to a Vietnamese station. He liked the singsong voices of the women singers. It was perfect background music for the procession of villagers passing in front of him on Highway One. The people would soon become a blur of color as Ruland stared straight ahead. He caught himself falling into a trance and shook his head. He pulled a paperback out of his pocket and tried to read, but couldn't concentrate, fascinated by the people passing in front of him. They always seemed to be in a hurry, but nobody appeared to be going anywhere. A constant parade of simple people without any purpose, he thought, except to move through another day. But then, Ruland thought to himself, maybe that was their purpose.

Ruland spent another hour on the wall before he noticed Sergeant Scroop conducting a class in the shade of the yellow building, so he walked over to see what was going on. It was a class on how to clean an M-1 rifle. Sergeant Scroop spoke Surfer English, so most of the time was spent with Sergeant Scroop repeating and explaining his words to Sergeant Tin so he could interpret for the Ruff Puffs. The soldiers couldn't understand why Sergeant Scroop said, "You know" after every sentence, and would all repeat "We know" in unison every time he said it. Since Ruland was the officer-in-charge of the MAT Team, he figured he had some obligation to observe the training session. But his mind kept drifting back to Thuy Van.

After the class, Ruland ate dinner in the mess hall with the rest of the American advisors. Sergeant Montague was missing, but according to Lieutenant Blossom, he seldom ate with the rest of the advisors. Sergeant Montague liked to eat with the other non-commissioned officers at

Camp Evans to get the latest information on the hottest poker games. It was quiet during the meal with the exception of an occasional belch from Major Hannah.

When he finished eating, Ruland went to the MAT Team's room. He set his alarm clock for two in the morning, deciding to get some sleep and get up for the World Series. After a couple of hours staring at the bottom of the top bunk, Ruland went back to the mess hall and collected an armful of beer and walked out to the sandbag wall. It was nearing sunset and the generator was running. The lights in the yellow building and Major Hannah's hooch were flickering behind the dark towels pulled over the windows for security.

Highway One ran north and south through Phong Dien. Ruland wanted to see the sunset over the mountains to the west. As the day came to an end, the flow of people on the highway turned into a trickle. Many young men left the village just before dark. Ruland figured they must have been going to join their Viet Cong units for night operations and take a shot at the bridge or Camp Evans. Ruland waved as they walked out of town and the young men waved back and smiled.

Ruland tuned his radio again to a Vietnamese station and sipped on his beer. Ruland decided to stay awake to listen to the World Series. He carefully plotted out his consumption of beer, not wanting to drink too much and miss the game.

The night passed pleasantly. Ruland sipped beer and was joined occasionally by Popular Forces soldiers, eager for a free beer. The Ruff Puff soldiers asked Ruland questions about the United States in broken English and Ruland patiently answered them. Between visitors Ruland listened to the Vietnamese music and watched an occasional fireball from a B-52 strike roll across the horizon to the west.

Ruland did pretty well spreading out his beer consumption until the baseball game started early in the morning. But he continued to drink during the game. By the middle of the ninth inning Ruland was drunk. His empty beer cans were stacked neatly in a pyramid beside him.

Ruland slowly got on his feet to stretch out. He hadn't stood up in a while so he didn't really know how drunk he was. He held a cigarette with one hand and can of beer in the other, weaving slightly as he maintained his balance. The Ruff Puffs on guard duty laughed and pointed at the American advisor.

His legs started to wobble so he sat down again on the sandbag just in time to hear the announcer say: "That's it folks. The Detroit Tigers have beaten the St. Louis Cardinals four to one in the 1968 World Series. Mickey Lolich held in there to defeat Bob Gibson for the win in one of the most exciting finishes in World Series history.

"Shit," Ruland said to himself. "I missed it."

Suddenly, off in the distance above Camp Evans, Ruland saw some signal flares rocket into the air. He figured some Tiger fans at Camp Evans were celebrating.

"We better acknowledge the victory," Ruland slobbered as he struggled to get up.

Ruland jumped off the sandbag wall and fell to the ground when he landed, forgetting how much beer he had consumed. He was a lot drunker than he thought. He ran over to the yellow building and disappeared inside. Within a minute Ruland burst out of the door with his hands full of signal flares. He ran as best he could back to the wall and tossed the signal flares on top of the sandbags, then ran back to the mess hall and returned with an armload of beer. He dropped the beer once and fell down when he tried to pick it up. Ruland made it back to the wall and threw most of the beer on top of it next to the signal flares. One of the cans of beer went over the top and rolled unto the highway. Struggling to get back on top of the wall, he fell back once, much to the delight of the Ruff Puffs on guard.

After he finally made it back on top of the wall, Ruland grabbed one of the cans of beer, opened it, took a drink, belched, then carefully set the can down so it wouldn't tip over, but it did anyway. Then he took a flare, removed the cap that contained the firing pin, placed it over the opposite end of the flare, and fired it by slamming it down on the sandbag.

It shot off in the air and lit up across the highway on the other side of the helo pad. The soldiers on guard began to appear from their positions along the wall. They laughed at Ruland and gathered around him. Playing to the audience, Ruland fired the flares two at a time, one in each hand. Each time Ruland set off the flares, the soldiers laughed and cheered. When he got down to the last four flares, Ruland took two in each hand and prepared them for firing. The soldiers stopped laughing and waited to see what the co-van would do. Ruland stood up on the wall to address the troops.

"It's the big finale, fellow freedom fighters," Ruland slurred to the soldiers. I send this glorious burst out in honor of the Detroit Tigers in their moment of celebration."

Ruland slammed the flares down on the wall with both hands and they shot off into the air. Three of the flares made graceful arcs above the highway. However one of the flares traveled about ten feet off the ground and landed on the thatched roof of one of the hooches across the highway. The roof burst into flames. A man and woman ran out of their home and began to beat on the roof with brooms. Their brooms quickly caught on fire and became torches. When the couple swung their brooms back, they set the roofs of their neighbors' hooches on fire. Within moments four of the hooches were on fire.

The Ruff Puffs on guard were all on the wall laughing. Ruland sat down cross-legged on the sandbags and looked at the soldiers and then at the burning home of their neighbors.

Then without anyone noticing, a man known in the village as Nguyen O'Bannon suddenly appeared from behind one of the burning hooches with a Chinese rocket launcher. He bent down on one knee and fired at the compound. The rocket passed just over Ruland's shoulder as he leaned over for his can of beer. The rocket hit the generator and exploded, igniting the gas cans beside the machine. Nguyen O'Bannon smiled and disappeared back into the dark.

Major Hannah appeared from the back of the yellow building wearing a pair of polka dot boxer shorts. His mouth dropped when he saw the burning generator.

"Bucket brigade! Form a bucket brigade!" Major Hannah screamed as Lieutenant Fujita joined him, wearing a light blue bathrobe.

The Ruff Puffs watching the burning generator didn't move.

"Di-di moi you fucking slopeheads before the fucking compound burns down!"

The Vietnamese solders casually walked up to the fire and stood around it. One of the men attempted to touch Major Hannah's face, amazed as it slowly turned bright red.

"A bucket brigade, god damn it you fucking slant-eyed gooks!" Major screamed, his voice cracking.

Lieutenant Fujita repeated the orders from the Major. "Di-di moi you fucking slant-eyed gooks! Form a bucket brigade!"

The Vietnamese soldiers looked at each other in confusion. Major Hannah reached down and scooped up a handful of sand and yelled at the soldiers.

"You sabe, you fucking gooks! Put the god-damn fire out!" Major Hannah screamed as he threw sand on the burning generator.

The soldiers looked at each other and nodded, then laughed and began throwing sand on the fire. One of the soldiers assumed command of the troops, and began yelling orders, mimicking the hysterical American.

"Bucket bligade! Di-di moi, gooks! Beaucoup bucket bligade!"

Ruland sat on the wall, too drunk to move, silhouetted by the flames of the hooches to his rear and the burning generator in front of him. He watched the Vietnamese soldiers and the two American officers fight the fire as the villagers behind him tried to save their homes. Ruland reached into his pocket and took out a cigarette and put it into his mouth and mumbled to himself.

"How about that. The Tigers won the World Series."

October 12, 1968

The charred remains of seven of the villagers' makeshift houses were still smoldering the next morning. Inside the compound, the top of the generator was barely visible under a pile of sand. Ruland was still on the sandbag wall, lying face-up among a pile of empty beer cans and flare casings. He had watched the melee the night before, too drunk to help or get involved. So after things calmed down, Ruland laid back on the sandbags and stared up at the night sky until he fell asleep.

Along Highway One the villagers passed by going to and from the village on their daily activities. Most of them looked up at Ruland and laughed at the sight of an American sleeping off a drunk so late in the morning. Thuy Van heard about the American on the sandbag wall so she got on her bicycle and rode out to the compound. She stopped beside the wall and yelled up at Ruland.

"Hey, Trung-uy! What you doing up there? You dead?"

Ruland began to stir. He raised his head a little, then let it fall back against the sandbag, increasing the pain in the back of his head. He covered his eyes from the sun with his arm, tilted his head up and looked around for the voice calling his name. Thuy Van yelled again.

"What's the matter, Co-van? You drink too much beer? Better you pay money and drink beer at my cafe. That way you no burn down village."

Ruland rolled over and looked down at the young woman, then noticed the smoking remains of the displaced farmers' shacks.

"Christ, I didn't mean to do that. I was just celebrating the World Series."

"No problem, Trung-uy," Thuy Van said. "That number one good deal for farmer. Make wife very happy. Now Americans in Danang come here and give farmer plywood and tin roof for new house. You make family very happy. You big hero in Phong Dien, Ruland. You make seven new houses for my village."

"What are you talking about," Ruland asked.

"Farmer can say Viet Cong attack village and burn house. That way American civilians from Danang come and give material to build new house." Thuy Van laughed. "But last night you only burn three houses. So four other houses burned by owners so they get new house from Americans too."

Ruland tried to laugh, but could only grimace with the pain in his head.

"Thuy Van," he said, rolling over on his elbows and slowly rising, "have you got a nice cold drink for me at your cafe? I could use a little hair off the dog."

Thuy Van looked puzzled. "Sure, Trung-uy," Thuy Van said, curling up the corner of her mouth in amazement. "I give you hair off dog. You come with me."

Ruland slid down off the wall and walked slowly beside Thuy Van as she pushed her bicycle toward the village. Both young people would look over at the other occasionally, quickly studying the other.

Two American MPs returning to Camp Evans from Quang Tri passed Ruland and Thuy Van in a jeep at the edge of the village. The senior MP motioned for the driver to circle back so they could check out the hung-over American and the beautiful Eurasian woman.

"You better not go in that village, Lieutenant," the driver of the jeep said as the jeep rolled to a stop in front of Ruland. "Viet Cong attacked it last night and burned part of it down. It's been reclassified from C to D."

"C to D?" Ruland asked, forgetting about Mr. Dryman's presentation on the new Hamlet Evaluation System.

"Hell, I don't know what that means, Lieutenant. But my Captain told me this morning that this village is now graded D after last night's VC attack, and that it's off limits to Americans night and day.

"It's OK," Ruland answered. "I'm with the Mobile Advisory Team assigned to this district. We're supposed to be in the village. It's our job. We can't advise if we can't go near the people we're supposed to be advising, can we?"

The two MPs looked at each other in confusion, so Ruland turned to the sergeant riding in the jeep who had not spoken.

"Sergeant, you can tell your commanding officer I'm assigned to this village and my job is to get to know the people. Right now this girl's going to take me to a barber shop."

"A barber shop? That don't mean nothing to me, Lieutenant," the sergeant managed to answer through a yawn. "But I wouldn't let no gook shave me…not in no village that just changed from C to D. But that's up to you, Lieutenant."

"I'll take my chances, Sergeant," Ruland replied.

The MP sergeant offered a half-hearted salute and the driver spun the wheels of the jeep in a U-turn as they continued on their trip back to Camp Evans.

"That good idea, Ruland," Thuy Van said. "I fix you up number one. Give you shave just like Chinese barber in Cholon…number one tho cao."

"How much you going to charge me?" Ruland asked.

"No be cheap GI, Ruland," Thuy Van said with a smile. "I give you special deal for making new houses in my village. You number one with farmers. Haircut cost two dollars. American money. No MPC."

Thuy Van handed Ruland the bicycle, then hopped on the handlebars. Ruland carefully straddled the bike. He managed to peddle the bicycle, but was obviously suffering from his hangover. He and Thuy Van wobbled down the main street of the village scattering the children that had gathered to join them.

Just before reaching Thuy Van's café, they passed Captain Moss, Mr. Dryman, and Mr. Priorto in a jeep. They were out surveying the damage done in last night's attack and writing down notes on clipboards. All three men looked at Ruland suspiciously as he managed to wave with one hand as he peddled by.

Thuy Van directed Ruland to go down a narrow alley at the side of her cafe. There was just barely enough room for Ruland and the bicycle between the two stucco buildings. Ruland leaned the bicycle against the rear of the whitewashed building as Thuy Van unlocked the back door with a key she had hanging around her neck on a dog tag chain.

Ruland was amazed at what he saw when he entered the building. The back room was a storeroom filled with PX items and American supplies. There were blankets, blue jeans, radios, field gear, and a variety of medical supplies. Everything was stacked neatly by category an elaborate shelving system like a department store. Most of the equipment was in its original package.

There was also an assortment of weapons and ammunition in the room. She had several old M-1 and M-30 rifles originally issued to the Popular Forces neatly lined up on the bottom shelf of a two-story gun rack. On the top shelf of the gun rack there were three Chinese-made AK-47 rifles. A variety of ammunition boxes of all types of weapons were stacked beside the gun rack. Hanging above the door to the supply room, as if on display, was a Soviet RPG-7 rocket launcher.

"You got any rockets for that thing," Ruland asked as he pointed to the rocket launcher.

"Sure do, Ruland," Thuy Van said. "It's no good without rockets."

"That's not the rocket launcher that takes a pot shot at the bridge every night, is it?"

"Don't know what you talking about, Ruland," Thuy Van said as she tidied up a shelf of C-rations.

The young woman then turned and laughed at Ruland's amazement. She motioned for Ruland to follow her, and smiled as she led him through her warehouse and into the main living room of the building. The room was light and clean with a dark brown tile floor. In the center of the room was a low rosewood table that reflected the light of narrow horizontal windows near the ceiling that created a constant cool breeze through the room. An elaborate fan hung from the center of the ceiling, waiting for electricity to return to the village.

"You wait here, Ruland," Thuy Van said as she put her hands on Ruland's shoulders and pushed him down to the floor. "I be right back." She disappeared into her warehouse.

Ruland sat cross-legged on the floor in the middle of the room on a straw mat. He could hear Thuy Van talking with another person. She returned with a new pair of Levi's, a knit polo shirt, and a pair of tennis shoes, all in original packaging with the price tags from the PX still on them. Thuy Van's mother followed behind her with a large bowl of warm water, a wash cloth and a towel.

"Here you go Ruland," Thuy Van said as she directed her mother to put the bowl of water in front of Ruland. "You wash and put on American clothes and I come back for shave and haircut. You wash now. I no watch you."

Thuy Van and her mother laughed and left the room. Ruland sat for a second, staring at the civilian clothes. They were just what he would wear back home. He hadn't worn any civvies in six months since his R an R in Hong Kong. He wrung out the washcloth in the warm water and pressed it against his forehead for a moment. The warmth of the cloth made him feel better already. Then he stripped down and washed. There was even a new pair of jungle green Jockey shorts for him. Ruland put the Levi's on and sat back down on the floor cross-legged.

Thuy Van immediately returned with a tray of shaving gear, a bowl of hot water and a can of cold Budweiser.

"How'd you know I was ready?" Ruland asked.

"Mama-san watch you. Then she tell me. I no watch you. I keep promise."

Ruland took a sip of beer to keep from blushing. Thuy Van saw this and laughed as she wrapped a sheet around Ruland's shoulders. She started to hum while she brushed the warm lather on his face.

"How long you been in Vietnam, Ruland?"

"Almost a year," he said. "I only got a couple of weeks to go."

Thuy Van was startled. She stopped and faced Ruland. "Couple weeks? Then you go back United States already? You short-timer, Ruland."

"That's right," Ruland answered.

"You go United States and never come back Vietnam?"

"No, probably not, not unless I stay in the Army. And I'm not planning on doing that."

"How about you, Thuy Van?" Ruland wanted to change the subject and know more about the woman about to shave him. "How did you learn to speak English so well living in this little village?"

"I no live in this village long time. I just come here last year. I live in Hue with uncle and go to Catholic school. I learn English and Francais in school. Then my uncle say it too dangerous to live in Hue, so last Christmas he send me back to Mama-san in this village. My uncle send me here before big battle during Tet. My uncle very smart. He know when battle begin so he send me here so I am safe. My uncle number one Viet Cong in Hue. So he know when it time for me to come to village. Now uncle hide in country after big battle."

"You know were he is?" Ruland asked.

Thuy Van looked surprised. "What? You some kinda spy Ruland? No tell you. It your job to find VC. Not my job to tell you."

Ruland was embarrassed that he even asked the question. He didn't care about her uncle's politics, or anyone else's politics in this country, so he changed the subject.

"Is that all your mother's stuff in the back room?" Ruland asked.

Thuy Van laughed and brushed some lather around Ruland's neck.

"No, that "stuff" belong to me. I know Americans at Camp Evans have beaucoup supplies and they like trade for things like souvenirs to take back United States. Since I only one in village who speak good English, I help my friends in village trade things."

"Looks like you do all right for yourself."

"That right." Thuy Van said seriously. "I learn about American free enterprise in Catholic school and university in Hue. I like to make profit."

"You went to the university in Hue?" Ruland asked.

"That right, Ruland. I am college student before Tet."

Ruland was not really surprised at the thought of this bright young woman learning about free enterprise system. He looked at the unopened cellophane package of the knit shirt beside him.

"Who do you sell all that stuff in your warehouse to?"

"I sell anybody who buy," Thuy Van answered, taken back at such a foolish question. "Sometime I sell to American GI when PX run out of things. Sometime I sell to Korean soldier, who then sell back to American GI. Sometime I trade things to people in village for more things to trade to American GI at Camp Evans. Sometime I sell to Viet Cong for American funny money…MPC, you know, Military Pay Currency."

"You sell to Viet Cong?"

"That right," Thuy Van said as she smiled at Ruland. "That free enterprise, right."

"I suppose so," Ruland conceded.

Thuy Van became very quiet as she started to carefully shave Ruland, holding a double-edged razor blade in her hand like all village barbers.

"Where'd you learn to do this?" Ruland asked.

"First time do this. It's OK, I watch barber in village."

Thuy Van shaved carefully Ruland's upper lip and moved down to his throat, and whispered.

"Ruland? How you know I not Viet Cong?

Ruland looked at the beautiful young woman he barely knew out of the corner of his eye and wondered if he had made a mistake being alone with her.

"I...I guess I don't." Ruland said, swallowing slowly.

"I can get beaucoup money from VC if I kill you."

Thuy Van shaved slowly around Ruland's throat and stopped and looked at Ruland seriously. Ruland instinctively looked for his rifle, but remembered he left it back in the compound. Thuy Van put her other hand on Ruland's shoulder.

"Ruland," she said sweetly, "I make deal. You marry me so I can go United States. You no have to stay with me. You take me California and I go away, you know, di-di moi...OK. Ruland?"

Ruland laughed nervously. "Uh...sure...There's a lot of paper-work...But we can do it."

Thuy Van shaved the last strip of lather on Ruland's throat with one final clean swipe, and burst out laughing.

"You crazy, GI. I not go United States with you, Trung-uy. I am Vietnamese. This is my cafe. This is my village now. What you think I am, Ruland, butterfly girl? Marry you just to go United States? You beaucoup crazy? Maybe you think I VC?"

Ruland grabbed his throat and exhaled. "I don't know what you are, but I wish you wouldn't mess around like that. Man, I don't know if you're VC or what?"

"Does it matter?" Thuy Van asked seriously.

Ruland and the young Eurasian both looked at each other a moment, wondering who the other person really was, then Thuy Van began to laugh and shake her head at the strange young American officer. Most of the officers she had done business with were always serious. Thuy Van took a moist towel and wiped the shaving cream from Ruland's face. Then she began to brush his hair gently and started to sing softly in Vietnamese. She backed away suddenly, startled when she realized she was daydreaming.

"You're a good barber," Ruland said, trying to break the mood.

Thuy Van relaxed and smiled, then leaned toward Ruland.

"Trung-uy, what you think it cost to pay American GI to take me back United States?" She asked seriously.

"I don't know, I'm sure there's someone around who would want to for the money."

"How 'bout you, Ruland? We say good-bye in California. I start business in Los Angeles. Beaucoup Vietnamese there. Very easy to find place to stay. No bother you."

"I guess it could be done. Sounds kind of complicated."

Thuy Van took Ruland's hand and leaned closer.

"OK, Ruland, you the one I gonna pay. Now you tell Mama-san we get married and go United States."

Thuy Van motioned toward the doorway with her head. Standing there were her mother and grandmother. The two women were carrying trays of food and beer. Both women were grinning at Ruland. The grandmother's teeth were black. Ruland immediately stood up and blushed.

"Good morning again, Mama-san." he said, with a rough bow to Thuy Van's mother. "And the other lady must be your mama-san, I bet." Ruland bowed in her direction. "Good morning Mama-san's Mama-san."

"Mama-san's mama-san," Thuy Van mimicked. "Where you learn speak Vietnamese so good, Ruland, from butterfly girl?"

Thuy Van laughed and took the towel and wiped off a bit of shaving cream on Ruland's ear. Ruland then put on the knit shirt and Thuy Van adjusted the collar in the back. Her eyes sparkled as she softly touched him. Meanwhile, the women set the food on the low table and took their places around it. Thuy Van motioned for Ruland to sit across from her, between the two older women.

Thuy Van handed Ruland a bowl of phu bo, noodles with some sort of meat in it. The ever-present nuoc mam, Vietnamese fish sauce, was also on the table. Thuy Van offered to pour some nuoc mam on Ruland's noodles, but he declined politely. He hadn't really been exposed to much Vietnamese cooking and wasn't ready for fish sauce yet. The old women began to eat in silence, watching Ruland carefully. They laughed as Ruland fumbled with his chopsticks. He managed to eat a little, but was still hung over, so the food was a little hard to get down. Thuy Van smiled as she watched him. Ruland returned the smile and indicated to the mother that the food was good by patting his stomach.

"Trung-uy," Thuy Van said, breaking the silence. "You like dog?"

"Another beer? You mean hair off the dog?"

"No, I mean you like dog."

"What do you mean 'dog'?" Ruland was puzzled.

"You know, 'dog'. One that go 'bark…bark!' You know, dog. You never eat dog before?"

Ruland looked down at his bowl. "You mean…"

"You say hair of dog make you feel better. So I tell Mama-san you want hair of dog. So…" Thuy Van smiled at Ruland, "Mama-san make you dog and throw away hair."

Ruland struggled to swallow what he was chewing, then took a long drink of beer, swished it around in his mouth and looked for a place to spit it. He had no choice but to swallow. The three women looked at him and smiled. Ruland took another long drink, closed his eyes and smiled.

"It was spotted dog, Ruland," Thuy Van said, not letting up. "They good dog to eat. But not as good as orange dog. Orange dog number one."

"Spotted dog?" Ruland began to laugh. "Old Spot." He looked at the grandmother. "Bark! Bark!"

"Bark! Bark!" The grandmother responded.

Thuy Van laughed and took Ruland's hand. "Come on, Ruland. Let's go for a walk. I show you village."

Thuy Van and Ruland walked through the village staying a respectable distance apart, but brushing each other slightly whenever they walked down a narrow alley, out of sight of the adult villagers. A crowd of children followed the couple, interested in both of the two strangers in their village. Thuy Van asked Ruland a constant stream of questions about his family and growing up in the United States. When Ruland tried to ask about Thuy Van's life before the village, she guarded her answers carefully. She mostly talked about life in the Catholic school, her classes at the university, and her Viet Cong uncle. She never mentioned her French father.

The next couple of hours passed very quickly. Ruland was amazed at the spirit of the villagers in the middle of a war. It was like nothing was going on around them. Most of the people had only known war, so they accepted it as part of their life. They survived as best they could. The hustle of Saigon was missing in the small village, but there was a sincere desire to go on about the business of living. Ruland liked this. He was a Midwesterner and he saw some of the character of his small hometown in Michigan in this village.

Ruland and Thuy Van returned to the café at the hottest part of the day. All the villagers had already retreated to their homes to escape the heat. Only the Americans in Vietnam continued working throughout the day. The streets were deserted except for a few Ruff Puffs on their way to the bridge for daytime guard duty. There were also an equal number of men in black pajamas on the streets, most likely on their way to someone's hooch to plan the night's attack on the bridge. The men would pass in the street and greet each other.

Ruland and Thuy Van sat at a small table in the shade of the awning at her cafe. They waved to the soldiers of both sides going to their duty stations. The usual sounds of the village were gone during this mid-day break. Occasionally they could hear the distant sound of artillery at Camp Evans. It was the H and I fire periodically firing at random spots in the countryside surrounding Camp Evans. After carefully nursing down a beer, Ruland got up enough nerve to move closer to Thuy Van. When he moved his chair in her direction, she got up abruptly and walked toward the door to her home. She reached inside the door and picked up a paper sack containing Ruland's fatigues and jungle boots. The fatigues had been cleaned and neatly pressed by Thuy Van's mother.

"I see you later, Ruland," she said as she handed the sack to Ruland. "I got work to do. I see you maybe tomorrow."

"How much do I owe you?" Ruland asked.

"You don't owe my nothing," Thuy Van quickly answered. "You just remember favor I do for you. You can help me get stuff when 1st Air Cavalry leave Camp Evans. I hear some of the soldiers are already moving out. They leave beaucoup things that I can sell. They just leave it behind and go."

Ruland had heard rumors that the 1st Air Cavalry was going to be replaced by the 101st Airmobile Division at Camp Evans, but he thought it was still classified information. However, he wasn't surprised that Thuy Van knew about the move.

"What are you doing the rest of the day? You got business with the Viet Cong?" Ruland jokingly asked, as he stood up and prepared to leave.

"Maybe," Thuy Van said coyly, then she turned and yelled over her shoulder as she disappeared into the dark door of her house. "See you later, Ruland. Don't forget you owe me favor."

Ruland stood under the awning of the cafe, a bit puzzled at the morning's activity. When he suddenly realized where he was, he took the paper sack in his right hand and walked down the empty street toward the compound. With the village shut down at the hottest part of the day, Highway One seemed very quiet. Most of the villagers were taking naps in their dark, cool houses. The only person left on the street was the local carpenter, Ngyuen O'Bannon, who was late returning from the hills to the west of the village. He had a load of bamboo on his back. He waved and smiled at Ruland as they passed. Ruland was unaware that Ngyuen O'Bannon was the person who fired the rocket into the compound the night before.

Many eyes followed Ruland from behind the shuttered buildings as he walked through the middle of the village down Highway One toward the compound. When he finally realized where he was, perhaps sensing the eyes following him, he began walking a little faster. When Ruland returned to his room he was relieved to see Stanley sleeping in the corner. He had hoped Stanley was not part of his noonday meal.

Ruland figured he should put in some time working on the firing range to keep Major Hannah out of his hair, so he changed into the clean jungle fatigues and spent the afternoon walking around the sandy flats south of the compound. He sketched out some plans for the layout of the range, just to have if Major Hannah asked him for a progress report.

In late afternoon, when it was finally a bit cooler, Ruland decided that a cold beer would taste good. He got a beer from the mess hall and took his position on the sandbag wall around the compound. Once again Ruland was drawn by the parade of people passing by on Highway One. Farmers walked quickly down the highway from a hard day's work in the rice paddies. An occasional village girl would pass by balancing two water pails on a stick balanced on her shoulder. The girls would walk with quick, short steps that kept the heavy water pails level as they hurried home.

Ruland heard some PFs laughing at the far end of the sandbagged wall and noticed two girls from the hooches across from the compound run giggling down the street from the village with Lieutenant Blossom in mock pursuit. Lieutenant Blossom noticed Ruland sitting on the wall, so he jumped up on the wall, sat down beside Ruland, and grabbed Ruland's beer. Lieutenant Blossom took a long drink and exhaled deeply.

"What's going on, Trung-uy?"

"Not much," Ruland responded. He looked at the young officer dressed in khaki Bermuda shorts and a madras shirt sitting beside him and wondered how this college kid ended up in this village on this pile of sandbags.

The Vietnam War was just a way of killing time for Ronnie Blossom. He planned on returning to the University of Tennessee and continuing his somewhat haphazard college career as soon as his service obligation was up. After high school, Lieutenant Blossom spent three and a half years at the University of Tennessee and managed to compile enough credits to be classified as a sophomore. He was not much of a student. His world was fraternity life.

Lieutenant Blossom was a member of Alpha Tau Omega, a white-only fraternity whose brothers aspired to become regional managers of national corporations. Their destiny was to live in the suburbs with a wife from some "decent" sorority raising some "decent" kids. The fraternity brothers looked upon college as a chance to find this perfect regional manager's wife and make some contacts, as they would call them even then. In their minds, these contacts were one of the main reasons for going to college. Finding the "decent" wife was secondary. However, partying and getting a "decent" lay was the unspoken primary reason for attending college.

During his third year at the University of Tennessee, Ronnie Blossom found a girl who would have made the perfect regional manager's wife. She was smart, good-looking, and ambitious. But unfortunately, it was rumored the girl was a mulatto who somehow managed to sneak into the all-white Chi Omega sorority. To compound the problem, Ronnie Blossom made her pregnant.

Most of the student body at Tennessee knew all about Blossom and the girl. He was treated as somewhat of a legend by the white boys, and was known as a cockhound among the white girls. The black students could care less about Ruland. They cared even less about the pregnant girl since she did not fit in their concept of being black in the sixties. The girl was not accepted by the either the whites or the blacks on campus.

Pregnancy was normally the way prospective regional manager's wives found their ATO husbands, but it usually wasn't until the spring of their senior year after they had exhausted all their options. University of Tennessee girls became amazingly fertile as it got closer to graduation time. Although Ronnie Blossom was more liberal about selecting a wife for his suburban future than his fraternity brothers, he just wasn't ready to marry a "nigra", as the ATOs at Tennessee called the black students in their secret meetings.

So Ronnie Blossom took his father's check for the spring semester's tuition and paid for an abortion for the girl in some back alley Memphis clinic. He also secretly completed all the paperwork and physicals necessary to enter the Army. Since there was a shortage of second lieutenants back in those days, the Army was recruiting just about anybody with at least one year of college for Officer Candidate School. Being an officer sounded pretty good to Ronnie Blossom, so he eagerly signed up for OCS.

Upon his return to Knoxville, Ronnie Blossom established his place in the history of the ATO house by announcing his intent to ship out for the "war in Indochina." Few of the fraternity brothers in the house even knew where Indochina was located. But that didn't matter, the phrase "war in Indochina" sounded good. Blossom promised to return to campus after he had done his duty. This brought cheers from the brothers. His farewell speech at the annual Greek Week party included something about not being able to stand by and allow a communist invasion of one of our Southeast Asia allies. Ronnie Blossom warned that to do nothing could start a "checkers effect", which was what he thought he remembered from the information supplied by the local Army recruiter. He had no idea where Vietnam was, or what was going on there.

But anyway, everyone at the party knew he was leaving school because he "knocked up that half-nigra girl." The brothers figured

Blossom would drop out of OCS at the first opportunity and return to campus as soon as the mulatto girl had transferred to another school.

But to the surprise of almost everyone, newly commissioned Second Lieutenant Ronnie Blossom returned back to campus a little sooner than anyone expected. After OCS, which he enjoyed, and described as a second-class fraternity hazing without paddles, Lieutenant Blossom was assigned to the Army ROTC unit at the University of Tennessee. This meant that every available off-duty moment was spent back at the ATO fraternity house as if nothing had happened. In fact, the brothers even let Ronnie Blossom keep his old room at the ATO house.

Lieutenant Blossom figured he had it made. He thought he could wait out his two-year obligation at the university, finish his degree and get his discharge at the same time. But with one year left to serve on active duty, he received orders to Vietnam. The night before he left for Vietnam, the fraternity brothers nailed the door to Lieutenant Blossom's room shut in a maudlin ceremony, complete with candles and a keg of beer.

Ruland and Lieutenant Blossom stayed on the sandbag wall until dark talking about home. Then, after they both realized they had no more to say for the night, retreated back to the MAT Team's room. Lieutenant Blossom reviewed his collection of Playboy magazines while Ruland listened to the top twenty songs back in the states on the Armed Forces Radio. Neither man spoke a word for the rest of the night. After a while, they just lay in their bunks and stared at the ceiling until they fell asleep.

October 13, 1968

The next day was Sunday. Ruland woke before sunrise. He couldn't sleep thinking about Thuy Van and the time they had spent together the day before. He dressed quietly so he would not disturb the other MAT Team members who managed to make it back to the compound from their night in the village, or wherever they spent the night. Lieutenant Blossom's bunk had not been slept in. Ruland figured Lieutenant Blossom spent the night at The Majestic.

Ruland slung his M-16 over his shoulder and walked to the plywood building that served as a mess hall for the advisors and found Lieutenant Blossom there eating a breakfast of canned pound cake and coffee.

"What are you doing up so early?" Ruland asked.

"Going fishing," Lieutenant Blossom answered, stuffing the last piece of pound cake in his mouth.

"Where do you go fishing around here?" Ruland continued, not really interested, but just making small talk over the morning coffee.

"Down at the river," Lieutenant Blossom said through a mouthful of crumbs, surprised at Ruland's dumb question.

Ruland nodded while he sorted through the box of C-rations. He found a can of chopped ham and eggs and a small can of cheddar cheese. He scooped out the cheddar cheese and placed in on top of the chopped ham and eggs. He then lit a candle that was stuck in a beer can in the center of the long table and heated the ham and eggs with cheese on top until the cheese melted over the eggs.

"Want to go with me?" Lieutenant Blossom asked.

"No thanks, I thought I'd walk around town for awhile. Get to know the people…hearts and minds and all that crap."

Lieutenant Blossom smiled over his cup of coffee.

"What particular heart and mind you want to get to know, Lieutenant?"

Ruland smiled foolishly at Lieutenant Blossom.

"The word down at The Majestic is that Thuy Van's not Viet Cong, but she's pretty fucking close." Lieutenant Blossom offered. "I personally think she's only out to make a buck out of this war, but I'd be careful if I were you. She could make beaucoup bucks settin' up your ass for some VC sniper."

"I'll be all right," Ruland mumbled.

Lieutenant Blossom looked at Ruland and nodded his head in understanding.

"Why don't you come with me for a couple of hours and go fishing?" Lieutenant Blossom asked. "Nobody in the village is going to move before nine. Most of these folks ain't Christian. They're Buddhist or something like that, but they still like to take Sunday morning off. It's probably because that Irish priest in the orphanage talked them into it. We'll be back by noon. You can see your new girlfriend then."

Lieutenant Blossom smiled over his cup of coffee.

Ruland thought it over and decided to go with Lieutenant Blossom. He took his can of lukewarm cheesy ham and eggs and followed Lieutenant Blossom out of the mess hall hooch to the MAT Team's jeep parked by the flagpole. Lieutenant Blossom had four bamboo fishing poles already rigged and in the back of the vehicle.

"I got a bag of dried shrimp from Thuy Van for bait," Lieutenant Blossom said as the men approached the jeep. Traded a pistol belt for it."

Ruland noticed Lieutenant Blossom's M-79 hand held grenade launcher and box of grenades in the back of the jeep.

"What are the grenades for?" Ruland asked.

"That's if things get a little slow. If I can't get fish the old fashioned way. I can lob a few grenades in the river and stun the fish. Then I just pick 'em out of the water. The method is not quite as sporting as traditional fishing, but pretty damn effective. I got this box of grenades from the ammo dump at Camp Evans. They're seconds or something. The EOD guys at Camp Evans were going to blow them up anyway, so they gave them to me. Those we don't use we can trade to Thuy Van for beer or something."

Ruland nodded his head and got into the jeep and laid his M-16 across his lap. The two men drove out of the compound and into the village. Ruland looked for Thuy Van as they drove by the cafe. The tables and chairs were not on the patio under the awning yet, and the front door to the building was closed.

Just past The Majestic Steam Bath and Massage Parlor, and right before the bridge, there was a trail leading along the river to the west. Lieutenant Blossom pulled off the highway unto the trail and put the jeep into four-wheel drive. They drove slowly down the trail for what seemed to be about two miles. Lieutenant Blossom would look over occasionally and smile at Ruland, knowing Ruland was nervous about traveling so far away from the village into the bush.

"Don't worry," Lieutenant Blossom said, "the VC do all their fishing at night. They're back home sleepin' by now."

Lieutenant Blossom pulled off the trail when he came upon a small clearing next to the river. He took the four fishing poles out of the jeep and inspected them. Two of the poles were rigged for bottom fishing. He placed three hooks with the small shrimp on them above the cluster of 50 caliber bullets he used for sinkers for the bottom fishing poles. He then threw the lines out in the river as far as he could and stuck the ends of the poles in the soft mud of the riverbank. Lieutenant Blossom then took one of the two remaining poles and baited the hook with two of the dried shrimp and placed a small cork bobber on the line. Ruland did the same with his pole. The two men threw their lines in the water and sat back on the riverbank, enjoying the last cool breezes of the morning before the dry monsoon heat would settle down on top of them like a hot blanket.

To no surprise to Ruland, Lieutenant Blossom was not a very patient fisherman. After a half-hour of squirming and pulling in his line every time the bobber twitched in the current of the river, Lieutenant Blossom got bored. Ruland looked over at his fellow lieutenant and smiled.

"I thought you liked to fish," Ruland said after watching Lieutenant Blossom squirm impatiently on the riverbank.

"I do, but this is too slow. I guess they're not biting. That's why I brought the grenade launcher. We'll pop a few in the river."

"Won't that bring in the VC?"

"Naw," Lieutenant Blossom said. "it scares them away. They figure the Marines are playing around in here. The VC don't like to operate with the Marines around. The Marines are too gung ho for the VC."

Lieutenant Blossom took the grenade launcher out of the jeep and loaded a grenade in the chamber. He walked slowly over to the river-bank to demonstrate his fishing technique for Ruland.

"You got to fire upstream," he yelled back at Ruland. "That way the fish float back down to us. Then we grab 'em while they're still stunned."

Lieutenant Blossom held the weapon high in the air and aimed it up the river. He fired the grenade and watched it go almost straight up in the air. Ruland grimaced, not sure where the grenade would come down.

"You got to put a lot of arch on it or the grenades won't detonate. You got to hit the water head-on."

The grenade landed about thirty yards upstream from where Ruland was standing. It exploded and created a narrow, ten-foot high geyser of water. In a few seconds two fish rose slowly to the surface and began to float downstream, belly up. Lieutenant Blossom watched the fish as they drifted passed. A few yards farther downstream the fish began to twitch then turned over and disappeared under the surface of the water.

"See," Lieutenant Blossom said to Ruland, "sure as hell beats trying to hook 'em."

He fired another grenade in the air. The grenade came down a few feet from where the first grenade landed. Lieutenant Blossom smiled and handed Ruland the grenade launcher.

"Here you go. Give it a try. I'll get the fish when they float by."

Ruland took the weapon and put a grenade in the chamber. He raised the grenade launcher to what he thought was the same angle that Lieutenant Blossom had used and pulled the trigger. The grenade arched gracefully into space and landed in the bushes on the far side of the river. It made a dull thump when it exploded.

"You gotta stick it almost straight up," Lieutenant Blossom said as he tried to retrieve a fish floating by the edge of the riverbank.

Ruland put another grenade in the chamber and raised the launcher almost perpendicular.

"More yet," Lieutenant Blossom directed.

Ruland raised the stubby weapon higher and squeezed the trigger. The grenade went straight up, disappeared briefly, then emerged as a black dot falling to earth on top of the two men. Lieutenant Blossom spotted the plummeting grenade and grabbed his hat with both hands.

"Shit, I think that's too much!"

The grenade struck the limb of a dead tree leaning over the river next to Lieutenant Blossom's retrieval spot. The explosion blew the branch off and it fell into the water. Lieutenant Blossom grabbed his chest and spun around and fell on both knees in the soft mud of the riverbank.

"Damn it! Damn it! Damn it!" Lieutenant Blossom screamed. "I've been hit!"

Ruland dropped the weapon and ran over to Lieutenant Blossom.

"Let me take a look," Ruland said nervously.

Lieutenant Blossom took his hand away from his chest slowly, studied the red spot of blood in the palm of his hand, and then grabbed his chest again.

"Shit. This burns like hell."

Ruland unbuttoned Lieutenant Blossom's fatigue shirt and pulled it back. A few inches from Lieutenant Blossom's left armpit was a small cut shaped like the letter C. Dark red blood was slowly oozing out and making a red trail down his chest.

"How deep is it?" Ruland asked.

"I don't fucking know," Lieutenant Blossom answered as he began to slowly stand up. "Hell, it stopped burning. It just sort of tingles."

"We better get to Camp Evans and let a medic take a look at you. No telling where that frag is."

Lieutenant Blossom smiled and took out a white handkerchief with a "B" monogrammed in the corner and pressed it against his wound.

"You know what this means?" he asked Ruland, smiling as he inspected the blood on the handkerchief.

"No, what?"

"It means a god damn Purple Heart. I always wanted one, but I didn't want to get hurt too bad to get it. This is just about right. Hell, I don't even feel it now. Wait 'til I write the brothers back at the house. Christ, I'm a hero."

Lieutenant Blossom walked over to the jeep and sat down in the passenger's seat. He looked again at his bloody monogrammed handkerchief and smiled. Ruland picked up the grenade launcher and put it on the back seat of the jeep.

"You sure you're all right?" Ruland double-checked as he got into the jeep.

Lieutenant Blossom smiled. "Sure, I'm OK. But we got to get our story straight for the medics. They're the ones who fill out the forms. Let's say we were riding along the trail searching for the place the VC use to rocket the bridge and the VC fired at us from the other side of the river, all right?"

"Sure," Ruland said as he started the jeep, "whatever you want to say is all right with me."

Ruland carefully guided the jeep along the river trail to make the ride as comfortable as possible for Lieutenant Blossom. There were children swimming at the bridge when they reached the highway. The children yelled at Lieutenant Blossom and he managed a quick royal wave with his left hand.

At the edge of the village Ruland saw Thuy Van talking to two Marine officers sitting in a jeep. She and Nguyen O'Bannon were selling them some woven reed baskets made by village craftsmen. Thuy Van waved and smiled at Ruland as he drove by.

Ruland drove south on Highway One to the field hospital at Camp Evans to get Lieutenant Blossom's wound treated. Once past the security at Camp Evans' main gate, Ruland raced down the roads of the camp for added effect, and slid to a halt at the emergency door to the field hospital. Lieutenant Blossom put his arm around Ruland's shoulder and managed to grimace as they entered the building. The two men walked past the roomful of morning sick call patients and other malingerers still waiting to be examined. The medic at the receiving desk looked up at the two junior officers, then back at his logbook

"Last name, first name, middle initial, and serial number," the medic routinely rattled off without looking up.

Lieutenant Blossom leaned over to speak to the medic, "Blossom, Ronnie T. 0-5244674."

"Unit?" the medic went on.

"Mobile Advisory Team I-24."

"What the hell's that?" the medic asked, still not looking up.

"CIA special operations," Ruland interjected.

"You the patient?" the medic asked Ruland, obviously not in the mood for games.

"No," Lieutenant Blossom answered. "I am."

"Problem?" the medic returned to his logbook again.

"Wounded in action," Lieutenant Blossom answered.

The roomful of sick call patients that were hoping to get out of the day's work looked up from their waiting room pornographic magazines to see an actual war casualty. The soldiers in base camps seldom saw someone who was wounded at morning sick call, at least no one with a wound that wasn't self-inflicted.

"Why didn't you say so," the medic said as he jumped to his feet.

The medic took Lieutenant Blossom gingerly by the arm and disappeared behind a canvas partition. Ruland waited at the check-in desk for a moment, then sat down in a chair at the end of the row of sick call patients. He picked up a tattered copy of Playboy and started thumbing through the magazine looking at the pictures and cartoons.

About a half-hour passed before Lieutenant Blossom and the medic returned. Lieutenant Blossom's left arm was in a green cotton sling. The two men stopped at the desk and started filling out forms.

"Can I see you a second, Lieutenant?" the medic asked Ruland. "I'll need you to verify this."

The medic handed Ruland a statement to sign. He had to verify the story Lieutenant Blossom had told the medic about being attacked by a Viet Cong squad. The report stated that the wound Lieutenant Blossom suffered was in the line of duty and was the result of hostile action. That was all the paperwork needed for Lieutenant Blossom's Purple Heart.

The two young officers walked out of the field hospital and got into the jeep.

"God, I feel great," Lieutenant Blossom proclaimed. "I was hoping to get a Purple Heart. You want to get something to eat at the Officers' Mess?"

"I'd just as soon get back to the village and eat at the café," Ruland answered.

"Aw, we're already here." Lieutenant Blossom whined. "Let's go over to the club and eat."

"All right," Ruland gave in, "but let's not stay all day."

"I'll drop you off at Thuy Van's café after lunch and you got the rest of the day with your new girl." Lieutenant Blossom laughed and shook his head.

Ruland started the jeep and drove to the Officers' Club.

Since the workday at Camp Evans started at six thirty in the morning, the Officers' Club mess hall was usually full by eleven o'clock with the lunch-time crowd. Ruland and Lieutenant Blossom arrived there just after eleven and had to wait in line for a table.

"This is no way to treat a wounded veteran," Lieutenant Blossom said to Ruland loud enough so everyone in line could hear.

Ruland knew then that Lieutenant Blossom's version of his war wound would get more serious with time, and the Viet Cong attack they supposedly repelled at the river would soon rival the siege at Dien Bien Phu.

The featured dish at the cafeteria-style mess was roast beef and mashed potatoes, so the two men took generous portions. This was a treat compared to the C-rations and food from the village cafes. Lieutenant Blossom spotted a tall, thin Donut Dolly sitting alone at a table for four. She had long, straight blond hair and was sitting up straight in her chair, apparently in some sort of meditation. Lieutenant Blossom led Ruland over to the table and sat down before speaking to the woman.

"Mind if we join you?" he asked as he took his arm out of the sling.

"No, I don't mind," the Donut Dolly answered, opening her eyes slowly. When she saw Lieutenant Blossom's sling, she gasped. "What happened to you?

"We got hit in an ambush this morning. NVA battalion caught us coming back from a reconnaissance mission across the DMZ. I caught a piece of shrapnel in the chest from a Chinese rocket."

The young woman closed her eyes and lowered her fork. She took a deep breath.

"Oh, this is too much," she said. "This is the first time I have really experienced the war. All of the parts of this total experience are finally beginning to fall into place. It's like, you know, that gestalt thing. Do you believe in Gestalt Theory?"

"Sure I do," Lieutenant Blossom answered, having heard the word once when smoking dope at a fraternity party.

"Like the parts falling into place and all that," Lieutenant Blossom offered, exhausting his knowledge of psychology.

"Like you have suddenly become part of my life script," the Donut Dolly continued, not hearing a word Lieutenant Blossom said. The Donut Dolly studied Lieutenant Blossom carefully. "How do you feel about yourself today?"

"I feel great," Lieutenant Blossom responded. "I was just telling my friend here just a few minutes ago that I felt a lot of gestalt today."

"I feel great too, ya know. Like it's very important for a person's being to take in the total environmental milieu of the day-to-day acts of a person's life-script, ya know. Like you have suddenly moved me a little closer to realizing my life script. Wow, like that's really too much. Let's share this moment together."

The Donut Dolly reached across the table and took the hand of Lieutenant Blossom's wounded arm. She looked into his eyes for a moment, then started feeding Lieutenant Blossom his mashed potatoes with a spoon, carefully wiping the corners of his mouth with her little finger. Ruland felt uncomfortable with this scene at the table, but managed to finish his meal. He watched as the couple across the table shared their life scripts by looking into each other's eyes and eating mashed potatoes with a spoon. When they had finished the pile of potatoes on Lieutenant Blossom's plate, the woman turned to Ruland with an exhausted look on her face.

"Will you drop me off at the Red Cross hooch. I feel like I need to lay down a while after this experience, ya know? Like this is too much."

"Sure," Ruland said, "just show me where you want to go."

"I would like that very much," the woman said as she carefully caressed Lieutenant Blossom's arm in the sling. "This experience is wild. Like a real wounded person became part of my life, ya know?"

Ruland nodded in agreement. "Like…I know."

Acting as if in intense pain, Lieutenant Blossom managed to let the Donut Dolly help him to his feet, discreetly grabbing her rear end for balance. The Donut Dolly put her arm around his waist and walked him out the door of the Officers' Club. Since the back seat of the jeep was filled with grenades and fishing tackle. Lieutenant Blossom got into the passenger's seat and motioned for the woman to sit on his lap.

"Too much," she exhaled as she placed her bottom in position on Lieutenant Blossom's lap, moving it slightly a few times for the proper fit.

The Donut Dolly directed Ruland through the roads of Camp Evans to her hooch by pointing out the turns when the jeep was already at the corner. As they passed the airstrip, nearing the Red Cross housing area, Ruland thought he heard the dull thump of a mortar being fired from the hills to the west. He figured it was one of the American firebases up in the hills so he drove on. Then he heard the unmistakable sound of an incoming shell. The mortar round landed to the left of the jeep on the airfield and exploded. The metal shrapnel whistled over the top of the jeep.

"Holy shit! We'd better get the hell out of here!" Ruland yelled.

"This is too much!" the Donut Dolly screamed as she threw her arms over her head. "This is like, ya know, war!"

Ruland spotted a small sand-bagged bunker on the other side of the airstrip. He cut across the runway as another mortar round hit and exploded behind them. The jeep slid to a stop on the metal runway in front of the bunker just as the base camp warning siren began to whine. Lieutenant Blossom pushed the Donut Dolly off his lap and she fell on the ground. Another mortar struck the middle of the airstrip and the shrapnel whistled over their heads. Lieutenant Blossom grabbed the woman's hand and pulled her into the bunker. Ruland got his rifle and the grenade launcher but no grenades and followed the couple to the safety of the bunker.

The bunker was a half-buried metal culvert covered with sandbags, one of several emergency bunkers along the airstrip. Rows of sandbags at both ends of the culvert kept out the shrapnel and most of the light. The mortar rounds were striking the airfield about every 60 seconds, so the three temporary prisoners of the bunker settled back and waited for the all clear siren. Like most mortar attacks, there wasn't much danger if you were in a bunker. The only real danger was when you received a direct hit. So, like all soldiers who had been through these types of attacks, Ruland would wait it out and hope the odds were in his favor.

After about five minutes and the fifth round hitting the airstrip, the Donut Dolly had her hands on the sides of her head and started chanting softly and rocking back and forth.

"Ommmm. Ommmm. Ommmm."

"You all right?" Ruland asked her.

She stopped chanting and took her hands away from her head.

"I can not believe this," she said. "Of all the variables that make up the psychodrama of, like, ya know, my life, this has got to be the most far out. What an experience."

The woman turned suddenly to Lieutenant Blossom. Ruland could see the whites of her eyes flash in the half-light of the bunker. She moved slowly toward Lieutenant Blossom.

"I want to share this moment with you, my wounded warrior," the Donut Dolly said to Lieutenant Blossom as she began to unbutton his pants. "It must be a total organismatic experience."

"I also want to experience this psychosomatic moment," Lieutenant Blossom said, not knowing what either she or he was talking about, but looking forward to what might happen next.

The Donut Dolly pulled down Lieutenant Blossom's jungle fatigues.

"Share this experience with me!" the woman yelled as she dropped her panties, pulled up her dress, and straddled Lieutenant Blossom.

"I will share! I will share!" Lieutenant Blossom answered in a high pitched voice as he tore the sling off wounded arm and flung it to the other side of the bunker.

The mortars continued to thump in the distance and explode in the base camp as the Donut Dolly and Lieutenant Blossom moaned and bounced in the half-light of the bunker. Then she suddenly pulled her brown Red Cross dress over her head and was completely naked. She began to slowly rise and fall on Lieutenant Blossom.

"Experience the moment!" she screamed as she pressed Lieutenant Blossom against the sandbags. Each time a mortar fell she screamed again.

Ruland was unable to stay in the bunker any longer. He slowly crawled outside on his hands and knees and sat with his back against the bunker, facing the hills and watching the American artillery counterattack.

The artillery from Camp Evans began to zero in on the suspected mortar position up in the hills. There would be a "thump" off in the distant hills, followed by the sharp blast of a pair of 155-millimeter howitzers from Camp Evans, then the boom of their shells exploding in the hills near the sound of the mortar. The moan of the Donut Dolly and the groan of Lieutenant Blossom followed each blast. The attack and counterstrike went on for another five minutes.

When the shelling stopped, Ruland knocked on the top of the culvert and looked in. The Red Cross woman was meditating naked in the full lotus position on the dirt floor of the bunker.

"Ommmmm...Ommmmm..." she repeated.

Lieutenant Blossom was hopping around on one leg, trying to put on his pants with his good arm.

"Hey," Ruland yelled in, "we're going to have to go now."

The Donut Dolly opened her eyes slowly and smiled. “This was a total experience, ya know. Wait ’til I share the experience with my encounter group.”

The two wartime lovers dressed quietly and got into the jeep. The Donut Dolly pointed the way to her hooch. She got out of the jeep at her SEA Hut without speaking, flashed the peace sign with her fingers, and ran barefoot into the plywood building holding her shoes and panties in her hands.

Lieutenant Blossom sat in the passenger seat smiling during the trip back to the compound. For the first time since Ruland had known him, Lieutenant Blossom was speechless.

After a stop back in their room to let Lieutenant Blossom get cleaned up, the two young officers drove into the village. The children in front of Thuy Van’s cafe told Ruland that Thuy Van had been at the café most of the morning, but left about noon to go up in the hills. The children pointed to the hills above Camp Evans in the direction of the mortar attack. They said Thuy Van was with Nguyen O’Bannon and two of his workers getting some mahogany to sell to the Seabees in Danang. Thuy Van had a contract for materials for a bar being built for the Chief Petty Officers Club.

Ruland never connected the mortar attack with Thuy Van’s trip to the hills. He sat in the café that afternoon and drank beer waiting for her return. Just before dark, Major Hannah and Lieutenant Fujita stopped in front of the cafe in their jeep. They had been up north to Quang Tri for a meeting with the district advisor there. Major Hannah motioned for Ruland to get in the jeep.

“You’d better come back with us, Lieutenant. Captain Moss says there might be another attack on the compound tonight.”

Ruland had been drinking too much and was too tired to argue.

“Yessir.” Ruland said, and he got in the jeep as Thuy Van watched him from the small window in the door of the café.

October 14, 1968

After the fishing expedition with Lieutenant Blossom, Ruland realized that he didn't have that many days left to accomplish his mission. He woke up determined to do something about building the rifle range. But as he was eating breakfast at the mess hall the next morning, Major Hannah walked in with a surprise.

"Ruland," Major Hannah proclaimed. "I got a little job for you today. You've been doing nothing since you arrived here, so I got something for you to do to earn your pay."

Ruland dropped his can of cheesy chopped ham and eggs.

"I'm working on that rifle range today, Major. I don't have time for other jobs."

"You ain't doing shit on that fucking rifle range. Fujita's got food poisoning or something and can't take the patrol out today. I want you to do it."

"Give me a break, Major. That's not what I was sent here for."

Major Hannah didn't like to discuss what he perceived as direct orders with junior officers.

"Don't give me any shit, Lieutenant. I know all about your assignment and all that crap. But as long as you're assigned to this district you come under my command and I want you to take the patrol out today."

Major Hannah felt his blood pressure rising and tried to relax.

"Hell, you'll be back before thirteen hundred. You know the SOP. I need an officer with each patrol and you're the only one left. So you got it, Lieutenant. Do I make myself clear?"

Ruland looked down at the table and sighed. "All right, Major. I'll do it, but don't blame me if the rifle range doesn't get built."

"I don't want to hear your problems, Lieutenant." Major Hannah said. "You didn't exactly jump into this project when you got here. I assume you know what you're doing and will have that range set up before you leave so that group of shitheads on your MAT Team can qualify these worthless slopes on their M-16s."

Major Hannah leaned forward and pointed his finger at Ruland.

"And if you don't get that range set up and running, you ain't going nowhere. I don't care if you are being discharged when you arrive in Oakland. I have to sign you out before you go anywhere and I ain't doing it if that fucking firing range ain't built. Do I make myself clear, Lieutenant?"

Major Hannah's face was flushed with blood again and he was in no mood to argue, so Ruland remained silent as Major Hannah stomped out of the mess hall and slammed the door behind him.

Later, Ruland learned the reason for all this urgency. Once a month all the district advisors in I Corps traveled to Danang to report on operations conducted in their districts. It got to be a game with all the district advisors competing to see who conducted the most patrols and night ambushes. At each meeting, one of the lieutenant colonel staffers working at I Corps headquarters would uncover a chart on an easel with the names of the district advisors on it. Along side the names were the total number of patrols and ambushes the district advisors conducted since the last report. The list was in order of the most patrols and ambushes conducted in some sort of elaborate weighting system only the briefing officer understood. All the advisors would check their standing and then check the face of the Corp Commander. The general would then turn to the district advisor with the lowest number and say, "Major, I don't feel that reflects your best effort. Don't you agree?"

The district advisor who was singled out by the general would then see the general's lieutenants scribbling in their note pads, just to be sure those same words spoken by the general would appear on the unfortunate major's next fitness report. Major Hannah had been singled out several times, so he was determined to run at least one patrol a day for the rest of his tour to stay ahead of the game.

Lieutenant Fujita usually went with the Popular Forces on their daytime patrols for Major Hannah. Since Major Vien wanted to avoid any actual firefights within his district, the patrols were always conducted in the safest possible areas surrounding the village. The patrols were often pleasant little walks for Lieutenant Fujita and the Ruff Puff platoon. Lieutenant Fujita enjoyed going on the patrols. It got him away from Major Hannah and the endless paperwork he had to do as the executive officer.

But for this day, Ruland had to take Lieutenant Fujita's place. He decided to take Sergeant Scroop with him on the patrol just for security. Major Hannah didn't care where the patrol went, just as long as it left in the morning and came back in the afternoon. Anything less than four hours didn't count as an "official" patrol, and wouldn't count toward the Major's monthly total of patrols being tallied up back in Danang.

The last thing Ruland wanted to do was run into some Viet Cong squad resting for the day. Knowing how Major Vien operated, Ruland asked him if he had any areas he wanted double-checked. Ruland also told Major Vien he would see about picking up the television set at the PX in Camp Evans that Major Vien had wanted. Major Vien knew what Ruland meant, so he picked a safe area along the river trail, near Lieutenant Blossom's fishing spot. Lieutenant Tram was assigned the task of pulling together a platoon of Ruff Puffs for the patrol.

Word was getting around the Popular Forces platoons that the new co-van wanted to avoid combat, so it was easy for Lieutenant Tram to get volunteers for the patrol. The Popular Forces soldiers weren't eager for any combat either. They just wanted to put in their time, just like Ruland. Sergeant Scroop suggested they walk down the river trail for about an hour, stop and have lunch, maybe take a nap for about two hours in the heat of the day, then return back to the compound. It sounded good to Ruland.

The people in the village were too busy during the day to pay any attention to the platoon as they left on patrol. A few children followed the soldiers as far as the Buddhist pagoda, but stopped when the monks chased them back to the village. The soldiers seemed a little more careful on this patrol compared with Ruland's night ambush. There wasn't enough time to get the word out in the village on where the patrol would be going, so the Ruff Puffs were afraid they might run into their VC neighbors by mistake and surprise them. Or even worse, run into some American unit.

The platoon moved cautiously down a well-worn path on the south bank of the river. The men moved slowly and deliberately, staying about ten feet apart just like Sergeant Scroop told them to do. A point man stayed about twenty feet in front of the platoon. He would disappear occasionally into the bushes and check for a possible ambush. The last thing the Ruff Puffs wanted was to surprise someone. Ruland walked next to Sergeant Scroop, much to the sergeant's discomfort. Sergeant Scroop knew it was unlucky to walk near officers because they were the favorite targets of snipers.

"Sergeant Scroop," Ruland said just to make small talk. "Why do you think Major Hannah's doing this to me? I'm too short for this shit."

"Like there's this Army rule, Lieutenant," Sergeant Scroop mused. "The rule is that the Army makes you do the thing you don't want to do most, at the time you don't want to do it." Sergeant Scroop was startled at his profound thinking, and nodded his head in agreement with himself. "Man, that's what makes the Army interesting."

"I'll never understand you lifers," Ruland said, knowing it was a jab at Sergeant Scroop.

Sergeant Scroop's jerked his head back, offended at being called a lifer.

"No way, man," he said, bobbing his head like a rooster contemplating scratching the ground. "I ain't no lifer." Sergeant Scroop then proceeded to tell Ruland, for the first time, his life story.

Sergeant Delta Scroop was pure Californian. His father was an aeronautical engineer whose specialty was the aerodynamics of wings. Since the elder Scroop was a proponent of delta-winged aircraft he felt it not only appropriate, but also an honor to name his first and only son after the often-tried and often-failed wing design.

Delta Scroop had spent most of his twenty-one years on the beaches of southern California while his father moved around the local aircraft industries in various engineering jobs. The only accomplishment of Delta Scroop before being drafted into the Army was also in the field of engineering. He designed and constructed, with the help of his father, a surfboard with a removable panel under the rear fin. This panel concealed a watertight box exactly the size of one kilo of marijuana. While growing up in Southern California, Scroop and his surfing buddies would visit Baja on surfing expeditions. On their way back home, they would stop in Tijuana and fill the secret compartment in the surfboard with marijuana. They found the border guards never bothered the elaborately painted surfboards safely strapped on top of Scroop's '57 Chevy.

Unfortunately, just when Sergeant Scroop's narrative got to the point of when he received his draft notice, what Ruland and the Ruff Puffs didn't want to happen, did happen.

The Ruff Puff point man wandered off the main trail a few yards and discovered a clearing. Just by bad luck, he happened to stumble upon three Viet Cong soldiers with AK-47 rifles squatting beside a makeshift shelter. Under the shelter was a woman in black pajamas, her face obscured by a straw hat. She was putting a dressing on the hand of a fourth man. Startled by his discovery, and regaining his senses somewhat, the point man let out a high-pitched scream of surprise and fired his rifle once into the air.

"VC! VC!" the soldier screamed as he ran back to join the patrol. Ruland turned to Lieutenant Tram. "Tell the men to stay put and don't do anything crazy. I'll see if we can get some artillery on top of them." He turned to Sergeant Scroop. "I don't want anyone running in like John Wayne if we don't have to."

Lieutenant Tram yelled instructions to the PF soldiers as Ruland reached for the hand mike from the radioman.

"Widow-mender six, this is Widow-mender six-two, over."

Major Hannah's voice immediately came back on the speaker. "This is Widow-mender six, over."

"This is Widow-mender six-two. We have contact. We have located Victor Charlie at..." Ruland looked at a map where Sergeant Scroop pointed out their position, "coordinates 454...886. How about some artillery to flush them out, over?"

"Roger, Six-two. Wait one."

There was a moment of silence on the radio as Ruland expected. He knew he could buy some time while Major Hannah sorted out the artillery support.

"Let's give ol' charlie every opportunity to get out of here," Ruland said aside to Sergeant Scroop.

Major Hannah's voice crackled back over the speaker. "Widow-mender Six-two, this is Six. That river's right on the damn border of two operation areas. I don't know if your target is in the Marine's op-area , or if it comes under Army artillery out of Camp Evans. Hang on a second I'll find out who's responsible for that area and get a spotter round out there ASAP. Standby...out."

Sergeant Scroop smiled and turned to Lieutenant Tram. "You'd better tell the men to relax, this may take awhile, man."

Lieutenant Tram yelled instructions to his men. They collectively breathed a sigh of relief and placed their rifles on the ground and squatted down. Two of the soldiers lay on their backs and pulled their jungle hats over their eyes for a quick nap.

"I think VC run away." Lieutenant Tram said to Ruland.

Ruland leaned against a tree. "That's OK with me."

"OK with me-too, Trung-uy," Lieutenant Tram said, understanding what was going on and equally pleased to be avoiding any contact. "We wait here."

Lieutenant Tram was a shopkeeper in the village who bought his way into the Popular Forces. His interest was staying close to his business and livelihood, not war. He was in no hurry to shoot anyone or get shot at.

After about five minutes, the radio crackled again.

"Widow-mender Six-two, this is Six, over."

Ruland took a deep breath and slowly reached for the radio hand mike.

"This is Six-two," Ruland answered.

"This is Six. We got a little problem here. Camp Evans says the Marines own that spot, and I think they're right. The problem is the Marines won't fire on the target unless an American's in trouble, over."

"This is Six-two. Did you tell the Marines I was here, over?"

"Roger, but they say advisors don't count. The Marines said if you want to live with the gooks, then use their artillery. They're saving their ammo for Americans, over."

"Roger, understand," Ruland replied, smiling at Sergeant Scroop as he talked into the hand mike. "What do you suggest, over?"

"Hell, from what I see on the map," Major Hannah responded, "there's a river up ahead of you. They can't get away without crossing the river. Our Intel folks think the VC you got there are the ones who hit the compound the other night and took out our generator. We don't want to lose them. So move out after them. You don't need no fuckin' artillery. Over."

Ruland closed his eyes and took a deep breath. "They're determined to get me killed," he said to Sergeant Scroop." Then he spoke into the hand mike. "Roger, Widow-mender, we're moving out after them."

"Roger," Major Hannah said, "Don't do anything stupid, out."

Ruland turned to Sergeant Scroop. "Let's move out slowly, but don't do anything stupid, says the major. Nobody knows for sure who's responsible for this area and the Marines won't fire their guns unless the American Legion is being attacked."

He then yelled to Lieutenant Tram. "Tell the men to spread out on line and move ahead toward the river…Slowly! Very slowly!"

Lieutenant Tram yelled at the men and they spread out perpendicular to the path. Ruland motioned with his hand and the platoon moved out. The soldiers began beating the bushes and shouting, ensuring their intended prey would hear them and escape.

"Jesus," Ruland said to Sergeant Scroop, "you'd think we were after tigers."

The Popular Forces soldiers moved slowly through the jungle growth whipping the undergrowth with branches. Ruland moved cautiously behind the radioman, stepping in his footprints, just in case the area was mined. The patrol came to a wall of thick vegetation at the edge of the riverbank. The bushes made a sort of barrier, hiding whatever was on the other side. The soldiers stopped in line and looked at Ruland. Ruland looked at Sergeant Scroop.

"They want the co-van to go first," Sergeant Scroop chuckled. "Man, that's why you get paid the big money for being an officer."

Ruland clenched his teeth, then motioned for everyone to get back. He put a round in the chamber of his M-16 and moved up to the thick bushes. He carefully spread them apart with his left hand, and released the safety on the black rifle with his right thumb. He eased slowly into the jungle growth, stuck the stubby barrel of his weapon through opening, and cautiously looked through the growth. Ruland fully expected to see a squad of Viet Cong rifles facing him on the other side of the river. Instead, he saw Thuy Van swimming in the river. She looked up at Ruland.

"Hey, Trung-uy," she yelled. "You sure make a lot of noise."

"Thuy Van," Ruland whispered. "What the hell are you doing here? Did you see anyone cross this river?"

"Sure, Ruland. Three, maybe four men with rifles swim across river. They run into brush on other side. Look like VC to me. You chase them, Ruland?"

"Not any more. I guess. This is as far as I go."

Thuy Van laughed. "How you going to get medals, Ruland, if you not chase VC?"

"You're confusing me with someone who cares, Thuy Van. I don't want any medals. I just want to put in my time and go home."

"That OK with me too, Ruland," Thuy Van said as she swam to Ruland's side of the river. As long as you put in time, you can put in time in river. You come and swim. Relax. It too hot to chase VC."

Ruland thought for a second and smiled, "I'll be right back."

He pulled himself out of the thick brush and walked back to the other members of the patrol. He took the hand mike from the radioman.

"Widow-mender Six, this is Widow-mender Six-two, over."

"This is Widow-mender," Major Hannah answered quickly.

"This is Six-two. I'm afraid charlie made it across the river. We lost them, over."

Major Hannah paused before he spoke. "Shit, Ruland, you let the gooks get away. I could've scored beaucoup points next month in Danang. Shit! Well, get your ass back here then. Widow-mender, out."

"Roger, Widow-mender. We're on our way back, out."

Ruland smiled and turned to Sergeant Scroop, "You and Lieutenant Tram go ahead and take the patrol back to the compound. If you see the Major, tell him I'm in the village buying some bananas or something. I'll see you in a little while."

Sergeant Scroop had gone in the bushes while Ruland was talking on the radio and saw Thuy Van. He returned and smiled at Ruland. "I can dig it, Lieutenant, but it can get a little hairy out here. You better watch your six."

"Don't worry about me," Ruland said. "I know what I'm doing."

The Ruff Puffs placed their weapons on their shoulders as if they had just finished a hunting trip. They began to walk slowly down the path toward the village. The men laughed and looked back at Ruland and made obscene gestures with their hands. They all knew what was going on.

Ruland waited until the patrol was well down the trail, then took off his clothes except for his green jockey shorts, and squeezed through the brush to the riverbank, holding his rifle at his side. He placed the weapon on a log on the bank and jumped into the river, going in over his head. When he surfaced, he looked around, but couldn't see Thuy Van.

"Hey," he yelled to no one in particular. "Where are you?"

On the other side of the river, four Viet Cong soldiers watched Ruland. One of the men, Nguyen O'Bannon, took his rifle and aimed at Ruland. As he sighted in, Thuy Van jumped from the bushes into the water, landing almost on top of Ruland.

"Where'd you go?" Ruland said, wiping the water out of his eyes. I'd thought you'd left me out here for the VC."

"I was just playing, Ruland. I not leave you." She held out her hand and motioned for Ruland to follow. "Come. Swim to side of river where sand is. I race you."

Ruland and Thuy Van swam to the low sandy shore on the far side of the river. They climbed on the sand bar and sat down, out of breath and not speaking. She was wearing a pair of blue gym shorts and a UCLA T-shirt. Thuy Van smiled and leaned forward slightly, brushing Ruland's arm. At Thuy Van's touch, Ruland suddenly lost all sense of where he was, or of any sense of danger.

On the other side of the river, Nguyen O'Bannon took aim again, but Thuy Van stood up and moved in the line of fire. Thuy Van's wet T-shirt was clinging to her and she crossed her arms, looking down in embarrassment. Ruland stood up and took her hand, pulling her gently toward him.

"Hey, Ruland," Thuy Van squealed as she pulled away. "What you doing? You beaucoup crazy."

"I just wanted to hold you," Ruland said.

Thuy Van pushed Ruland away slightly and smiled at him. "Take it easy, GI. You act like you crazy or something. You think I butterfly girl?"

"No," Ruland countered, "I think you're someone who's a little out of place here."

"That so, GI." Thuy Van said as she pushed Ruland farther away.

"Maybe you think I your girlfriend, too?

Ruland shook his head. "I hope so."

"Trung-uy? You think we had date the other day you come my house?"

"Well," Ruland answered, puzzled. "If you want to call it that, then we did. Why do you ask?"

"If VC know I have date with you, maybe they kill you. Probably no kill me. VC my friends. I make good business with them. Sell them beaucoup rice. You better be careful, GI. VC no care if you my friend. Their job is to kill Americans."

She bowed her head down shyly, wanting to change the subject. "You know what, Ruland. I like go on date like American movies I see in Hue. Like Sandra Dee. Maybe go to dance or something."

Ruland knew what she was getting at. "I can do better than that. I'll take you on a date tonight. We'll go on an official, regulation-style date. We'll even dance. How's that sound?"

Ruland reached out and tried to hold Thuy Van again, but she jumped away and jumped back in the river. She swam quickly to the other side and yelled back when she climbed up the riverbank.

"Then I go to get ready for date! See you tonight, Ruland! Seven o'clock. Don't be late, GI."

She picked up her knapsack on the far riverbank and quickly disappeared into the bushes.

On the other side of the river Ruland stood alone as Nguyen O'Bannon took aim again and followed Ruland in his sights. Ruland suddenly looked around and felt very alone. He quickly jumped into the water and swam to the riverbank. He got out of the water, grabbed his rifle and moved quickly into the bushes. Nguyen O'Bannon lowered his rifle and smiled. On the other side of the bushes Ruland hoped to see Thuy Van, but she had disappeared. Ruland dressed quickly and walked back to the village.

Later that night, Nguyen O'Bannon would confess to the Catholic priest in the village, the man who raised him as an orphan and whose last name Nguyen took as his own, that he had sinned. Nguyen confessed that his sin was thinking evil thoughts about his fellow man, but deep down Nguyen wondered if his real sin was not eliminating his enemy.

Ruland returned to the compound and prepared for his date. Just before dark, Ruland drove the MAT Team's jeep into the village pick up Thuy Van. He arrived at the cafe at exactly seven o'clock. The children who always gathered in front of the cafe swarmed around the jeep and called Ruland by name. The children liked to stay around the cafe in hopes of an odd job or errand they could get from Thuy Van.

Ruland knocked on the door of the cafe. Thuy Van's mother opened the door and motioned for Ruland to enter. She led him to the main living room and pushed on his shoulders to set him down. No sooner was Ruland firmly settled on the floor than Thuy Van's grandmother placed a cold beer and a small dish of peanuts in front of him on a tray. Then both women disappeared.

The freshly starched and pressed set of jungle fatigues Ruland was wearing creased sharply at the knees. Ruland pulled the fabric in the legs apart where they were stuck together from the starch. He picked up the cold beer and ran the bottle across his forehead. He was slightly sunburned from the day's patrol, and the cold beer and the cool room felt good.

The beads in the doorway leading to the sleeping area rattled, and Ruland looked up to see Thuy Van standing in the room. She was wearing a Red Cross dress and had her hair pulled back and tied in a ponytail. She looked like she stepped off a Donut Dolly recruiting poster. She was beautiful and had a freshness about her that made Ruland feel very good.

"Thuy Van," Ruland said. "You look terrific. Where'd you get the dress? You look just like a number one Donut Dolly."

"What do you think?" She turned around for Ruland to see. "Sergeant Montague say he has other sizes if this not fit. I trade him VC hand grenades for dress. He say base camp warriors pay good money for VC stuff."

"You'll be the best looking girl at the club," Ruland said. "Just wait 'till the other Donut Dollies get a load of you."

Thuy Van laughed and shook her head. She was not quite sure what Ruland was talking about. But she was eager to go with Ruland to Camp Evans.

"Ruland," Thuy Van said coyly, "you do me small favor after dance?"

"Sure, what is it?"

"Stop by hospital. I got some business there. I have some things for trade. Make good deal with medics. OK, Ruland?"

"Sure," Ruland agreed, "we got all night."

The mother and grandmother looked in from the sleeping area and giggled. Ruland put out his arm and Thuy Van placed her hand on his arm with great ceremony and smiled at her mother. They walked out of the cafe and got into the jeep. A box of hand-carved water buffaloes was already in the back seat, placed there by one of Thuy Van's helpers. The carvings were standard trading material in Thuy Van's business.

It was just getting dark and the street was nearly empty except for the Popular Forces and the Viet Cong soldiers passing in the street on their way to work. Ruland had to drive past the compound to get to Camp Evans. The usual crowd of Ruff Puffs was sitting on the sandbag wall as the jeep passed. They remained quiet and did not whistle or call out to Thuy Van like they normally did. The soldiers were beginning to like Ruland, and they also knew from Thuy Van's stern glance when to be quiet. Captain Moss was standing at the entrance to the compound smoking his pipe. He watched the jeep drive by and stroked his mustache as he scrutinized the couple in the jeep.

Two guards were on duty at the main gate of Camp Evans when Ruland's jeep approached. When the jeep was within twenty yards of the gate, one of the men stepped in the middle of the road leading into the camp and halted Ruland. He walked slowly over to Ruland and looked at the wood carvings in the back seat of the jeep.

"You're out a little late, ain't you, Lieutenant?"

"We're just getting back from Quang Tri," Ruland said, tilting his head toward Thuy Van. "She was with the Marines up at Quang Tri."

The guard looked at Thuy Van. "I thought I knew all the girls at this camp. You with this Red Cross unit here at Camp Evans, ma'am?"

"Hue," Thuy Van answered.

"She's transferring from Hue," Ruland interrupted. "Her boss sent her up to Quang Tri to let her see what it's like near the DMZ."

The guard looked puzzled. "You sure look familiar. You ever been here before?"

Thuy Van laughed and threw her head back. "I was born here."

"I know what you mean," the guard agreed. "Seems like I've been here forever too.

The guard saluted and stepped out of the way. Ruland drove through the main gate and into the camp. When the jeep was well down the road, the second guard walked over to his partner.

"Man, that was one of the best looking Donut Dollies I've seen in a long time. I'm going to have to look her up before the officers find her."

"She ain't bad," the first guard said. "But she looks half-gook or something. Must be from California."

"Ya," the second guard agreed. "I hear they got a lot of good looking American gook women out there."

Ruland cruised through camp slowly showing off Thuy Van to the soldiers. She appeared to like it, smiling back at Ruland when some GI would stop in his tracks and stare at her. He parked the jeep in a row of other jeeps in front of the Camp Evans Officers' Club. The other shiny jeeps belonged to the commanders of support units based at Camp Evans, or the executive officers of units in the field. Enlisted men slept or listened to the radio in the jeeps belonging to the commanders. They were the drivers for the commanders. The executive officers drove themselves to the club.

The Officers' Club was crowded with men dressed in freshly laundered jungle fatigues. A Philippine rock band was playing on a small corner stage. The band featured two girl singers dressed in mini-skirts. On the dance floor five Red Cross women danced with officers. Each woman was aware that her every move was watched by the men in the club, and they loved it.

The band and dance area seemed apart from the noise and confusion in the bar area of the club. Officers were three deep at the long mahogany bar. They were all involved in animated war stories, each trying to outdo the other. All of the men's stories were partially true. Usually they were based on something they had heard or experienced. They were usually embellished with bits and pieces of stories from a common core of stories that formed a genre. The officers would go home and repeat the stories as truth for years afterwards until their friends got tired of listening.

When Ruland and Thuy Van entered the club, all the men at the bar turned to look. For a moment, it seemed every man at the bar exhaled when he saw Thuy Van. She glanced at the bar and each man felt she looked into his eyes, and for another moment each man felt he had met the girl of the Orient he had always dreamed about. In that one moment, the Philippine band and the dance floor were off in a distant world. A silence fell over the men at the bar and they forgot about the war, their job, and their women back home.

Ruland spotted a table in a corner near the dance area. He led Thuy Van by the hand to the table and sat down. The men at the bar returned to their war stories. They thought they had seen a vision, and went back to their own thoughts.

"This isn't your average American date," Ruland said to Thuy Van. "But it's as close as we can get for now. You stay here while I get something to drink. I'll be right back."

Thuy Van grabbed Ruland's hand. "What about all these men?"

"Tell them we're engaged," Ruland said.

Immediately after Ruland left for drinks, two men headed for Thuy Van. One man was older and obviously senior, so the younger, junior man returned to his table. The older man sat down with Thuy Van.

"Hello, Miss. I'm General H.M.S. Cooley. It's nice to see you here tonight. I'm up north on an inspection tour for MACV and I wanted to talk to some of you Red Cross girls and see how you're doing. But first, let me tell you that you girls are doing a great job here in-country."

"Thank you," Thuy Van said.

"What do you think of your tour so far?" the general asked.

"Number ten, sir," Thuy Van answered.

The general sat back, startled, then laughed. "I love the way these expressions catch on with you young people. It's a little crude, but to the point. Do you think that expression will become part of the American language?"

Thuy Van shrugged her shoulders.

"Say, you're not very talkative," the general said as he put his hand on Thuy Van's knee. "But I'd bet you'd like to dance with me."

Ruland recognized General Cooley as he arrived back at the table with a beer and a Pepsi. He reached between Thuy Van and the general and set the drinks on the table.

"We're engaged," Thuy Van said to General Cooley.

"General," Ruland interrupted, not knowing what Thuy Van would say next, "there are some of your advisors at the bar who would like to talk to you. I told them you were here. It's those guys at the far end of the bar."

Ruland pointed out what appeared to be the drunkest officers in the bar thinking they would listen to General Cooley's speech about being carried back on a shield. They would have to be carried out soon anyway.

"Fine…Fine…Lieutenant, very well," the general mumbled. "Well congratulations, Lieutenant, and to you too, Miss. I guess I have some business to attend to. I have to talk to the troops, you know."

Thuy Van smiled and shook the general's hand as Ruland pulled her onto the dance floor. The band played a slow song to give the two Philippine go-go girls a rest. Ruland took Thuy Van to the middle of the dance floor. He held Thuy Van at a respectable distance as they danced, slowly, in one spot. One of the older Red Cross girls led her drunken partner over to Ruland and Thuy Van.

"Say, honey," the Donut Dolly said. "Are you checking in here at Camp Evans?"

"Sorry, sweetheart," Ruland interrupted, "we're not talking shop tonight."

"Listen, stud," the Donut Dolly snapped back, "I don't want any of my new girls taken for a ride until I can get them set straight in the saddle."

Ruland didn't want to get involved but he couldn't resist. "You got a thing for horses with all that saddle talk, sweetheart, or do you always talk like a cowboy?"

The Donut Dolly stuck her chin out and stopped dancing. "Fuck you, Lieutenant. I don't know who you are, but just see if you ever talk to another Donut Dolly around here."

The Red Cross volunteer spun around and walked off the dance floor with her partner. When she passed one of the other Red Cross girls, she leaned over and whispered in her ear. Ruland ignored all this, and continued dancing with Thuy Van.

"American girls talk dirty," Thuy Van said.

"Just your average, All-American Girl," Ruland commented.

Ruland and Thuy Van kept dancing to the music of the Philippine band, getting closer together with each dance. Thuy Van loosened her hair and let it fall around her shoulders. All the men at the bar saw this, and were lost in their own thoughts as they watched the beautiful Eurasian woman. Nobody bothered Ruland for the rest of the night.

The Philippine band quit playing at midnight and an old jukebox took in quarters from the homesick men, playing slow country songs. Some of the senior officers found a few ballads from the early fifties and played them. Only Ruland and Thuy Van were left dancing. Most of the Donut Dollies had paired up for the night and left earlier. Some of them had even returned to have a quiet beer with the semi-sober junior officers their own age. The young officers had just left the field and had a hard time getting drunk. The regular base camp officers at the bar were either facedown asleep or slobbering out maudlin stories about home or baseball.

When the bartender rang the bell for last call, he also pulled the plug on the jukebox. It surprised Ruland and Thuy Van. They left their drinks on the table and walked out of the club arm-in-arm. They got in the jeep and rode to the perimeter of the camp using only the blackout lights on the jeep. Ruland found a defensive tank position between two sandbagged bunkers just off the perimeter road. He pulled in the spot and turned the engine off.

"Why we stop here, Ruland?" Thuy Van asked surprised.

"We're parking," Ruland answered.

"What for?"

"Because this is what you're supposed to do on an American date."

"Sit in jeep? You go sit in jeep and look for VC in America?"

"No, you park and make out," Ruland said.

"What you mean 'make out'?"

"I put my arm around you like this," Ruland said as he put his arm around Thuy Van, "and then I kiss you." Ruland leaned toward Thuy Van and tried to kiss her, but she turned away so his kiss landed on her cheek.

"Then what we do," Thuy Van said, playing it straight as if nothing had happened.

Ruland sat back in his seat. "Well, hell, I don't want you to get carried away. And you don't need to analyze everything we do."

Thuy Van laughed. "Just tease you, Ruland. I know about dates. I see beaucoup American movies...like Annette Funicello. I know when to be quiet. I no more talky-talky."

Thuy Van kissed Ruland on the cheek and put her head on his shoulder. They watched the stars over the black shadow of the mountains in the west while Thuy Van talked about growing up in Hue. They talked and watched the red glow from a B-52 strike on the horizon and waited for the rolling thunder ten seconds later.

They could have been two college students parked on a college campus except for the periodic blasts from the 105 howitzers' H and I fire and the glow of arclights in the distance. Thuy Van would jump when the artillery went off, then laugh at the way she acted, as if she had never heard it before.

After a while, Thuy Van sat up straight and said to Ruland, "OK, time to pick up supplies and then go home."

Ruland stopped by the medical building. Sergeant Montague had arranged Thuy Van's trade with the night duty staff the day before. Thuy Van took her box of hand-carved water buffaloes and traded them for some bandages and antiseptic and fifty dollars in Military Pay Currency.

After the transaction, Ruland drove back to the village. It was two o'clock in the morning, and the five-kilometer stretch of Highway One between Camp Evans and the village was usually no place for an American vehicle to be in the middle of the night. But Thuy Van told Ruland that it was safe with her in the jeep. Ruland was beginning to understand.

They rode back to the village slowly. The full moon lit up the rice paddies and sandy flats so they could see an occasional shadowy figure rise up to watch the young couple, then disappear in the night.

Ruland pulled up in front of Thuy Van's café and turned off the engine of the jeep. When he turned to face Thuy Van she quickly kissed him and jumped out of her seat and grabbed the box of medical supplies.

"See you later, Ruland. Thank you for good time." She said as she ran through the front door being opened by her mother, never looking back.

Ruland sat in the jeep a moment, then started the engine and drove back to the compound.

Ruland felt comfortable with Thuy Van. He enjoyed talking to her and being around her. She confided in Ruland that night parked on the perimeter of Camp Evans. She told him how desperately out of place she felt in the village. Although she was born in Vietnam, it was difficult for her to fit in. The villagers were distant to her, not only because she looked different than the other village girls, but because she was an educated, city girl from Hue. For the older people in the villagers, she was also a reminder of the French occupation, a time most of them wanted to forget.

Nevertheless, Thuy Van was dedicated to the people of the village. She was influenced by the compassion of the nuns at the Catholic schools in Hue during her school days, almost as much as the American movies she saw every Saturday. From both of these influences, she was a capitalist in the truest sense of making money, and a socialist in her desire to help the villagers. She lived with the war, not against it, and made the most of it. The war was just something that provided her with an opportunity to do the bartering and trading she loved.

Thuy Van was a typical college student from the cultural capital of Hue before the Tet Offensive. She and her friends talked about art, music, literature, and of course, the American presence in Vietnam. In that sense, she was no different than most college students in the United States back in 1968. Of course, Thuy Van and her friends were all against the war, just like American students. After her uncle, a Viet Cong leader, sent her back to her mother's village after Tet, she discovered that by helping the people of the village she could be a part of the revolution for change in Vietnam. It was a practical arrangement in her mind.

That night, Thuy Van told Ruland that the government that the people would choose after the Americans left would be the government she would accept. If that meant the government of North Vietnam, then she would work with the communists and adapt her brand of entrepreneurial socialism to fit the situation. If the American-backed government maintained power, she could also adapt her particular brand of benevolent free enterprise.

Thuy Van was flexible and durable, and Ruland liked her independence. Ruland also realized that after their night at Camp Evans, he was becoming more and more attracted to her. But he wasn't sure how she felt about him.

October 15, 1968

There was a note on Ruland's door when he woke up the next morning. Lieutenant Fujita informed Ruland, in very precise printing, that Major Hannah wanted to see him ASAP. Ruland took his time and dressed. He then walked out of the yellow building and discovered a different jeep parked by the flagpole. A young American soldier wearing the yellow scarf of an armored cavalry unit was sitting on the wall surrounding the flagpole. The soldier raised a cigarette to his lips as Ruland approached. He saluted Ruland while remaining perched on the concrete blocks, the cigarette still dangling in his lips.

"Have you seen Major Hannah?" Ruland asked the young soldier, not expecting a straight answer or any semblance of military courtesy.

Ruland knew that the commanding officers' jeep drivers were usually the problem children of the company. They were usually assigned these cushy jobs because it placed these soldiers directly under the control of the first sergeant. It didn't take long for the word to spread that if you didn't want to go to the field, and were smart enough not to risk a court martial, then just act like you had the potential to cause trouble. You would either be transferred to another unit or assigned to headquarters staff as a driver.

The soldier inhaled the smoke from his cigarette and thought about Ruland's question. He exhaled, and the smoke escaped through one nostril as he looked up at Ruland.

"I don't know. Who is he?" answered the soldier.

"He's the district advisor here. He's the top man here in Phong Dien."

"I don't know one phong from another, Lieutenant."

"Then you haven't seen Major Hannah?"

"I don't even know where I am, Lieutenant. I just drive the jeep where the Captain tells me. The reason I drive the jeep is because the Captain wants to keep an eye on me because I smoke dope and cause trouble. That way I don't have to be in the bush. In other words, Lieutenant-sir, I don't really care where this Major is or his phong ding."

"In that case," replied Ruland, "I thank you for your support and undying devotion to duty. Just by chance have you seen anybody around that happens to look like a major, regardless of where you are or why you're here?"

The soldier smiled at Ruland with a corner of his mouth and took another drag on his cigarette.

"All the lifers are around back in one of those plywood hooches."

Ruland nodded to the soldier, and walked off. The armored cavalry soldier gave a mock British salute when Ruland's back was turned.

When Ruland entered the plywood building, he discovered that some sort of official hearing was going on. Major Hannah was sitting beside Major Vien at the long mess table covered with green felt, signifying a tribunal of sorts. Captain Moss sat at one end of the table, stroking his long, stringy mustache, watching Ruland carefully as he entered the room. He smoked a yellow stone pipe with a metal lid over the bowl. Another Army captain sat at the opposite end of the table from Captain Moss. He wore a yellow scarf and spurs on his jungle boots, signifying the uniform of an armored cavalry officer.

In front of this board of officers stood a Vietnamese couple. The man was dressed in black pajamas with mud around the cuffs. His wife was squatting beside the man, also dressed in black pajamas, chewing on a betel nut. She would take the nut out of her mouth occasionally to examine it, then put it back on her tongue.

Major Hannah ignored Ruland and looked over the top of a blue folder at the farmer and his wife.

"Three-thousand dong. That's all I can pay!" Major Hannah shouted, believing they would understand English if he yelled at them. He then put his cigar in his mouth and folded his hand across his belly, covering the spot where a button had popped off.

Sergeant Tin translated Major Hannah's statement for the farmer. The farmer shook his head and spoke softly to Sergeant Tin.

"He say boy number one," Sergeant Tin relayed to Major Hannah. "He bery good worker. Three-thousand dong not enough."

Major Hannah removed his cigar from his mouth and leaned forward on the table.

"You tell the son-of-a-bitch that the United States government has a flat rate of this sort of thing, and it's three-thousand dong."

Major Hannah paused to catch his breath, then shouted at Sergeant Tin.

"Tell him he can take it or leave it."

Sergeant Tin quietly translated Major Hannah's words for the farmer as everyone watched the old man tremble. The farmer then spoke softly to his wife, who shook her head. He turned to Major Hannah and shook his head.

"He say no," Sergeant Tin said.

Major Hannah began to turn red. He took a stack of Vietnamese money from the blue folder and handed the money to Major Vien.

"Here's three thousand dong. Tell the bastard to take it or leave it or he's not getting anything."

Major Hannah pointed to the cavalry officer.

"The Captain here can't hold up a convoy just because one of his tanks runs over some goddamed slope kid."

"That's right," Lieutenant Fujita added from behind the table where he was furiously taking notes on a yellow legal pad.

Major Hannah paused to puff on his cigar, exhaled a series of smoke rings to calm himself, then addressed no one in particular.

"We're here to help these goddamn people be free from communism. Doesn't he know that? Goddamn slope kid shouldn't have been on the road anyway."

Major Vien took the money from Major Hannah, reached in his pocket and added some American military pay currency, and held it out for the farmer. Major Vien spoke softly, like a father, to the couple. The woman stood up, went up to Major Vien and took the money. She handed it to her husband, who quickly turned and walked out of the room. His wife followed two steps behind him. When the door closed behind the couple, a smile slowly appeared on Major Hannah's face.

"There," Major Hannah shouted to Captain Moss, "the son-of-a-bitch took fifty bucks for his number one son. Wonder how much he'd take for his old lady? Man, I get a kick out of these little people."

Major Hannah laughed at his wit and put his cigar back in his mouth. Then in a rare moment of reflection for him, he repeated what he said earlier.

"Damn kid shouldn't have been in the road anyway…We're here trying to help these people."

He turned to the cavalry officer.

"There you go, Captain. We're all settled up. I'd wish you'd tell your troopers to stop running over these damn gooks. We can't win the hearts and minds of these people after a fifty-ton tank runs over them."

Major Hannah and the cavalry officer laughed loudly at the Major's joke. Lieutenant Fujita looked up from his notes and joined in when he heard Major Hannah laugh. Captain Moss managed to snicker a little.

"Yes sir, Major," The cavalry officer said as he stood up and saluted. "You're exactly right, sir. I'll tell the troops."

The cavalry officer picked up some papers in front of him and shook hands with Major Hannah and said: "See you next week, Major." He then walked quickly out the same door the farmer and his wife just used.

Major Hannah took another long drag on his cigar, and appeared lost in thought as he exhaled on the burning tip. The white ash of his cigar turned a glowing red. Suddenly, Major Hannah remembered why Ruland was in the room and turned to him. He had another patrol for Ruland.

Major Hannah knew Ruland had spent most of the night in Camp Evans, so he figured Ruland was just drinking at the club and wanted him to pay for his sins by taking out another patrol that day. Ruland knew this was coming as soon as he saw Major Hannah smile at him, so he accepted the assignment without an argument.

Captain Moss had found out from his spook buddies that the current hiding place for the Viet Cong who half-heartedly attacked the bridge every night was in a tunnel system just east of the village, in some higher ground just before the dikes of the rice paddies. The VC lived there during the dry season relatively comfortably. Captain Moss had marked the site of the suspected tunnels on a map that he had prepared for Ruland.

Captain Moss was assigned to the district as part of the Phoenix Program. He was the sort of person that made people uncomfortable at first meeting, and would never really make people feel comfortable around him. Like most intelligence officers Ruland had met, Captain Moss was tight-lipped and offered little information about himself. Lieutenant Blossom claimed that Captain Moss was a West Point graduate who had spent his first assignment in Germany as a tank platoon leader. But his troops hated him so much they staged a sit-down strike the day before a major inspection. The brigade commander, also a West Point graduate and eager to protect one of his own, assigned Captain Moss to his intelligence staff before the troops fragged him.

Captain Moss developed an interest in the secret world of intelligence gathering so he requested a change of military designator from an armor officer to an intelligence officer. Since the Army had so much money invested in his West Point education, and knew from his officer fitness reports that Captain Moss would never make it in actual command of combat troops, the transfer was approved. When Captain Moss arrived in Vietnam, he learned of the Phoenix Program and, using his West Point influence once again, was assigned to the program.

The Phoenix Program was named for the mythical Vietnamese creature Phung Hoang, a bird that heralded peace and prosperity. The closest English translation of Phung Hoang was Phoenix, so for the Americans it was the Phoenix Program. The purpose of the program was to identify and "neutralize" the Viet Cong Infrastructure, or the infamous VCI. The word "neutralize" meant to take out of action either by arrest or execution, whichever was more convenient. Without the knowledge of Ruland and the other MAT team leaders across the country, the Popular Forces units would become one of the principal agents in the Phoenix Program's intelligence gathering. However much Ruland wanted to remain uncommitted in this war, he would soon be a part of this assassination program.

Ruland wasn't in the mood to argue with Major Hannah about the patrol, so he listened to his assignment, responded with a hasty "yes sir" and walked out of the room and returned to his room. There he quietly got his things together for the patrol.

The Popular Forces troops always liked to patrol in the rice paddies because they were open areas, safer than patrolling in the dangerous, heavy brush. Also, they preferred the open rice paddies because there was less of a chance of crossing paths with an American unit. The U.S. troops could navigate better in the open areas. It was too easy for the inexperienced Americans to get lost in the jungle areas to the west of the village and stumble on a Popular Forces patrol, thinking they ran into a Viet Cong unit.

A new platoon leader was in charge of the Popular Forces platoon for this patrol. His name was Second Lieutenant Nguyen Tu Dong. Lieutenant Dong was a man of few words who, like the other officers in the district, bought his commission in the Popular Forces to avoid the

South Vietnamese Army draft. He sold household goods as a traveling salesman in the northern provinces and only came around the compound when he had an assignment.

Ruland teamed up with Lieutenant Dong and the PF platoon by the flagpole and got their final instructions from Major Hannah. Lieutenant Dong looked at the red dot on the map drawn by Major Hannah, nodded his head, and saluted Major Vien. He yelled at his men, motioned for them to follow, and began to lead the platoon out of the compound.

Just as the patrol was about to go under the concrete arch, Captain Moss ran up to Lieutenant Dong and handed him a piece of paper with a list of names on it. Captain Moss motioned for Sergeant Tin to come over and translate a few words that Ruland could not hear. Lieutenant Dong nodded again, and walked stoically out the gate. The platoon straggled out behind him in single file without saying a word. Sergeant Tin then joined Ruland and they took their places at the tail end of the file.

Lieutenant Dong seemed to be familiar with the search area. He led the patrol quickly out of the village to the rice paddies. He was all business. The platoon moved carefully down the dike system, knowing this was an area likely to be heavily mined by the Viet Cong. The platoon would stop occasionally while Lieutenant Dong ordered one of the men to investigate a suspicious looking area where the grass or dirt was disturbed. Lieutenant Dong was methodical and cautious. Ruland liked the way he operated. A few old hiding tunnels that appeared to be unused were uncovered during the first three hours. Lieutenant Dong would throw a grenade down the hole for good measure, then move on down the dike.

Just before noon, when the necessary amount of time had been spent for Major Hannah to receive credit for a complete patrol, Ruland began to relax and prepare for the return trip to the compound. But to Ruland's frustration, Lieutenant Dong found an area of high ground that didn't seem quite right. One edge of a dike seemed to be farther out from the rice paddy than was necessary to hold in the water during the monsoon. He told a Ruff Puff private to jump on the sod until it broke away. It revealed a narrow hole that appeared to lead back under the dike. Lieutenant Dong smiled at the soldier on his discovery. It was the only display of emotion by the Vietnamese officer Ruland had seen. Lieutenant Dong then jumped into the rice paddy and took his .45 caliber pistol out of the holster. He fired three shots into the hole.

Ruland and Sergeant Tin watched the action as they walked toward the activity. They got to the scene just as Lieutenant Dong began to shout down the hole.

"Thieu-uy think VC in tunnel," Sergeant Tin, the interpreter, said to Ruland.

Lieutenant Dong looked up at Ruland and smiled as he pointed down the hole.

"VC! VC!" Lieutenant Dong screamed to Ruland.

One of the soldiers jumped onto the dike to join Lieutenant Dong. He held a grenade ready to throw into the tunnel. Lieutenant Dong motioned for the soldier to wait. Then the lieutenant fired three more shots into the hole with his pistol, and put his ear near the opening to listen. After a moment, Lieutenant Dong shrugged his shoulders and motioned for the soldier beside him to throw the grenade in the hole. The soldier pulled the pin on the grenade and threw it into the hole. He and Lieutenant Dong took a step back away from the opening. Ruland moved quickly behind a nearby dike, and dropped down under cover, hoping the grenade hadn't landed on a Viet Cong ammo dump.

After a long seven-second wait, the grenade exploded with a dull thump. Ruland took a deep breath and relaxed. The private looked at Lieutenant Dong and smiled. The Lieutenant put a new clip in his pistol and handed it to the soldier. Another soldier gave the man a flashlight and pointed toward the smoking hole. The soldier moved without hesitation into the tunnel. In less than a minute the soldier backed out of the hole with the pistol pointed at the head of a man in black pajamas. The man was shaking his head and holding his ears. His right arm was bleeding but he apparently didn't know he was wounded.

"I'd better call Major Hannah," Ruland said to Sergeant Tin. "Tell the radioman to come over here."

Sergeant Tin motioned for the radioman to go to Ruland. The soldier reported to Ruland and handed him the handset.

Lieutenant Dong had already started questioning the man in black pajamas. He didn't recognize the wounded man as a local Viet Cong, so he figured he must be from one of the larger Viet Cong units or even a North Vietnamese advisor. The Lieutenant questioned the prisoner in the standard Ruff Puff interrogation process. Lieutenant Dong yelled at the temporarily deaf man, then slapped him because he wouldn't answer.

Ruland tried reaching Major Hannah on the radio. "Widow-mender six, this is Widow-mender six-two, over."

The radio crackled with static.

"Six-two, this is six, over."

The radioman had turned the PRC-25 radio to the speaker so most of the soldiers in the area could hear the exchange. The Ruff Puffs recognized Major Hannah's voice and laughed at this electronic marvel.

"This is six-two," Ruland continued. "We have one Victor Charlie. We are beginning to question him at this time. The man is about mid-twenties."

"Roger, six-two. Do you have a name yet? Phoenix is right beside me. He thinks your victor charlie may be high level cadre. Get his name, over."

"Wait, out," Ruland answered, and turned to Sergeant Tin. "Did you get that? Find out his name."

Sergeant Tin walked over to Lieutenant Dong and the frightened prisoner. Ruland followed along behind. The prisoner's eyes showed intense fear when he saw Ruland. The private returned Lieutenant

Dong's pistol and the pointed the flashlight back in the tunnel and sputtered something to Sergeant Tin.

"He say dead VC in tunnel," Sergeant Tin translated.

"Fine. We'll take care of them later. See if we can get this guy's name," Ruland said to Sergeant Tin.

Sergeant Tin spoke to Lieutenant Dong. Lieutenant Dong yelled at the prisoner. The prisoner held his ears and didn't answer so Lieutenant Dong slapped him on the side of his face again. Ruland noticed about half the Ruff Puffs were staying away from the scene, quietly talking and smoking. They were either not interested, he thought, or sympathetic to the prisoner. The other half of the platoon were excited and enjoyed the show put on by Lieutenant Dong. The prisoner noticed his wounded arm for the first time and gasped. Lieutenant Dong slapped him again.

"Widow-mender six-two, this is six, over," Major Hannah's voice boomed over the speaker box.

"This is six-two, we just pulled a probable VC out of a tunnel, over," Ruland answered.

"Did you get that gook's name, over?"

"This is six-two. We're working on it, over."

"Well, hurry up, Lieutenant. We need the name for Phoenix, over."

"Roger, wait one."

Ruland shrugged his shoulders and looked at Lieutenant Dong. The Vietnamese lieutenant took the pistol and put it to the prisoner's head and screamed at him. The prisoner looked Ruland. His eyes pleaded for Ruland to stop Lieutenant Dong.

"Tell Lieutenant Dong not to get carried away," Ruland said to Sergeant Tin. "We want to keep this guy for questioning."

Sergeant Tin looked at Ruland. "VC kill Lieutenant Dong brother. I don't think he listen very well."

"Tell him anyway," Ruland ordered.

Sergeant Tin spoke quietly to Lieutenant Dong. When he was finished, Lieutenant Dong slapped the prisoner across the head with the pistol. A small cut opened in the man's eyebrow. The blood began to trickle over the man's eye. Then Lieutenant Dong took the list of names given to him by Captain Moss out of his pocket and yelled at the prisoner again.

"What's he saying?" Ruland asked Sergeant Tin.

"Thieu-uy now ask his name."

The prisoner began to mumble something as Ruland keyed the hand mike.

"Widow-mender six, this is six-two. Standby, I think we are going to…"

The crack of Lieutenant Dong's pistol interrupted Ruland. A dark wet spot appeared on the side of the prisoner's head as he slumped down on his knees and fell backwards into the water of the rice paddy. He floated half-submerged, face-up in the water.

Ruland was stunned. He had seen dead men when he was in the Central Highlands with the infantry, but they were lump figures that were lying around after a firefight. He had never been this close to an actual killing. He had also never been in a position to save someone before. He suddenly felt like he should have done something.

Major Hannah's voice came over the PRC-25 again.

"Widow-mender six-two, this is six. What the hell is going on? I'm waiting for this fucking slope's name."

Ruland took the handset from the radioman and inhaled deeply.

"This is Widow-mender six-two. I'm afraid his name was on the list. We've just had a bit of the Phoenix Program administered on the spot, over."

"What the hell you talking about?"

"The POW is now confirmed KIA, over."

There was a moment of silence as everyone looked at the speaker box on the radio.

"Six-two, this is six. Bring the unit back to bravo charlie. Chalk one up for Phoenix."

"Wilco," Ruland acknowledged the order.

"Widow-mender six, out." Major Hannah closed the conversation.

The private who went back in the tunnel was slowly emerging again. He was pulling on the legs of another person in black pajamas. The soldier pulled the body clear of the tunnel entrance and pushed it up on the dike. It was a young girl of about fifteen or sixteen. Her face was very peaceful and unmarked. Ruland felt a sickening in his stomach.

"Let's get the hell out of here," Ruland said to Sergeant Tin.

Sergeant Tin dutifully translated for Lieutenant Dong. The lieutenant yelled to the soldiers. Most of the men began to walk back to the village. Three of the Ruff Puffs were occupied with the girl. They had pulled the black pajamas off the girl to examine her. There was a small slit under her left breast but no blood. One of the soldiers started to molest the girl with a stick but another man stopped him. Another soldier pulled the dead man out of the water and stripped the clothes off the body. Then he placed the man's body on top of the girl and his friend pulled the girl's legs up around the dead soldier. Several of the men laughed at this.

The nervous laughter stopped suddenly, as if the men finally realized what they were doing. Then they turned and began to join the tail end of the procession back to the village, leaving the bodies in the hot sun.

Ruland looked back and saw this. He started to say something to the men, but then figured it was their war and said nothing. Sergeant Tin noticed Ruland was upset and walked over beside him.

"These men fight war long, long, time. Sometime make fun of VC. Sometime VC kill family. VC kill Lieutenant Dong brother. Lieutenant Dong kill man. You see, Trung-uy?"

"I guess so," Ruland said. He didn't feel like talking about it.

Things were pretty much routine on the way back to the village. The Ruff Puffs casually sauntered along with their giant M-1 rifles resting comfortably on their shoulders. Lieutenant Dong let the point man carry his .45 caliber pistol, which was considered an honor for the soldier.

The point man was the only one concerned with security because they had left the rice paddies and entered the brush area on the trail back to the village. He set a slow pace, walking as if to a gunfight with his hand outstretched with the .45 caliber pistol aimed ahead. Sergeant Tin had completely put the killings out of his mind. He was trying to describe to Ruland with his hands and broken English the size of the breasts of the American women he had seen at the USO Show at Camp Evans. Suddenly the two men heard the point man yell at the head of the line. This was soon followed by the unmistakable sound of M-16 rifles being chambered.

The Ruff Puffs scrambled to the sides of the trail and began searching their pockets and lunch bags for their ammunition. They had put it away earlier since they figured their day was finished with a successful patrol and two VC to their credit. Ruland and Lieutenant Dong looked at each other, each person hoping the other one would take some action. But before that was necessary Ruland heard someone yelling up ahead.

"What the fuck are you? You speak American! What the hell you doing out here? Who the hell are you?"

Ruland knew they had run into an American unit. It was now his job to fix the problem before the Americans shot the point man and opened fire on the rest of the platoon.

"Hey, up ahead!" Ruland shouted. "We're friendlies! Hold your fire!"

"Hold my fire, shit!" a voice came back. "Let me see your ass before I hold anything! Identify yourself!"

"I'm an advisor! This is a South Vietnamese unit! My name's Lieutenant Ruland! This is a Popular Forces platoon."

There was silence up ahead as both sides hugged the ground. Then the voice came back through the brush, "What's the capital of California?"

Ruland's head dropped, then turned to Sergeant Tin. "Oh no, this loony's seen too many war movies."

But this was a real problem. Ruland didn't know the capital of California. He thought for a moment, then countered with his own question.

"Who won the World Series this year?"

The American voice came back. "That's too easy! I asked you first!"

"I don't know," Ruland yelled ahead to the bushes. "I think it's Sacramento."

There was a pause up ahead. "That's a lucky guess. What's the capital of South Dakota?"

Ruland's head dropped again. He knew this one but wasn't in the mood to play these John Wayne scenes.

"Hold your fire!" Ruland shouted. "I'm coming up front! Don't shoot!"

"OK," the voice said, "but move slow or we'll blow you away."

Ruland heard several more M-16s being chambered up ahead. He took a deep breath and stood up cautiously. He walked slowly toward the front of the file on the trail, between the Vietnamese soldiers crouched off to each side. Ruland held his rifle high over his head.

When Ruland saw the American lieutenant he knew there would be trouble. The young officer had a haircut much shorter than was necessary and wore a blue bandana wrapped around his head like some sort of commando. Ruland moved slowly toward the American as the muzzles of a platoon of M-16s pointed at him from the bushes. They had walked into a classic L-shaped ambush.

"We're from the village," Ruland said to the platoon leader. "These are Popular Forces troops. We're just going back after patrol. Are you from Camp Evans?"

"That's affirmative," the young officer shouted.

The man's response confirmed Ruland's suspicions that he was dealing with a zealot and had to be careful. The American lieutenant had the Popular Forces point man face down on the trail with his M-16 pointed at his head.

"He's one of mine," Ruland said, pointing to the man spread out on the ground. "He's my point man."

The American thought for a few seconds, then raised his rifle. "I guess you're OK, or else you're an awful tall fuckin' VC?"

Laughter rose from the bushes on the American side.

"We got about twenty people who need to pass through," Ruland said. "I'll stay here until they're all through."

"OK, go ahead," the American conceded.

Ruland motioned for the Ruff Puffs to move on through the ambush site. He hoped there were no more than twenty because he knew the American platoon leader would probably shoot the twenty-first Ruff Puff who passed. The Vietnamese paraded past the American soldiers with some trepidation, never sure about their allies' ability to distinguish between Viet Cong and South Vietnamese allies. The fate of the Popular Forces platoon, of course, rested upon the American platoon leader. If he had determined the Ruff Puffs were Viet Cong, he would fire without hesitation. It was a popular philosophy for many American troops that was often written on their helmets: "Kill 'em all and let God sort it out."

The platoon passed through the ambush site, carefully watched through the rifle sights of young American soldiers. When the last Vietnamese soldier passed through. Ruland said nothing to the American platoon leader and took his place at the end of the file with Sergeant Tin.

The American shook his head as Ruland passed by. "You wouldn't get me working with no gooks. The only good one is a dead one."

There was laughter again from the unseen American soldiers in the bushes as Ruland disappeared on the trail back to village.

When the patrol got back to the village, Ruland stopped at the café. Sergeant Montague was sitting there waiting for him. Ruland asked about Thuy Van. Sergeant Montague said he hadn't seen Thuy Van all day. Her mother said she went to see her uncle. Ruland wondered if the patrol had gone near Thuy Van's uncle's hiding place, or if Thuy Van was in one of those tunnels. It made him uncomfortable to think that he knew about Thuy Van's uncle. This was information Captain Moss would want to have as he pieced together the district's Viet Cong Infrastructure, and target them for execution.

After a couple of beers, Ruland began to relax. He and Sergeant Montague talked a little about the day's operation and the killing of the man and the young girl. Ruland knew it would be best if he talked to someone about it.

"It ain't pretty," was all Sergeant Montague would say. He'd been in this business a long time.

"No," Ruland agreed. "It's not pretty."

The two men stayed at the café until dusk, then walked down Highway One back to the compound. Sergeant Montague left Ruland off at the compound and continued on to Camp Evans for a poker game. Ruland took his place on the sandbag wall and watched the people until Highway One was deserted. He then went back to his room and tried to read, but his thoughts kept going back to Thuy Van.

October 16, 1968

The following morning Ruland went to the cafe to have some coffee and a bowl of rice. Ruland was disappointed when he learned Thuy Van wasn't there. The most information Ruland could find out from her mother was that Thuy Van was still in Hue with her uncle, and would be back later that day. That relieved Ruland to think that the man they had killed yesterday was probably not Thuy Van's uncle. So after breakfast Ruland went back to the compound.

Ruland was lying in his bunk smoking a cigarette when Sergeant Scroop stuck his head in the room. Ruland could hear the sound of a helicopter in the distance.

"Hey, Lieutenant," Sergeant Scoop shouted. "The Major wants everybody out by the flagpole ASAP!"

Ruland listened to the helicopter approach but did not move until he heard it land at the LZ across the highway. Then he slowly got up and grabbed his fatigue shirt off the back of a chair and walked out to the front of the yellow building. Major Hannah and the rest of the Americans were standing around the base of the flagpole. Captain Moss was squatting on the ground next to the jeep. He watched Ruland over the top of his yellow pipe.

Ruland walked up to Lieutenant Blossom. "What's going on here? The war over or something?"

"Don't know for sure," Lieutenant Blossom said. "We just got word from headquarters to have all U.S. personnel ready for some visitors."

Ruland watched as a silver Air America helicopter slowly descended onto the LZ pad. The two Department of Defense staffers, Mr. Dryman and Mr. Priorto emerged from the helo and ducked low as they shuffled to the edge of the LZ. Both men were still very pale from long days and nights spent in closed intelligence centers. They were dressed like they were about to go on a safari. Mr. Dryman was wearing an Australian Army bush hat and carried a briefcase. Mr. Priorto wore a green beret with a DOD lapel pin replacing the Special Forces insignia. He carried a shotgun and wore a silver plated revolver in a side holster. He also had a bandoleer of shotgun shells hanging around his chest like a Mexican revolutionary.

"Christ," Major Hannah snorted when he recognized the two men. "It's those REMFs."

A REMF was what was known as a Rear Echelon Mother-Fucker. These were staff officers and civilians who remained at base camps and headquarters. They remained in the relative security of the rear echelon camps, venturing out into the combat areas only long enough to be eligible for medals and key phrases in their fitness reports, like: "participated in paramilitary operations at the hamlet level to generate rural support in pacification efforts." This meant the REMF hitched a ride on a helicopter to spend 20 minutes talking to members of a combat unit and scribbling notes in a notebook. These REMFs were looked down upon by the combat troops.

Major Hannah turned to Captain Moss. "Hey Captain Phoenix, it looks like some more of your spook business. Get out there and see what these staff pukes want. You're the only one around here who speaks their language."

Captain Moss slowly unfolded and walked over to the approaching men. When the men met, they exchanged a few words that the others could not hear. Captain Moss pointed to Major Hannah and the civilians nodded. They walked over to the Major, carefully looking around the compound at the Popular Forces soldiers watching them.

"Major Hannah," Mr. Dryman said, "I'm here on Project Greenbucks."

The man showed his identification card to Major Hannah, smiled, and waited for a reaction.

"I know who the hell you are," Major Hannah grunted. "You've been here before, remember? What the fuck is going on?"

"Sir?" Mr. Dryman asked, appearing to be startled.

"What the fuck is Project Greenback?" Major Hannah pressed.

"Green buck, sir." Mr. Priorto offered. "It's green buck. The word should have reached you via MACV OPORDER SIX-EIGHT ZERO ONE THREE, dated 18 September 68. It was classified secret, Major."

"I guess it was," Major Hannah said. "I never saw anything about any fucking project greenback."

This time it was Mr. Dryman's turn to correct the Major. "It's green…buck, not back, Major."

Mr. Dryman then turned to Mr. Priorto. "Vern, give the major the message."

Mr. Priorto handed Major Hannah a piece of paper with the word SECRET printed in red on the top and bottom. Major Hannah immediately handed it to Lieutenant Fujita without looking at it.

"You ever see anything like this, Fujita?"

Lieutenant Fujita glanced at paper and looked back at the Major. "This is classified, Major. Do I have a need to know?"

"Just read the fucking paper, Fujita! Of course you got a need to know, you idiot!" Major Hannah yelled.

Lieutenant Fujita held the piece of paper as if it were about to explode and looked at it. "I think this is Captain Moss' business, sir."

He handed the piece of paper to Captain Moss.

The two CIA men formed another huddle with Captain Moss and talked quietly. Major Hannah shook his head and tried to light the stub of a cigar he had held in his mouth since breakfast. The huddle broke up and Captain Moss turned to Major Hannah.

"Major, in accordance with this directive, I'm going to respectfully request that you to confine all the Americans under your command to the compound for the next twelve hours."

"Oh sweet Jesus," Sergeant Montague exclaimed. "We're having another money exchange."

"What's that?" Ruland asked.

"They're going to replace the red Military Pay Currency with something else to try and control the black market. They do this every year or so. It's probably going on all over the god damn country."

The two CIA men and Captain Moss looked at each other and smiled.

"I'd like all of you men to turn in all the MPC in your possession to me," Mr. Priorto said. "We'll be back later today with an equal amount of MPC in the new green series."

He held up a crisp one dollar MPC. It was the same design as the red money, only a lighter, pea green.

"It's that time again, huh?" Sergeant Montague asked. "Viet Cong making more on the market that the local officials?"

"For those of you who haven't been through this, the aim of Project Greenbuck is to control the black market. We've done this periodically, and I must say it is quite effective. When all the PX's and servicemen's clubs closed last night, they were ordered to stay closed until this operation was completed. They will remain closed until 0800 tomorrow morning, at which time all the red MPC you now hold is worthless."

Mr. Priorto smiled at Mr. Dryman and said quietly, "We got to make it up to Quang Tri before 1500." He then turned to Major Hannah, "Major, if you and your men would turn over your red MPC at this time, we'll be out of here and back later today with the same cash value in the green series."

"All right," Major Hannah yelled out. "You heard the man. Get all your red MPC and turn it in to these gents here. And don't nobody leave the compound today. That's an order. Everybody understand that?"

Mr. Dryman opened his briefcase on the concrete block wall surrounding the flagpole. Major Hannah and Lieutenant Fujita lined up and pulled out their wallets. They always kept all their money on them. Sergeant Montague and Lieutenant Blossom went back to their rooms and returned quickly. Lieutenant Fujita only had a few bills of the MPC. Sergeant Montague had a large roll of money in his hand.

"Where'd you get all that money, Sergeant?" Major Hannah asked.

Sergeant Montague was tight-lipped. "Won it in a poker game, Major."

"What poker game? In Las Vegas?"

"No sir. Two days ago at Camp Evans at an all-night poker game. Won most of it from some airborne guy doing advance work for the 1st Airmobile's move to Camp Evans." Sergeant Montague smiled. "It just proves that anyone who jumps out of a perfectly good airplane can't be that bright at the poker table."

Major Hannah grunted and turned away as Sergeant Montague winked at Ruland.

The men silently went through the line and turned in their red money and received a receipt from Mr. Dryman. Ruland took his receipt and stuffed it in the front pocket of his fatigues. He then walked over to the main gate and climbed up on the sandbags and lit a cigarette. He crossed his legs and watched the people passing by on the highway.

He suddenly noticed Thuy Van riding her bicycle toward the compound, obviously upset about something. She stopped at the wall in front of Ruland. He slid down off the wall and put his hand on her handlebar to steady her bicycle.

Thuy Van smiled and caught her breath. "OK. I made it. Ruland, I want you do big favor for me, OK?

"Sure," Ruland said. "What do you need?"

Thuy Van pulled a large business envelope from under the vest of her ao dai. "I want you get new money for me, please."

She showed Ruland the envelope full of red military pay currency.

"Jesus, Thuy Van," Ruland exclaimed as he looked in the envelope. "How much you got there?"

"I got three thousand five hundred fifty dollars."

She pushed the envelope toward Ruland. "You take it and give to CIA men. They not know it my money. Here, Ruland, hurry, please."

"I'm sorry, Thuy Van. I already turned in my money. I signed a piece of paper saying that was all that I had." Ruland pulled the piece of paper out of his pocket and showed Thuy Van the receipt. "I can't give them any more. It's too late. I'm sorry."

"What you mean 'too late'?" Thuy Van pushed the envelope into Ruland's hands and smiled. "You get me new money, please Ruland."

Ruland looked at the CIA men by the jeep. "I can't do it. You should have given it to me yesterday. Sergeant Montague is turning his money in now. He's the last one."

Thuy Van was almost in tears. "You take, Ruland. Please get me new money. I give you half."

"You know I'd do it for nothing, Thuy Van, but it's too late."

Thuy Van ripped the envelope out of Ruland's hands and screamed.

"You number ten, Ruland! I no want to see you ever! You go drink beer with butterfly girls by bridge! I no want to see you ever! You number fucking ten GI!"

She dropped her bicycle and started running back to the village in tears. Some of the Ruff Puffs sitting on the wall whistled and laughed as she ran by. Thuy Van stopped and yelled at them.

"You number fucking ten gooks!"

The soldiers yelled even louder as she began walking toward the village with her head in the air. Ruland stood helplessly beside the main gate. Lieutenant Blossom was watching all this and walked up to Ruland.

"What happened, Trung-uy?" Lieutenant Blossom asked. "Miss a chance to make some easy money? Looks like you lost your girlfriend too."

Major Hannah saw the two lieutenants outside the compound and yelled at them.

"I told you two shitheads to stay in the compound and I meant it!"

The Major walked over to the two young officers and met them as they strolled back inside the sandbag wall that surrounded the compound.

"Ruland," he said, pointing his finger at Ruland's chest, "one of the staff pukes told me that them new M-16s for this district are locked in some MACV warehouse down in Danang. I want you to get down there tomorrow and check it out. I want you to find out when they're supposed to get here. Then I want you to get back here and build that goddamn rifle range you were sent here to build. I want it built before those fucking rifles get here. Am I perfectly clear, Lieutenant?"

Major Hannah stopped and put his face close to Ruland's and squinted his eyes.

"Cause if there ain't no firing range when those rifles arrive, I'll screw up your transfer papers so bad you will stay on administrative hold until I feel like fixing them. And it will take a fucking long time for me to do it. You understand me, Lieutenant?"

"Yes sir. It'll get done," Ruland said.

Major Hannah turned and looked up and down at Lieutenant Blossom standing at attention in his madras shorts and T-shirt, shook his head, and turned and walked away.

"Jesus H. Christ," Ruland said to Lieutenant Blossom. "Why is everything getting all screwed up. I thought all I had to do was put in my time up here and go home. I didn't plan on things getting this complicated."

"Don't worry about the Major," Lieutenant Blossom said. "He's just blowing smoke. He can't hold you here for not building nothing. He's just trying to get you rattled. Don't worry, we'll get you out of here. I know how to get a rifle range built. No sweat, Trung-uy."

"Well, that's only part of the problem," Ruland said. "I've been thinking about putting in for a six month's extension. Hell, I don't have any plans for when I get out. Another six months won't hurt. Besides, I'd like to see more of Thuy Van."

"Oh shit," Lieutenant Blossom exclaimed, his mouth dropping. "You're getting too involved here, good buddy. Thuy Van's nice looking and all that, but she's pretty tight with the VC. You got to be careful, man. You need to come on down to The Majestic with me tonight and forget about Thuy Van. I still think she's Viet Cong, man. You got to be careful with her. The VC watch who's makin' friends with who. And I'm not talking about these local part-time commies. I'm talking about the hard-liners sent here from up north. They'll make Thuy Van set you up and blow you away, man."

Lieutenant Blossom paused and studied Ruland's face, and lowered his voice.

"Thuy Van's a real fine lookin' woman, but no piece of ass is worth gettin' blown away for. This is as good as time as any to put a stop to this shit. You have to call it quits with her sooner or later. You might as well do it now with a clean break. You couldn't take her back to the world, man. This money exchange thing's the best thing that could happen to you."

Lieutenant Blossom looked at Ruland for a response.

"Ya, I guess you're probably right," Ruland said. He stared at the passing villagers. "But I'll be honest with you. I'd take Thuy Van back with me if I had a chance. Then if things didn't work out, we'd split. She says she wants to go the States and maybe I could help her."

"It ain't that easy, man," Lieutenant Blossom countered. "You couldn't pull it off with all that paperwork." He looked at the ground and started making circles in the sand with his penny loafers. "Besides, the Majestic's got some good looking girls workin' there. You come with me tonight. You don't have to have a girl or nothing if you don't want to. Just have a steam bath and massage. Relax a bit. You need to get your head straight, man."

Ruland nodded in agreement and both men walked back to the MAT Team's room to wait for Mr. Dryman and Mr. Priorto to return with the new MPC. All four Americans from the MAT Team spent the day playing cards in the room.

At about six o'clock the Air America helo landed with Mr. Dryman and Mr. Priorto. The pilots gave the two men just enough time to get off the helo, then took off. The full amount of money in pale green MPC was returned to all the men in the compound. The two civilians told Major Hannah they would lay over at the compound that night to work with Captain Moss on some things. Major Hannah didn't want to know or even care about the work they did, so he set them up in his SEA Hut for the night.

Just after dark, when Major Hannah had settled in for his nightly drunk, Ruland and Lieutenant Blossom walked to The Majestic Steam Bath and Massage Parlor. Both men had the crisp, new green military pay currency in their starched jungle fatigues.

A gray Navy truck was parked in front of the white picket fence surrounding the abandoned bunker. It was unusual for an American truck to be at The Majestic after dark. Smoke was rising from the wood furnace that provided steam for the bath house section of the whitewashed concrete building. Lieutenant Blossom put his hand on the gate and rattled it. Nothing happened so he put his fingers to his mouth and whistled. Ruland flinched and looked across the river into the jungle brush along the far bank, expecting to see a Viet Cong rocket launcher zeroed in on his head.

"You know there's a war on," Ruland said.

Lieutenant Blossom smiled and whistled even louder. An old woman dressed in black pajamas scurried out of the shadow of the front door of the bunker. She unbolted the gate and motioned for the two men to follow her.

The old woman entered the bunker with Ruland beside her and Lieutenant Blossom following close behind. The main room had a makeshift bar along one side. Two young girls were sitting on barstools at the bar. They noticed Lieutenant Blossom and waved.

"Hey, Lieutenant Blossom. It about time you bring Ruland here," one of the girls said. The girl leaned back seductively on the bar and watched Ruland carefully.

A Navy medical officer from Quang Tri was seated at one of the small tables. He had his foot in a cast. He kept looking at his watch and squirming in his seat. Two Vietnamese men in tiger fatigues without rank or unit insignia were sitting at another table with two other girls, sipping their beer and looking around nervously. Ruland nodded to all the customers and sat down at one of the two empty tables. He noticed a large wooden altar with a gilded statue of Buddha at the far end of the room. He figured the door beside the altar led to the sauna and bedrooms. Lieutenant Blossom went straight to the bar and moved between the two girls, patting both of them on their rear ends. He whispered to one of the girls and she walked to Ruland's table and sat down.

"Hello, Trung-uy," the girl said. "You fine-a-ry come to Majestic."

Ruland nodded to the girl. "And good evening to you, too."

"My name Yvonne," the girl said. "What you want, Trung-uy?"

"I'll just have a cold beer, please. What would you like, Yvonne?"

"I want Saigon Tea, preese."

"At least your honest about it," Ruland said. "How much does Mama-san charge for Saigon Tea here?"

"Two buck for Marine. Three buck for Korean soldier." Yvonne smiled. "And one buck for co-van. Special deal for advisor."

"That's fine, Yvonne. Get yourself what you like and bring me a cold beer. I want an American beer. No ba muoi ba, OK?"

"OK, Trung-uy. Mama-san buy best American beer from Thuy Van."

"That figures," Ruland said.

Yvonne leaned down so her dress fell open. "What else you want, Rurand?"

Ruland looked down the cheap cotton dress at the flat-chested girl. He figured she was about sixteen at most.

"I'll just have another beer when I'm done with the first one, thanks anyway," Ruland answered.

Yvonne laughed and went for the beer. The Navy officer at the other table watched Yvonne go for the beer, looked down at his watch, then yelled in the direction of the backrooms.

"Hurry up, Preston! It's getting dark out."

Yvonne brought the beer and a small glass of tea to Ruland's table. Mama-san followed close behind. Ruland paid the old lady a ten-dollar bill of the new green military pay currency. The woman smiled with her black teeth and pulled change in the new currency from a small bag she had hanging around her neck on a yellow cord. She apparently had already exchanged her MPC.

"How long you been Vietnam," Yvonne asked Ruland.

"Eleven and one-half months," Ruland answered.

"Ah..." Yvonne said, biting her lower lip. That why you no come here to Majestic. American GI not come here before go home. Afraid take clap back American girlfriend. But first come Vietnam, fucky-fucky all time."

The girl laughed and made the same obscene gesture with her hands used by the Ruff Puffs. "Don't worry, Trung-uy, Mama-san girl all clean here. No clap. No catch nothing here. You have girlfriend back United States, Trung-uy?"

"No," Ruland answered.

"Maybe you have girlfriend in village, Trung-uy?" the girl asked with a sly smile.

"No, not now," Ruland said.

"Good," Yvonne said grabbing Ruland's hand. "You get steam bath and then can stay with me. All night. Give you good price. Beaucoup cheap."

Before Ruland could answer, Mr. Dryman and Mr. Priorto burst through the front door, startling the Navy officer sitting at the table. They staggered up to the bar, knocking over a chair on the way, and grabbed the girl sitting next to Lieutenant Blossom.

"C'mon, honey," Mr. Dryman said, slobbering his words. "Leave that kid for a real man. I'll make it worth your while."

"Lieutenant Blossom grabbed the man's arm. "Take it easy, partner. The girl's with me. And you're a little too drunk to punch in the nose."

Mama-san rushed from behind the bar and started beating Mr. Dryman on the shoulders with a broom.

"You number ten drunk!" Mama-san screamed. "Di di moi! You beaucoup drunk!"

"OK, Mama-san," Mr. Priorto said, grabbing Mr. Dryman and pointing him toward the front door. "We'll get out of here. This is probably a clap joint anyway."

The two men stumbled toward the door in almost a caricature of two men who get drunk only once a year. Before the men left, they stopped and took a careful look at Ruland and the others in the room. Mama-san pushed them out the door, then took her place behind the bar, sputtering in some blend of Vietnamese and English obscenities.

"Do they come here often?" Ruland asked Lieutenant Blossom.

"First time I've seen them here. They probably got a little horny because the Donut Dollies won't have nothing to do with those headquarters pukes. These guys are making ten thousand dollars a month and feel like they own the place. They come over for a six month boondoggle and make a bundle."

"C'mon, Preston!" The Navy officer sitting at the table yelled again. "We got to get out of here."

The two Vietnamese soldiers sitting at the table still said nothing as they sipped their beer, cautiously watching the Americans.

Yvonne turned her attention back to Ruland as Lieutenant Blossom and the other girl disappeared into the back rooms.

"I used to have American boyfriend back Saigon," Yvonne said in an attempt to start a conversation with Ruland.

"He Air Force sergeant. He make me have baby. He say he marry me, but one day he gone. Move back to United States. He just go. He never come get me and baby like promise. I move back Hue with family, but they no want GI baby. No place to go. Mama-san give me job here."

"Is that right?" Ruland said, not wanting to get involved.

"That right, Trung-uy. I have American baby. You no believe me? You come. I show you."

Yvonne took Ruland by the hand and led him past the Bhuddist altar and through the door to the back rooms. It took a few seconds for Ruland's eyes to adjust to the dark. They entered a large, square room, with no partitions for privacy. At the far end of the room was the door to the sauna. There were candles on the table next to the door to the sauna marking the entrance in the dark room.

The rest of the room was partitioned into cubes. Each cube contained a bed. Large sheets of semi-transparent mosquito netting hung over the opening to each cube, making the people behind the netting look like ghosts. Ruland saw a naked girl through the hazy netting, sitting upright on the bed. The Navy officer named Preston, wearing only his shirt, was sleeping on her lap. Lieutenant Blossom and the other girl had already disappeared into one of the darker corners.

"Hey, Lieutenant Ruland," the naked girl said. "It about time you come Mama-san's. When you finish Yvonne, you come fucky-fucky me. I fourteen. Yvonne seventeen. She old mama-san."

"I like older women, sweetheart," Ruland said to the naked girl.

Yvonne took Ruland to a bed by the far wall and pulled back the mosquito netting. A small child about three years old with reddish blond hair was sleeping on the bed. Yvonne picked the child up and placed her on the far side of the bed.

"There," Yvonne said. "Now you stay with me all night."

Yvonne walked to the end of the bed and slipped her cotton dress off. She carefully put it on a hanger and placed the hanger on one of the ropes holding up the maze of mosquito netting. She wore a pair of red panties that had the words: "I left my heart in San Francisco" printed on the back. Yvonne walked back to Ruland and leaned against him and put her hand on his leg just as Mama-san appeared from the shadows.

"Trung-uy," Mama-san said. "Twenty dollar. All night. Ten dollar short time."

"No thanks," Ruland said. "Not tonight, Mama-san. I'm just here with Lieutenant Blossom for a steam bath and massage. Then I'll just relax with a beer."

"I give you good massage," Yvonne squealed as she began to unbutton Ruland's shirt.

"You special, Trung-uy," the old woman said. Special deal. Fifteen dollar. All night."

"Beaucoup MPC. I give you two dollar for just steam bath and massage," Ruland countered, starting to get in the spirit of the game.

Mama-san laughed and shook her finger at Ruland. "No can do, Cheapy Joe. My girls number one fucky-fucky."

"But I'm not here for that, and besides, I'm protecting your village. You give me special deal. Ruland took two dollars out of his wallet and handed it to Mama-san.

"Two dollar for steam bath and massage, you cheapy joe GI."

"All right," Ruland said, figuring the sauna would be a good way to relax while waiting for Lieutenant Blossom to finish his business.

Mama-san took the two dollars and disappeared into the darkness as Yvonne started to undress Ruland. Ruland looked over at the naked girl watching from behind the mosquito netting with the Navy officer on her lap. She smiled back as her Navy officer's friend yelled again from the bar room.

"Hurry up, Preston! For Christ's sake!"

"Look's like you did old Preston in, honey."

Ruland pointed to the Navy man sleeping on the naked girl's lap.

The girl blew Ruland a kiss as Yvonne carefully took Ruland's clothes, folded them, and placed them beside her sleeping daughter. Yvonne then wrapped a towel around Ruland's waist and quickly pulled off his underwear from underneath the towel as she looked away in surprising embarrassment. She led Ruland past the candles at the entryway to the steam room and opened the door. Ruland took one step in the mahogany-paneled room and Yvonne quickly pulled the towel off him and giggled.

"You no need this, Trung-uy," she said. "I come back for you in ten minutes then you maybe you feel like fucky-fucky."

She pushed Ruland into the sauna and closed the door. There was only a faint light coming through a steamed windowpane from the candles on the outside tables. Ruland paused for a second to get used to the sudden heat, and realized there was a Vietnamese man in the sauna with him. Ruland nodded and sat down on the wooden bench beside him.

"Chao ong," Nguyen O'Bannon said, holding out his hand.

"Chao ong," Ruland responded and shook the man's hand, not knowing he was sitting beside the man who had him in his rifle sights two days earlier.

Both men sat in the silence that men often have when meeting for the first time. The naked men would occasionally glance at each other and smile, not knowing what to say. Nguyen O'Bannon wiped his head once and shook it, indicating what they already knew, that it was hot in there.

Suddenly Mama-san pulled the sauna door open.

"MP. MP. Beaucoup MP." the old woman whispered.

Yvonne ran in the steam room, grabbed Ruland and pulled him out of the sauna, stuffing his clothes in his arms.

"Hurry up, Trung-uy," she whispered. "You come with me."

Ruland fumbled with his clothes as he and Yvonne ran out of the room. The naked girl frantically tried to revive Preston. Yvonne stopped at the Buddhist altar and slid open a panel on the side of the large rosewood cabinet and motioned for Ruland to get inside. She pushed Ruland under the altar and threw his clothes inside on top of him. Yvonne then motioned for Ruland to move farther over and she pushed in a naked Nguyen O'Bannon with his tiger fatigues bundled in his arms. Lieutenant Nguyen O'Bannon, local Viet Cong cell leader, smiled at Ruland as Yvonne put the panel back on the side of the altar.

Ruland looked out from a slit in the intricate carving of the front panel of the rosewood altar and saw the Navy officer with the cast on his leg looking out the front door window, then hop on his good leg back to his table and sit down. The door burst open, splintering the wooden latch. Mr. Dryman, Mr. Priorto, Captain Moss, and two MPS walked cautiously into the room. Mr. Dryman and Mr. Priorto were not drunk, but appeared to be in charge of the raid. Inside the altar, Ruland looked over at Nguyen O'Bannon who held a .45 caliber pistol at the ready. Nguyen smiled again at Ruland.

Mr. Dryman spoke to the Navy officer sitting at the table. "You know this place is off limits, Lieutenant? I'm afraid you got some explaining to do to your boss. You know this is a good place to get the clap."

"It's also a good place to have a beer. There's nothing wrong with that, is there?" the Navy man asked, sensing he was in trouble. But he was a little drunk and didn't know when to shut up. "And I'm sure glad the same friends and neighbors who sent me over here also sent you here to make sure I couldn't have a beer in local cafe."

"There should be a couple more out back," Mr. Priorto said to Captain Moss, ignoring the Navy officer. "There are a couple of your advisors around here somewhere."

Captain Moss turned to the two MPs.

"Go get 'em. And remember, they're officers, so no funny stuff."

The two MPs shuffled into the bedroom. Captain Moss smiled at Mr. Dryman. The MPs returned quickly carrying the other Navy officer by both arms. He was half-asleep and still naked from the waist down, trying to cover himself with his hat. Lieutenant Blossom's girl, the naked girl with the Navy officer, and Yvonne, who was wearing only her souvenir of San Francisco panties, followed along behind.

"What's going on," the drowsy Navy officer asked his fellow officer.

"Our friends here are running tonight's Daughters of the American Revolution patrol," the officer with the broken leg said.

Mr. Dryman asked Captain Moss. "Is that one of your boys, Captain?"

Captain Moss shook his head but did not speak.

"They must have gone out the back some way," one of the MPs said to Captain Moss. "We lost them. Let's get out of here. I don't like being out after dark this far north."

The raiding party guided the two Navy officers through the front door. As Mr. Dryman walked away he turned and winked at Mama-san. The old woman gave him the finger. When the men had driven away, Yvonne ran to the altar and opened up the side panel. Ruland and Nguyen O'Bannon got out of the altar. The two men laughed as they quickly put on their clothes, leaning on each other for balance as they put on their pants.

Lieutenant Blossom casually walked out of the bedroom area, wearing only a pair of plaid boxer shorts, and greeted the men.

"Where the hell were you," Ruland asked.

"Down in the wine cellar. You didn't expect the French to build a bunker without some way to keep their wine cool, did you?" Lieutenant Blossom said as he reached to shake Nguyen O'Bannon's hand. "How's it going Nguyen, you old commie you?"

Nguyen laughed and shook Lieutenant Blossom's hand.

"I'm OK, Trung-uy. How are you?"

"I'm fine. Let me introduce you to Lieutenant Ruland here. He's the new advisor here."

Nguyen bowed and shook Ruland's hand, "I know who Lieutenant Ruland is, Trung-uy. I see him many times."

Lieutenant Blossom turned to Ruland. "I pretty sure ol' Nguyen here is VC. He's always around when something happens, if you know what I mean."

Lieutenant Nguyen O'Bannon and Lieutenant Blossom both laughed and slapped each other on the back.

"Are the MPs gone for good?" Ruland asked, pulling his green T-shirt over his head.

"Everybody gone, Trung-uy," Yvonne answered. "They no come back same night."

"I think Captain Moss is after you, Ruland." Lieutenant Blossom said. "You'd better watch your step. I don't trust those Intel spooks. They take this war too seriously."

"What do we do now," Ruland asked, looking around the room. "We can't go back to the compound. Captain Moss will ask too many questions."

"As long as we're here," Lieutenant Blossom said, his eyes lighting up. "Let's have a beer. I'm buying. Mama-san, put these on my account."

Mama-san and the girls squealed with glee. Within moments she produced cold Vietnamese beer for the men and lukewarm Saigon tea for the girls.

"You know," Lieutenant Blossom waxed philosophically as he opened his beer. "This war ain't such a bad deal, really. Pretty women…Cold beer…Good friends…What the hell more does anyone need?"

Lieutenant Blossom toasted the group with the two naked girls hanging on each arm. He tipped his bottle up and poured it down just like he was back on the campus of the University of Tennessee. The girls giggled with delight and clapped their hands.

Nguyen O'Bannon, local VC leader, raised his bottle to return the toast.

"To Ho Chi Minh," he proposed.

"To Ho Chi Minh," the group responded.

"Hell's bells," Lieutenant Blossom pronounced solemnly, "I may never go back to Knoxville."

October 17, 1968

Major Hannah cornered Ruland the next morning in the mess hall and told him to take the shuttle down to Danang. He wanted Ruland to check on the status of the M-16 rifles. The Major was getting excited about the new rifles, and was eager to have his Popular Forces be one of the first units in I Corps to receive the new weapons. He figured he could earn some points with the I Corps staff. He also gave Ruland another speech about some sort of administrative hold. Major Hannah said he would hold Ruland for "administrative technicalities" until after the new rifles arrived and all of the Popular Forces platoons qualified on them on the rifle range yet to be built.

Ruland didn't know whether Major Hannah was serious or not, but he didn't want to take any chances. So later that morning, Ruland found Lieutenant Blossom at the Majestic and asked him to drive him into Hue to catch the shuttle to Danang.

The two men left in the MAT team's jeep around mid-day just as the heat was settling in. A team of Army EOD experts were just south of Camp Evans on their daily sweep of Highway One when Ruland and Lieutenant Blossom passed them. The EOD team's truck was moving slowly down the center of the road with two enlisted men walking ahead of the truck balancing long aluminum poles with mine detectors on the ends of the poles. Lieutenant Blossom drove the jeep on the shoulder of the road in the soft sand to pass the truck. The wheels of the jeep kicked sand on the two leading men as they yelled warnings about the danger of driving on a road before it was cleared.

Lieutenant Blossom laughed and leaned over and yelled at Ruland over the whine of the jeep's engine as he sped down the road.

"There aren't any mines in the pavement. I don't know why they do this every day. You just got to watch for a new patch of blacktop or something strange-looking and go around it."

He swerved to avoid a piece of soggy cardboard stuck in the center of the highway.

"Like that there," he yelled. "You can never tell what's hidden under shit like that. But I figure if you go fast enough, you'll be over the explosion and only get a glancing blow."

Ruland nodded at Lieutenant Blossom's logic and raised his feet off the floor and put them on the dashboard of the jeep. Ruland felt uncomfortable riding with Lieutenant Blossom because he tended to drive too fast and too close to the pedestrians walking along side of the road. The fact that the road had not been cleared that morning didn't make Ruland feel any safer. As they increased the distance from the mine clearing team plodding along behind them, Ruland's anxiety didn't get any better.

The trip to Hue took about forty-five minutes with Lieutenant Blossom driving. Ruland was dropped off at the MACV liaison office and was told he would be the only passenger on the Danang shuttle. The sergeant in charge of scheduling the shuttle flight took Ruland to the soccer field and dropped him off in the middle of the field. After about a half an hour sitting at mid-field, a green deHavilland aircraft appeared from the north, having made an early morning run to Quang Tri. The plane clipped the trees at the end of the field and landed after one long graceful bounce.

The sergeant unloaded two mail sacks and ten gallons of light green paint. He exchanged this cargo for a mail sack that he tossed through the open door of the aircraft. He handed Ruland a courier package he was to deliver to MACV headquarters. All officers were assigned instant courier duty on flights in-country.

Ruland got on the airplane and strapped himself tightly in the seat. He wondered how this flying box could ever take off from such a short runway. The boxy airplane taxied to the far end of the soccer field, then lumbered toward the trees at the other end at full power. At the goal line the plane lifted off and rose sharply and ran headlong into the top three feet of the trees. The deHavilland plowed through the tops of the trees as if passing through a cloud. The chopped leaves and branches formed a green salad outside the passenger window before the blue sky appeared. The pilot and co-pilot looked at each other and laughed at their maneuver, then they turned and smiled at Ruland.

The flight from Hue to Danang was fairly smooth. Ruland was glad he had a chance to eat breakfast that day. He never got airsick when he had a little food in his stomach. On the flight Ruland thought about Thuy Van. He had the uneasy feeling he was being used but he didn't care. Thuy Van was beautiful and smart. Ruland thought about her proposal to take her back to the states, but quickly ruled out the idea as unrealistic. It would mean a lot of red tape and a six-month extension for Ruland to pull it all together. Ruland dismissed the idea, but he couldn't keep Thuy Van out of his mind. He thoughts kept coming back to Thuy Van the entire trip. He was too tired to fight off his feelings.

The plane landed at the Danang airfield and jolted Ruland out of his dilemma. Ruland had made good time so far that day and he hoped to get the business about the rifles straightened out and go to some decent restaurant in town. He thought about the Stone Elephant officers' club and ruled it out, remembering his first visit to the club. Ruland really hoped that Kate Maddock-Smythe had left the country and taken her anti-war movement back to the states.

The MACV mail truck was waiting at the airfield for the shuttle's arrival. Ruland told the truck driver he had a courier package, so the truck driver gave Ruland a ride to headquarters where he dropped off his courier package. The driver then took Ruland to the MACV supply building. That was where Major Hannah said the paperwork for the rifles was being processed. Ruland walked into the supply building and saw a soldier sitting behind what appeared to be an old post office counter. He walked up to the window that said LOCAL DELIVERIES and asked the clerk behind the small window if he could see the supply officer. The clerk stuck his head up to the bars and pointed with his chin to the closed door to his left.

"You can go in now if you want," the clerk said. "Captain Chin has an open door policy."

Ruland walked to the door and knocked twice, then entered. A short Chinese-American officer was standing behind an ornately carved oriental desk. He was standing on his toes while leaning on his fingertips. Ruland stopped short of the desk and saluted. He always hated to salute captains because they were only one grade higher than he was, and usually younger.

"Captain," Ruland announced. "I'm Lieutenant Ruland from the Mobile Advisory Team at Phong Dien. I'm here to check on the status of the M-16s for our Popular Forces troops."

Captain Chin saluted very quickly and placed his fingertips back on the desk.

"Where are you from again?" he asked.

"I'm up at Phong Dien, with the Ruff Puffs," Ruland answered.

"Ah so, the Popular Forces." Captain Chin said. "And you want to know about the date of delivery for your M-16 rifles, is that why you're here?"

"That's right," Ruland answered, determined not to say 'sir' to an officer one grade above him.

"Please sit down," Captain Chin barked, more of an order than an invitation. Then, speaking very deliberately, he continued. "If my memory serves me right," pausing, still leaning on his fingertips, "the rifles, I believe one hundred twelve in all, destined for Phong Dien Popular Forces are due to be shipped by truck convoy on 19 October. Does that answer your question, Lieutenant?"

Ruland was amused at Captain Chin's formality.

"It sure does, Captain," Ruland said.

"As of this moment, the one hundred and twelve M-16Al weapons are in my property book. Who will sign for them on behalf of the Popular Forces? Would that person be you, Lieutenant?"

"No, that person would be a Major Hannah, the district advisor, Captain."

"Does he intend to come here and sign for the rifles, Lieutenant?"

"No, he probably intends to sign for them when they are delivered in Phong Dien, Captain."

"Ah so," Captain Chin said, tapping his fingers on the desk. "then we have a problem, Lieutenant."

Ruland waited while Captain Chin carefully thought out what he was going to say next.

"I will not release the weapons from my warehouse until someone signs for them. I cannot be responsible for the weapons while they are enroute to your district. What do you propose we do about this, Lieutenant?"

Captain Chin smiled and rocked back and forth on his fingertips.

Ruland suddenly felt the heavy hand of bureaucracy settling on his shoulders. It was the old CYA game- Cover Your Ass. Captain Chin was not about to ship the rifles until someone had signed his property book, thereby removing the rifles from his responsibility. A smile grew wider on Captain Chin's face as he continued to rock forward and back on his fingertips, still leaning on his ornate desk.

"All right," Ruland said. "I'll sign for the rifles. But I'm not riding the convoy up with them."

Captain Chin slowly sucked air between his clenched teeth. "That's up to you, Lieutenant." He paused and tilted his head. "But if I signed for these weapons, I wouldn't let them out of my sight. You will be held financially liable if any are lost or stolen. You do understand this, Lieutenant?"

"Ya, I know all about how the game is played, Captain."

"Very well, then. The weapons will be loaded on the trucks at zero eight hundred tomorrow morning. You can sign for them at that time. The estimated time of arrival at Phong Dien is approximately ten hundred on nineteen October. That's two days from now. There are some other deliveries before your destination." Captain Chin finally took his fingertips off the desk and stood up straight. "That is all, Lieutenant."

Captain Chin turned quickly and started shuffling computer printouts on a matching credenza behind his desk. Ruland saluted Captain Chin's back with his left hand and left the room. He had been sucked into something he was trying to avoid. Not only was he becoming involved with Thuy Van, Ruland made a command decision and became entangled in the Army's supply system with only a few days left to go.

Like most command decisions in the military, it was made only after being backed in the corner by someone who had something you wanted. Ruland could have gone back to Phong Dien and told Major Hannah that he would have to go to Danang and sign for the M-16s, but that may hold up Ruland's departure. Nevertheless, Ruland was mad at himself for buckling under to Captain Chin just for the sake of efficiency.

"It's only a paperwork drill," Ruland said to himself as he left the supply building. He figured Major Hannah would sign for the rifles when they got to Phong Dien. And if the truck were lost in the convoy, it wouldn't be his fault.

After he had rationalized his decision, Ruland looked at his watch and realized he had done what he was sent to do in less time that he expected. He felt like he was setting a bad precedent for the rest of the MAT Team because Lieutenant Blossom had once stretched out a week in Danang signing for the MAT Team's jeep. Lieutenant Blossom used the bureaucracy to his benefit, bribing clerks to hold up paperwork so he could explore the nightlife in Danang. Unfortunately, once he got the jeep the canvas top and spare tire were stolen while he spent the night at some whorehouse.

"You should never do a job in a reasonable amount of time in the military," Ruland mused. "It screws up the system. You should add at least one day to your anticipated completion date for the sake of tradition."

On his way out of the supply building, Ruland noticed a flier on the bulletin board advertising all-you-can-eat spaghetti suppers at the MACV officers' club that night. One of the clerks told him that MACV had its own officers' club on the top floor of the headquarters building but he hadn't checked it out. The headquarters building was only a block away from the supply building so Ruland ruled out a return engagement at the Stone Elephant and walked to the MACV club. He was wearing the black advisor's beret with the South Vietnamese lotus blossom insignia on the front, signifying first lieutenant. The people on the street knew he was an advisor and greeted him as "Trung-uy", or First Lieutenant.

It was the beginning of happy hour when Ruland walked in the MAVC officers' club. Three officers were already standing at the bar, so drunk they leaned on each other for stability. They were singing along with the country music on the jukebox. Ruland found a table next to a window with a good view of the street and sat down. The Vietnamese waitress managed to explain in her broken English that the all-you-can-eat spaghetti supper wouldn't be ready until six o'clock. Ruland told her that he understood and ordered a small pitcher of beer and one glass. The waitress brought two glasses but Ruland knew it was easier to just let her pour two glasses than try to explain to her that no one else was going to join him.

Ruland let the extra glass of beer go flat as he finished the small pitcher of beer. He didn't touch the other glass because it looked like there was someone else going to join him and it kept the three drunken officers at the bar away. After a second pitcher of beer, a few more officers and some American civilians began to show up and take seats at the small café tables. At six o'clock exactly, the small Vietnamese waitresses began serving spaghetti. Ruland ordered a third pitcher and the spaghetti special.

The dining room quickly filled with men in a variety of uniforms and civilian clothes. The crowd was mostly Army officers, but there were a few men from the other services there. Many of the men were advisors to various Vietnamese regular and reserve units in the Danang area and wore a variation of that unit's uniform, tailored to fit the larger Americans.

The bartender turned the jukebox up to overcome the growing noise of the growing crowd. A lot of the advisors that had been in combat operations that day in the area surrounding Danang. They were now arriving at the club as if dropping in at a bar after a day in the accounting department at an insurance company.

The waitress served the spaghetti to Ruland and he dove right in, not realizing how hungry he was. He hadn't eaten anything since breakfast so the hearty meal really tasted good, especially after the two pitchers of beer. Ruland had his head down twirling his spaghetti on his fork when he noticed the dress of a woman standing in front of his table.

"Hello, Lieutenant," Kate Maddock-Smythe said as she pulled out the chair opposite Ruland, spun it around, and sat down straddling it. "Mind if I join you?"

Ruland looked up, and suddenly regretted not signing for the rifles that day and taking the last shuttle back to Hue.

"How you doing, Kate," Ruland said, resigned to the fact that the woman was going to join him. "I already got a beer for you."

"I'm sure you do. You never expected to see me again, did you?"

"No. I didn't," Ruland said as he poured the stale beer into the pitcher and refilled the empty glass with the foamy beer. "But somehow it doesn't surprise me."

Kate leaned forward and let the front of her dress fall open, almost completely uncovering her left breast.

"I promise...No more speeches," she said, crossing her left breast slowly with her finger. "I know you're almost ready to go home, so let's just celebrate your DEROS."

"Good idea," Ruland said as he touched his glass to Kate's in a toast.

Kate sipped the beer and quietly watched Ruland eat the spaghetti. When he finished the meal, Kate asked Ruland about his college and his hometown. They talked casually over the beer and Ruland began to enjoy Kate's company. There was no mention of the Army or the war or the protests back home. Periodically they would dance a few slow songs to the music of the overworked Rockola jukebox being fed quarters by homesick officers.

At nine o'clock the bartender rang a ship's bell for last call. The club closed early because the MACV general didn't really like the idea of a club in a headquarters building, but he knew enough not to try and get rid of it during his tour. The general decided to leave that decision to his relief, just as all the other generals had done. Besides, most of the men had an early commute the next morning back to their units for their workday in the war.

Many of the advisors for the Danang area Vietnamese forces commuted to work. They stayed in apartments around the MACV headquarters, ate and drank at the officers' club, were picked up each morning by a jeep and driver, and delivered to the field to work with their assigned Vietnamese units. After a day at the office, which ranged from patrolling the surrounding hot spots to conducting classes on combat operations, they would return to their apartments, get cleaned up, and go to the club. Most of them thought it was a very civilized way to fight a war.

Ruland and Kate were dancing when the last call bell rang. They had become very quiet and their dancing had become very close and warm and drunk.

"Have you been to the steam bath here?" Kate asked.

"No," Ruland chuckled, remembering last night's visit to the Majestic's sauna. "Is there one nearby?"

"There's one in the basement of this building for advisors. A lot of folks go there when the bar closes to take a steam bath and sober up. MACV advisors can take a guest. I can be your guest, Ruland."

"You mean it's coed?"

"At this time of night it is," Kate answered. "It's open until midnight. Come with me. I'll show you where it is."

Kate led Ruland down the stairs of the building and out the front door. The entrance to the steam room was around in back of the building in what looked like a service entrance. Two young Vietnamese girls at the front desk were disappointed when they saw Ruland with an American woman. This meant a loss of income for their massage service and the other unadvertised services they provided.

One of the girls directed Ruland and Kate to a row of stalls used as dressing rooms. Ruland and Kate each went into their own stall. There was a stack of towels in each stall and a small lock box with a key for valuables. Ruland got undressed and tightly wrapped a towel around him and stepped out of the stall. He didn't bother to use the lock box. Kate joined him in a few seconds with her towel loosely wrapped around her so it hung low on her breasts.

The young Vietnamese attendant led the couple past a series of wooden doors. She opened one door and motioned for Ruland and Kate to enter. The room was filled with steam with one dim light bulb hanging from the ceiling. When they were inside, the girl motioned with her hand toward Ruland and spoke in Vietnamese.

"She wants our towels," Kate said as she pulled her towel off and tossed it to the girl. The girl caught the towel and smiled at Ruland. Kate reached over and slowly unwrapped his towel and handed it to the girl.

Kate was the model of the sixties American woman. She was lean and a bit muscular with full breasts, already beginning to sag because she gave up wearing bras years earlier. Kate reached up with both hands to unloosen her hair and proudly displayed her unshaven armpits. She made a point of displaying her unshaven armpits to men. The Vietnamese girl giggled at the tall, hairy American woman, then closed the door to the sauna.

"You ever made love in a steam bath," Kate said, getting right to the point as usual.

"I've never been in a steam bath with a woman before. Hell, I only take steam baths with my Viet Cong friends."

Kate laughed and stepped closer to Ruland. "You have to take it real easy because it's so hot," Kate said as she moved her hands down Ruland's hips, and slowly lowered herself to her knees, running her tongue down Ruland's stomach as she descended.

"Let's see if we can raise the flag in Danang," Kate said as she looked up at Ruland. When Ruland's flag was up, Kate moved to the long wooden bench along the side wall and laid on her back, pulling her knees back so they touched her shoulders in some sort of stretching exercise.

"Remember now, nice and easy," she said

Ruland started to laugh when he saw Kate's warm-up calisthenics, but held it back when the steam seared his lungs. He thought it was a little strange to warm up in a sauna.

Kate motioned for Ruland to come to her. He went to Kate, walking tenderly across the hot concrete floor and lay down on top of the American woman. Kate immediately turned and locked her legs around Ruland's waist so he couldn't move. She was very strong, or experienced, probably both, Ruland concluded as he began to move up and down.

All the time this was going on, Kate whispered: "Slowly…nice and easy…we got all night."

Ruland thought she may have had all night but it was getting awfully hot and he started to speed up to get this ordeal over with. All of a sudden it was becoming hard work. Yet the faster he went, the deeper he breathed, and the more hot air he would take in. His lungs felt like they were on fire and it was becoming harder to stay on top of Kate because of their perspiration and her gyrations. Ruland grabbed unto the sides of the bench for stability as Kate began bouncing higher and higher on the hard bench. When the climax came, Ruland was sure it was his lungs bursting in flames. Kate was apparently an old hand at steam room screwing for she was not even out of breath.

"There," she said matter-of-factly when they were finished, "that really flushes out the old system, doesn't it? You can't beat that after a night of beer, can you Lieutenant Ruland?"

Ruland tried to answer but could only gasp. She laughed and grabbed Ruland by the shoulders and slid him down her wet body and off the end of the bench on his knees. Then she went into a series of post-coital exercises, which to Ruland, now that he had lost all interest in sex, looked particularly gross. Ruland was still on his knees gasping for air and watching Kate in bewilderment when the Vietnamese attendant knocked hesitantly on the door to the sauna.

"I told the girl fifteen minutes," Kate said. "You don't want to do too much of this at first. You've got to work up to it."

The girl handed Ruland and Kate two towels to wrap around them. Ruland wrapped his towel around his waist but Kate tossed her towel over her shoulder. The attendant led the two Americans to a small room with two tables arranged next to each other. Ruland and Kate got on their tables and faced each other.

Two different Vietnamese girls entered the room and quietly began to massage Ruland and Kate. Ruland relaxed under the gentle touch of the girl's small hands. He was almost asleep when Kate swatted his butt and announced it was time to go. Ruland paid the girls and he and Kate got dressed and walked out into the night air. The monsoon rains would be starting soon and it was starting to get humid at night.

Kate took Ruland back to her apartment near the MACV Headquarters. Ruland fell asleep almost immediately and Kate stayed up late to write the day's event in her journal, just as she did every day since her arrival in Vietnam.

October 18, 1968

Kate had coffee with eggs and bacon ready for Ruland the next morning. Kate talked as Ruland ate. She told Ruland about her life as the daughter of an Air Force brigadier general, prep schools, and two years at Brown University before dropping out and joining the antiwar movement of the American Mobilization Committee. She went to work for the small radical magazine, Bold Challenge, as her contribution to the protest effort. The magazine enabled Kate to get press credentials and entry into Vietnam as a reporter. She didn't have the money to pay her way to Vietnam, so her brigadier general father paid Kate's way, hoping she would mature a little and return to Brown and finish school.

Kate had been in Danang a little over a year now, spending her time talking to officers and enlisted men, hoping to persuade them to desert to Canada through an underground network with an office in Hong Kong. She would try and persuade soldiers and Marines to go to Hong Kong on R and R where arrangements could be made to fly them to Canada. Kate talked to a lot of military men, but was never sure of her success rate. When most of the men arrived in Hong Kong, they had such a good time that they were eager to return to Vietnam in hopes of getting another R and R.

Kate's knowledge of the war was based on coffeehouse discussions she had as a college sophomore. However, after her second year at Brown she realized the most anti-war activity any of her classmates would ever do, would be to talk about the war, so she dropped out of college and became a genuine active pacifist. She enjoyed her role as an activist/pacifist/reporter, and felt her cause was just. Ruland could care less about the war since both the war and the Army were almost over for him. The only thing about Vietnam that interested Ruland now was Thuy Van, and it looked like she was history.

After breakfast Kate asked Ruland about what it was like being an advisor to the Popular Forces for an article about Phong Dien and the negative effect of the American presence on the people of the village. Like a lot of reporters during that war, she had already decided on the story line. She rattled off to Ruland her premise of how the war and the American occupation ruined a peaceful village full of innocent peasants. She persuaded Ruland to take her back to Phong Dien, promising she would live in the village and not bother him. She just needed to gather some material. With an uneasy feeling in his stomach, Ruland agreed to take her back to the village.

Ruland stopped by Captain Chin's office and signed for the rifles before checking in with the MACV transportation dispatcher. The sergeant scheduled Ruland for an Air America helo that was on its way to Quang Tri. Ruland knew it would be hard getting Kate onboard the CIA helo with just her press credentials, so he decided to try and get them on the Army shuttle to Hue. Once they got to Hue, they could then find a ride from Hue to the village.

The Army pilots who flew the shuttle runs were usually 20-year old warrant officers who were easier to work with than the older CIA pilots. The Army pilots would let almost anybody fly with them as long as they had room. So when Ruland and Kate went to the airfield in Danang, Ruland bypassed the manifest clerks and talked directly to the pilots of the deHavilland shuttle and easily got Kate a seat.

The trip from Danang to Hue was smooth and relaxing. Kate slept most of the way. The boxy plane landed at the soccer field in Hue right on schedule, clipping the tops of the trees on the final approach. Ruland had not made any arrangements for Lieutenant Blossom to meet him, so he and Kate got a ride on the civilian bus that made the Hue to Quang Tri daily run. The bus was packed with people, so Ruland and

Kate rode on top of the brightly painted vehicle, along with a few farmers and their chickens. It was cool on top of the bus, and provided a much better view of the countryside. It also provided a layer of passengers beneath them to provide a little additional protection from a land mine.

The bus stopped in front of Thuy Van's cafe around noon. Ruland and Kate climbed down the ladder at the rear of the bus and were greeted by the village children immediately. Sergeant Montague was sitting at one of the small tables under the awning having a bowl of noodles for lunch.

"Welcome back, Lieutenant," Sergeant Montague yelled holding a glass of tea up in a toast.

Ruland and Kate walked over to the table. Sergeant Montague pulled out a chair for Kate and ordered cold cokes from Thuy Van's mother. Ruland told Sergeant Montague that Kate was going to stay in the village for a while to write a story and asked him to set her up with a place to stay.

"No problem, Miss," Sergeant Montague said, "I know a place with a room that will be just the thing for you. I think it's free too. I'll fix you right up."

Kate said she wanted to look around a bit and get some pictures of the village so she left her duffel bag at the table and took her camera and walked around the shops on the street. She was followed by a gaggle of children yelling and tugging on her denim shirt, all eager to have their picture taken.

Sergeant Montague watched Kate photograph the children, then turned to Ruland.

"What's happening with the M-16s, Lieutenant?"

"They should be arriving in a couple of days," Ruland said as he looked at the door leading to the house. "Anything going on around here?"

"Not much, but Major Hannah's getting a little uptight about that rifle range. He's determined to have it ready when those rifles arrive. He wants to invite some brass here for the big day. The Major's up for Colonel, you know, so he's out to make some points."

"Ya, I know," Ruland said with a sigh of resignation. "We got to get going on that thing. I was looking at that area south of the compound the other day. All we really need is a pile of sand for a berm so these Ruff Puffs don't shoot up the farmers out in the rice paddies. We can mark off 25, 50, and 100-meter firing lines and we're ready for qualifications. It's not that big a deal. We can do it in a day."

"Then we'll get on it, Lieutenant," Sergeant Montague said with smile. "You won't get your Bronze Star if you don't get that range built. Got to make sure all you officers get your end-of-tour Bronze Star. They just give us poor black folk an airplane ticket out of here."

Ruland smiled at Sergeant Montague. "Spare me the speeches, Sergeant. You'll need more than one airplane for you and that cargo box full of money you've collected from your after-hours work."

Ruland looked around the café, searching for Thuy Van. He then turned to Sergeant Montague and tried not to appear too eager.

"You seen Thuy Van around here?"

"She's around back in her Army-Navy Store."

"She get some new things?" Ruland asked.

"She got a whole pallet load of Cold Power laundry soap from a convoy yesterday. She plans on selling it to the Marines. They like to wash in cold water. They think it makes them tough." Sergeant Montague leaned toward Ruland as Kate was crossing the street, returning to the cafe.

"I think Thuy Van would like to see you, Lieutenant. She was a little upset when she heard you spent the night at the Majestic."

"I didn't think she wanted to see me again."

"All that money changing business is cleared up," Sergeant Montague said as Kate sat down at the table. "Why don't you go back and see her and I'll take care of this reporter here."

Ruland walked around to the rear of the building. Thuy Van was in front of the back door seated in a chair. She was treating an infection on the arm of a small boy. She saw Ruland and smiled as she finished wrapping a bandage on the boy's arm, then sent him away. She motioned for Ruland to follow her as she carried her chair into the back room. Ruland followed her into the room and Thuy Van closed the door behind her.

"How you doing, Ruland. I thought you never come see me again. I get mad at you. Now I know why you no change MPC for me. But everything number one now. I fix everything. I buy beaucoup cameras from Korean soldiers before they know red MPC no good. Then sell cameras to American GIs because there are no cameras in PX. Korean soldiers buy them all. GIs get cameras and I get new green MPC. Korean soldiers buy metal bracelets from Montagnards with old red MPC so they can sell bracelets to American workers in Saigon. Montagnards take old MPC to CIA. CIA give new money to Montagnards so they stay on Saigon and American side. Everybody OK. Everybody make money except CIA, but they no care."

She paused and stepped up to Ruland and put her head down. "You mad at me, Ruland?"

"No. I'm not mad. I'm just sorry I couldn't help you. That was a lot of money you had to change."

Thuy Van looked up at Ruland and pretended to be upset. "Ruland, why you go Mama-san's by bridge and see butterfly girls? You no like me?"

"I didn't think you wanted to see me anymore," Ruland stammered. "Besides, I didn't do anything there. Just had a couple of beers with Lieutenant Blossom."

"And Nguyen O'Bannon. He tell me you now become Bhuddist. You hide under Buddha."

She laughed and put her hands on Ruland's arm as Sergeant Montague knocked on the door and opened it. Thuy Van quickly stepped back from Ruland.

"How many VC you got back here, sweetheart?" Sergeant Montague said, winking at Thuy Van.

Thuy Van smiled at Sergeant Montague. "Just me, Trung-si."

Sergeant Montague looked around the storeroom, stocked high with all types of supplies. Thuy Van smiled at Ruland, proud of her warehouse.

"Sergeant Montague and me been talking," she said to Ruland. "We like to help people in village. Everyone fight in war. But I help people in village. I have soap and cloth and bandages. Sell everything else. Many people think I butterfly girl because I spend beaucoup time with GIs and Koreans, but I not care. I make beaucoup money and help people. You want to help me, Ruland?"

"What do you need?" Ruland asked, knowing he was being pulled in again.

"Maybe you take me next time you go Camp Evans. You buy for me, what you call, antiseptic in PX. Children in village get many infections. Very hard for me to get alcohol. Please, Ruland. And please get me other things I can sell. I can sell anything. First Cavalry is moving out and they throw away beaucoup good things I can sell. You go to ammo dump, OK. Lots of things there I can sell. GI throw away beaucoup bullets and ammo. No place to store bullets on trucks when they move, so they throw away."

"Ammo dump?" Ruland asked. "Who you going to sell ammo to?"

Thuy Van looked surprised. "I sell anybody who buy. Who you think? Then I take money and help people in village. What you think, Ruland?"

"Lieutenant," Sergeant Montague interrupted. "I think we can fix her up fine. Let's all go to Camp Evans right now. You can talk to the folks at the engineer battalion about getting a bulldozer to build the berm for the firing range. I'll go see an EOD friend of mine who's got access to the ammo dump. He owes me one. Then we'll cruise around and see who's pulling up stakes and see what we can find."

Ruland thought for a second about how supplying surplus ammunition to Thuy Van so she could sell it to the Viet Cong fit in his mission of helping the people of the village and concluded it made sense in a convoluted way.

"All right," Ruland announced. "I'll see if we can get some heavy equipment out here and build that firing range. Then we can swing around some of these 1st Cavalry outfits that are leaving and see what we can get. Let's do it today."

"But first I make you lunch," Thuy Van said to Ruland and reached for his hand.

Sergeant Montague got the message, so he smiled and said, "I'll go out front and take care of that reporter, Lieutenant. Looks like you two want to talk." Sergeant Montague left the couple to help Kate find a room in the village. He yelled over his shoulder as he went out the door. "I'll be back in about an hour, then we'll head for Camp Evans."

Thuy Van led Ruland into the main room and sat him down at the long, low rosewood table. Thuy Van sat beside him and brushed against him. Ruland smelled the sweet smoke of the joss sticks in her hair. All that he thought about on the plane ride to Danang came back. He made up his mind.

"You know what I'm going to do?" Ruland blurted out.

Thuy Van sat up straight, surprised at his outburst.

"What you do, Trung-uy?"

"I'm going to put in for an extension," he announced.

"What you going to extend, Trung-uy?"

"It means I can stay here for another six months."

Thuy Van pulled back from Ruland and looked at him. "You going stay here? Why you do that, Ruland?"

Ruland shrugged his shoulders. "I guess it's because I got nothing else to do."

Thuy Van leaned forward in disbelief. "Maybe it because you want to be with me. Is that reason, Ruland?"

"Ya, that's part of it I suppose," Ruland conceded. "I don't mean all the time, but I can be with you a lot of the time. All I got to do is get Major Hannah to approve my request and forward it to MACV in Saigon. He'll do it if I get that firing range built and the PFs qualified. They're always trying to get people to extend over here so why wouldn't they approve an extension. It's cheaper than flying in new people."

"Ruland," Thuy Van continued to press him. "You maybe stay because you like me?"

Ruland felt commitment closing in around him. "That could be," he said, with some effort.

Thuy Van laughed and punched Ruland in the stomach. "You know I right," she said. "And I tell you something else, Ruland. I will be your number one girlfriend for next six months so you not want to leave."

The young woman laughed and threw her arms around Ruland, knocking him over on the floor. They wrestled and laughed for a minute, then the two young people looked into each other's eyes and were silent. They were world's apart, yet something was pushing them together. With the prospect of another six months together sinking in for both of them, the feelings they had tried to hide were coming out. Ruland was not sure what was going to happen. He had hoped he wouldn't get involved. But it was too late.

Sergeant Montague arranged for Kate to stay at the Catholic orphanage in a room that was used for visiting priests. Kate thanked Sergeant Montague profusely, excited about the opportunity to write a photo-feature on the Irish priest and the children of the orphanage.

After Sergeant Montague got Kate settled, he picked up Ruland and Thuy Van in the jeep and they headed to Camp Evans. He dropped Ruland off at the headquarters of the engineer battalion, and continued on with Thuy Van to the ammo dump. The engineers' headquarters was a simple frame building in a row of similar buildings. The sign in front of the building said: 445 ENGINEER BATTALION. Ruland got out of the jeep and walked into the building. Sergeant

Montague and Thuy Van drove on down the dirt road to visit his EOD friends at the ammo dump.

There was a clerk sleeping at the front desk just inside the door at the engineer battalion. Ruland walked past the man and down narrow hallway until he saw a wooden sign with COMMANDING OFFICER intricately carved on it. Ruland knocked on the door and walked in. A second clerk tried to stop him, but Ruland walked on past him. He went straight to the desk of a Captain Prbyzc. Ruland stopped in front of the captain's desk and saluted.

"Captain, I'm Lieutenant Ruland from the Mobile Advisory Team I-15. I'm assigned to the village just north of the camp.

"I don't think you got an appointment, Lieutenant," Captain Prbyzc said. "What exactly do you want here?"

"Well Captain," Ruland began his request, "in a couple of days the Popular Forces in the village are going to be issued new M-16s…Part of the Vietnamization program. You probably heard about that. I need to build a rifle range so my advisor team can train the Ruff Puffs on their new rifles. We're required to qualify them as soon as possible. It's as MACV requirement."

Ruland paused to let his words sink in.

"We got an area picked out for a firing range just south of our compound, but it so flat around there that there is nothing to shoot into. What I need is one of your bulldozers to push up a pile of sand into a berm as a backdrop behind the targets. We need to build a berm for an impact area so we don't shoot up the farmers who work in the nearby rice paddies. You see what I'm getting at, Captain?"

Captain Prbyzc rubbed his chin and thought. "The United States Army combat engineers are concerned about their image in this war, Lieutenant." He stroked his handlebar mustache. Are there going to be any press people there to cover this Vietnamization shit?"

"Yes sir," Ruland said, thinking of Kate Maddock-Smythe, reporter for Bold Challenge magazine.

"I see," Captain Prbyzc mused. "The press likes these human interest stories, you know. But, a rifle range has got to go pretty low on our priority list when it comes to public affairs. It's too…too…warlike, if you know what I mean…too many guns. Right now we're rebuilding a schoolhouse some Navy pilot bombed by mistake. It's beautiful…beam ceilings…matching outhouse. The Division Public Information Officer thinks it's going to make all three networks. Of course we didn't tell the press about the Navy's screw-up. We said the VC blew up the school. You got to take advantage of this stuff, you know what I mean, Lieutenant?"

"I think so," Ruland said, knowing he was going to have to endure a speech before he got an answer.

"We engineers try not to show guns," the Captain continued. "We want to show the good things about this war. The American public sees the bad things on television every night thanks to the left-wing liberal press back in New York. Hell, we got more reporters over here than infantrymen. We got to fight fire with fire, you know. It's a PR battle now. So you see, we can put your rifle range on our work schedule, but there's no telling when we can get to it. We got a lot of projects ahead of you…projects that make for better press, if you know what I mean, Lieutenant?"

Captain Prbzc suddenly laughed uncontrollably for no apparent reason, then continued.

"These Navy guys flying off carriers will bomb anything. They get bored floating around the South China Sea all day. They don't have little gook whores waiting for them back at the barracks like the Air Force pilots do. So the Navy guys let off steam by bombing everything they see. Hell, they're blowing up so much shit up we're getting behind in our work."

"War is definitely hell," Ruland said.

"We've put in for a full-time public information officer to be assigned just to us."

Captain Prbyzc paused and drifted into another thought, then he remembered Ruland was standing in front of him.

"Go ahead and fill out an F-681 Alpha and we'll keep it on file. But it'll be a long time before we can get to it. A rifle range…damn bad press during a war. You can see what I mean, can't you Lieutenant?"

"I understand, Captain," Ruland said and saluted. He knew there was no use arguing with Captain Prbyzc.

"Sorry I can't help you out," Captain Prbyzc said as he returned Ruland's salute.

Ruland did an about face and left the building the way he came in. The clerk at the front desk was still sleeping, face down on his green blotter. A small dark spot was just under his mouth.

Ruland waited in front of the building for Sergeant Montague to return. He noticed Captain Prbyzc's jeep. It had a bumper sticker on it, which read: COMBAT ENGINEERS-REBUILDING VIETNAM ONE HOOCH AT A TIME.

After about a ten-minute wait in front of the engineer's building, Ruland was picked up by Sergeant Montague and Thuy Van. They had the back of the jeep filled with boxes containing hand grenades. The grenades had been issued to enlisted men then collected again by the Military Police when fragging officers started to become popular. The base commander decided not to reissue them to the troops in the field, justifying his decision by claiming that some of the grenades had their explosives removed, ready to be mailed home as souvenirs of the war.

Sergeant Montague's cache was scheduled to be blown up by the Explosive Ordnance Demolition team on the base the next day. The EOD team usually set aside one day a week to detonate artillery duds so the Viet Cong wouldn't get their hands on them and make them into booby traps. Most of the duds were collected by Vietnamese children and sold to the CIA for cash.

"You did better than I did," Ruland said to Sergeant Montague. "I struck out with the engineers. We're on their project list for a bulldozer, but it's not going to happen any time soon."

"Hell, Lieutenant, I knew you wouldn't have any luck with that damn Captain Prbyzc. I play poker with his first sergeant, and he told me the captain won't do anything that won't help his career. Hell, that man's jeep's too clean, for openers. It's obvious he's not going to get out in the field if he can help it. Especially, if it means doing something they can't put in his fitness report."

Sergeant Montague thought about the problem as the trio drove down the dusty road of the base camp. He suddenly brightened up with an idea.

"But you know who can help, Lieutenant? Ol' Lieutenant Blossom. He's in tight with some Sea Bees up at Quang Tri. Hell, they got a bulldozer, and they will do anything for a little booze."

Before leaving Camp Evans, Sergeant Montague stopped at a small plywood building near the field hospital that was used for storage. One of the medical support units had already packed up and left Camp Evans and the replacement unit from the 101st Airmobile Division hadn't arrived yet. The building contained all sorts of medical supplies that were considered expendable and too much of a bother to pack. So the medics just left them. Thuy Van was excited about the cache of supplies, free for the taking.

Ruland and Thuy Van loaded up the jeep with as much as they could while Sergeant Montague walked over to the field hospital. He returned with an official looking document on the field hospital's stationary. The document announced that the small building and all its contents were the property of MAVC. The document was signed by Sergeant Montague in an elaborate, unreadable signature.

"I got a buddy over at the hospital," Sergeant Montague said as he thumbtacked the letter on the front door of the building. "This letter will keep this stuff safe for us until I send Sergeant Scroop back here to collect it. In this man's Army, just as long as you have some sort of official looking paper on the front door, no one is going to mess with it."

The trio climbed on the jeep, now overflowing with supplies, and slowly made their way back to the village. They unloaded the supplies at Thuy Van's café just as Sergeant Scroop was returning from an afternoon massage at the Majestic. Ruland asked Sergeant Scroop to return to Camp Evans and collect the rest of the supplies. Sergeant Scroop was eager to do it because he liked Thuy Van. She was also one of his business partners. She was one-third of a business Sergeant Scroop started with Nguyen O'Bannon. They had a little shop in the village making mahogany surfboards that Thuy Van sold to the Special Services supply officer down south at the China Beach Rest and Recreation Facility.

When Sergeant Scroop returned later that day, he not only had the jeep filled with supplies from the medical building Sergeant Montague liberated, he had the entire building. It was dismantled and loaded on the back of a deuce-and-half truck that followed the jeep. He figured the building was just what was needed for his growing surfboard business. Sergeant Scroop unloaded the supplies in Thuy Van's warehouse, then took the dismantled building to Nguyen O'Bannon. Sergeant Scroop and Nguyen O'Bannon then spent the rest of the afternoon attaching the building onto their small carpenter shop. It was a major capital improvement for the home of Scroop-O'Bannon Surfboards, Inc.

At the end of the day's work, Thuy Van hosted the Americans to free beer and bhan trang cuon ton, shrimp rolls made from fresh shrimp. Sergeant Montague managed to get the shrimp from the cook at the Camp Evan's Officers' Club. Kate Maddock-Smythe and the Irish priest joined the party about halfway through the meal. Nguyen O'Bannon wasn't able to join the party. Sergeant Montague figured it was his night to fire a few rockets at the bridge.

The party lasted to about ten o'clock, when the sound of two small rockets could be heard exploding on the bridge. That was the unofficial curfew signal for the village that it was time to go to bed. Thuy Van gave Ruland a shy, goodbye handshake in front of the priest and other guests and quickly disappeared into her house. Sergeant Montague took the jeep and dropped Sergeant Scroop off at The Majestic, then returned to Camp Evans for another poker game. Kate and the priest went back to the orphanage. Ruland walked slowly back to the compound thinking it had been a pretty good day, more or less.

October 19, 1968

The M-16s arrived around noon the next day. Ruland and Lieutenant Blossom were having lunch at Thuy Van's cafe when Lieutenant Tram walked by and told them the rifles were on a truck now parked in the middle of the compound. Major Hannah wanted Ruland to sign the shipping order, then transfer the rifles over to Major Vien and the government of South Vietnam. Neither Major Hannah nor Lieutenant Fujita wanted to put their name on the document, even for a short period of time.

Lieutenant Blossom drove Ruland to the compound and dropped Ruland off at the main gate. There was a crowd of villagers around the gate, all looking in at the truck that brought the M-16s to town. Lieutenant Blossom was not interested in staying around for any type of paperwork either. He had to get back to the Majestic for his regularly scheduled afternoon massage and nap.

When Ruland entered the compound Major Hannah was standing in the back of the truck wearing a shoulder holster with a .45 caliber pistol. Around forty Ruff Puffs were milling around the truck waiting to receive their new black rifles. They carried their M-1 rifles and .30 caliber carbines with them, more than eager to trade these old weapons for the sleek M-16s. The new rifles meant that they would carry the same weapons as the Americans and the Army of the Republic of Vietnam. They would gain status as near equals, even though the Popular Forces were a pretty loose-knit military organization, and thought to be near the bottom of the military pecking order.

The American truck driver who brought the rifles to Phong Dien had all the paperwork ready for Ruland. It was a simple matter for someone to sign his name in two or three places for receipt of the rifles, replacing Ruland as the responsible officer. Major Hannah had spent a considerable amount of time the last few days developing an elaborate distribution system for the rifles. Major Vien would accept the rifles from Ruland and enter them into the district's property book. Then each Popular Forces soldier would trade in his M-1 or carbine, and sign for his new M-16. Major Hannah figured the soldier would then be accountable if the rifle was lost, stolen, or sold to the Viet Cong.

Lieutenant Fujita sat at one end of the long table used in the mess hall for the transfer ceremony. He had a new green ledger book, three sharpened pencils, and an ink pad in front of him. He had carefully drawn columns in the green ledger for the serial number of each rifle, and space for the Popular Forces soldier to either sign or put his thumbprint beside Major Vien's signature.

This system, in traditional U.S. Army fashion, would indicate for legal purposes, both the accountable officer and the responsible soldier. To make it harder for the Ruff Puffs to sell the rifles, Lieutenant Fujita was ready to stencil the letters "PF" with a can of yellow spray paint on the butt of each black plastic stock. When each rifle was marked with the yellow paint, it was given to the soldier. Many of the soldiers held the weapon at arm's length, like a strange, black snake.

The distribution began after Major Vien made some sort of short speech to his troops. All the Americans thought the speech had something to do with appreciating the contribution of the United States to their security. Actually, Major Vien told his troops to not ask questions and just sign or mark where they were told. He had plans for some of the new rifles.

The transfer was all very orderly. The old M-1 rifles and the .30 caliber carbines were collected from the soldiers and put on the truck. Then the brand new Colt M-16s were issued to the troops. Most of the

PF soldiers put their thumbprint beside Major Vien's elaborate signature and smiled broadly as they were handed their new weapon.

Major Vien stood to make a little money from the arrival of the new weapons. Like most District Chiefs, Major Vien's military pay was supplemented by what were known as ghost soldiers. Ghost soldiers were the names of soldiers on the Popular Forces who had deserted, been killed in action, or who were simply fictitious. The names of these ghost soldiers were listed on Major Vien's troop roster along with the actual members of the Popular Forces. This was the roster that was sent back to Saigon for pay purposes. The Saigon government would then allocate pay for each man on the roster, and Major Vien could pocket the pay of these ghost soldiers. This was an accepted practice throughout the country, and a way for the underpaid district chiefs to make a little extra money.

The number of M-16s allocated to Phong Dien District was also based on the pay roster Major Vien submitted to Saigon, ghost soldiers and all. Therefore Major Vien received one brand-new M-16 rifle for each real soldier and one for each ghost soldier on his roster. Although Major Hannah was standing beside Major Vien as each of the Popular Forces soldier received his new weapon, just to make sure all weapons were accounted for, he was not aware of what was happening. Since all Asians looked the same to Major Hannah, several soldiers reappeared in line representing Major Vien's ghost soldiers. They would accept the rifles, put their thumb print on the district property book, go in the yellow building and turn these extra rifles over to one of Major Vien's lieutenants.

After the administrative business was completed, Major Vien collected the extra rifles and stored them in his room in the yellow building. Major Vien knew the new M-16s were in demand on the black market, and would fetch a good price. Thuy Van knew this too, and had already negotiated a sale for several of the ghost soldier's rifles.

Only one thing was missing from making this a smooth transition. The decision was made at MACV Headquarters to ship the rifles and ammunition in separate trucks in separate convoys. This was to prevent both rifles and ammunition from falling into the hands of the Viet Cong in the event one of the convoys was ambushed on Highway One.

Unfortunately, and quite predictably, the ammunition truck was delayed in Hue because the truck driver was too hung-over to join his convoy. The ammunition truck wouldn't arrive for a day or two. This not only left the compound defenseless for a couple of days, but also frustrated the Ruff Puffs who were eager to try out their new weapons.

But it didn't take long before the underground supply network took over. Three cases of M-16 ammunition appeared in the compound within a couple of hours, purchased from Thuy Van by Major Vien. Major Vien felt uncomfortable with his Popular Forces not having any ammo for the night. Although most everyone in district liked Major Vien, most Viet Cong included, there was still a price on his head and the PFs were his first line of defense. Nobody knew what Major Vien paid Thuy Van for the ammo, and it didn't matter when the shooting started.

It all began simply enough. Major Vien passed out the ammunition to his soldiers and told them it was for defense of the compound, and that it would be a couple of days before more ammo arrived. After each soldier received eighty rounds of Thuy Van's ammo, enough for four clips, Major Vien then went to Camp Evans with Major Hannah for a meeting. Major Vien dispatched his lieutenants to the village to get some supplies for a party that night. He never passed up an opportunity to have a celebration, and the arrival of the M-16s was as good a reason as any to have a party.

After the trucks left and Ruland settled down in the security of the yellow building, a few of the braver Ruff Puffs couldn't resist the temptation. They began to fire single shots into the air just to get the feel of their new weapons. Then a couple of the soldiers fired their rifles on full automatic to see how they compared to the old .30 caliber carbines. This sporadic firing went on for a couple of hours.

At around mid-afternoon, arguments sprung up around the compound concerning the accuracy of the new rifles. Some of the older soldiers were convinced that their old M1 rifles were more accurate than the modern M16s, which was true. And as usually happens in most arguments, two sides formed and the debate became quite heated. Then as would be expected, the main point of the discussion became lost in the rhetoric. Gradually the discussion turned from the merits of the M-16 rifle to the virtue of some of the wives of the men.

Since all the Popular Forces soldiers were more or less on the same side in support of the war, although about half of the Popular Forces unit would probably join the Viet Cong if they were offered a better deal, nobody actually really wanted to hurt anybody. So the two arguing factions soon dispersed to their respective bunkers in the sandbag wall surrounding the compound to cool off.

Then when boredom set in, each side began taking shots at the eating utensils of the opposing debate team. The metal rice bowls and platters drying in the sun outside the little cubicles of the soldiers built into the sandbag wall were too hard to resist. And if a soldier's favorite rice bowl was hit in this target practice, the soldier would retaliate by running from his bunker with his new weapon on his hip like a miniature John Wayne and strafe the opposing sandbag bunker with a burst of five to ten rounds. All the soldiers would laugh wildly at this and things would settle down for about 10 minutes until someone started shooting pots and pans again. The villagers who were watching from Highway One thought it was quite a show.

During this exchange of friendly fire, Major Hannah and Major Vien were safe inside the thick walls of a sandbag briefing room at Camp Evans. Lieutenant Fujita was in the mess hall hooch nervously checking and counter-checking the green ledger, not quite sure why there always seemed to be fewer Ruff Puffs around than the number of weapons delivered that day. He heard the shots but now figured the soldiers were just eager to try out their new weapons, and would save a few rounds for the night.

Sergeant Montague had left the compound as soon as he saw the truck pull in. He knew from experience what would happen when the Ruff Puffs finally got a toy-like weapon that was more their size. Sergeant Scroop locked himself in one of the small rooms in the yellow building with his Popular Forces marijuana supplier and smoked a couple of pipes. Ruland watched all this through the window of his room while crouched on the floor of the yellow building.

Luckily, no one was killed during this debate on M-16s versus M-1s, and the follow-up discussion on the virtue of women. One PF soldier did lose a piece of his thumb, however, when he leaned on his rifle with the muzzle in dirt. He accidentally pulled the trigger and the rifle blew up in his hand. This provided a forty-five minute break to treat the wounded man, and it gave the two opposing sides time for tea. After this, the battle of the rice bowls resumed.

Ruland managed to escape from his room and slip away during the tea break. Thuy Van had promised to take Ruland to show him the local Bhuddist pagoda that afternoon. He took his rifle and put a magazine of ammunition in each pant leg pocket, more for balance than anything else, and walked into the village.

Thuy Van's mother sent Ruland directly into the living room when he arrived at the cafe. Thuy Van was standing in the middle of the room dressed in a traditional white ao dai. The young women in the cities would wear the all-white outfit on special occasions, but it was rarely seen in the villages. Nearly all the women wore black pajamas with a loose, colorful blouse for everyday wear. Thuy Van looked at Ruland with strong, serious eyes as he walked toward her. He stopped across from her in front of the long wooden table. Thuy Van held her left hand out for Ruland to take.

"After we go to pagoda," she said softly," we come back here to eat. I fix you special Vietnamese dinner."

She waited for Ruland to speak, carefully studying the American she barely knew. Standing there in the white ao dai, Thuy Van was in complete control. Ruland was interested in the attractive Eurasian girl from the first time he saw her, but she was more of an exotic curiosity than anything obtainable. Now, seeing her standing before him as a beautiful woman, Ruland felt himself being drawn to her, and closer to the one thing he was trying to avoid- commitment.

He suddenly felt compelled to immediately reevaluate his reasons for leaving Vietnam. He never thought this would happen. It had always been just a matter of putting in his time. Then with a little luck, he would leave the country, the war, the Army, and put it all behind him. Suddenly, things were not that simple anymore.

"Do you listen," Thuy Van asked as she shook Ruland's hand to rouse him from his thoughts.

"Sure, we'll spend the day together," Ruland announced.

"And the night?" Thuy Van said, sticking her bottom lip out to mimic a pouting schoolgirl.

"Oh, I'm sorry," Ruland fumbled, quite unprepared for this, "I meant that…as long as you want to…"

"You beaucoup crazy, Ruland," the young woman said, laughing at the American. "What kind of girl you think I am?"

Thuy Van stepped lightly around the low table and put her hand on Ruland's arm. She leaned her head on Ruland's shoulder as they walked out of the living room and into the kitchen area of the cafe. As they stepped out onto the patio of the cafe, in public view, Thuy Van gently pulled her arm away and assumed the proper distance for a Vietnamese city girl and a young man.

The afternoon seemed a little cooler to Ruland as he and Thuy Van walked to the Bhuddist pagoda. He knew that the monsoon rains would soon be arriving. The young couple walked together through the village huts and the people smiled and bowed to Ruland. Every once in a while a group of two or three children would start to follow along, but Thuy Van quickly sent them back with selected phrases of American GI English.

The pagoda was in a cool cover of banyon trees in the middle of a grassy area about a block off Highway One. An ornate yellow wooden fence surrounded the quiet, green spot. The fence also kept in two large water buffaloes, calmly grazing beside the stucco building. Thuy Van opened the gate to the pagoda grounds as the two water buffaloes looked up at Ruland and snorted. Ruland hesitated for a moment and Thuy Van smiled and pulled him by the arm.

"Come on, Ruland. Don't be afraid of little cows."

Ruland let Thuy Van get between him and the water buffaloes as they walked to the pagoda. He watched the animals carefully, knowing they had a nasty habit of chasing Americans for no reason at all. Thuy Van laughed and shook her head.

A bald monk in a saffron-colored robe greeted them at the doorway of the pagoda. The monk bowed and shook Ruland's hand after a brief introduction in Vietnamese. Thuy Van took four joss sticks offered to her by the monk and put some green MPC in a collection jar near the entry. She motioned for Ruland to stay by the door, then walked with the monk to an altar and placed her joss sticks in a vase on the altar. She lit the four joss sticks and stood in front of the burning incense with head bowed and her hands folded under her chin.

After a few moments Thuy Van turned and smiled at Ruland over her shoulder. She placed some more green MPC in an offering dish on the altar, bowed to the monk, and walked back to the doorway where Ruland was standing.

"Is that it?" Ruland asked.

"What you expect Ruland, big ceremony?"

"You got all dressed up for two minutes at the altar?" Ruland teased.

"Why not, Trung-uy. I'm not Buddhist."

"You're not Buddhist?" Ruland asked.

"No, I'm Catholic. What you think, Ruland? I like pagoda. And I have business with monks. They carve small water buffaloes for trading. I buy and sell to GI."

Thuy Van stuck her lower lip out again and went into her pouting act.

"You don't know I get dressed up for our dinner?"

Ruland got carried away and leaned over to kiss Thuy Van on the cheek. The young woman gasped and turned her head to the side, glancing at the monk. She put up both hands to cover the blush in her cheeks.

"Let's go, Ruland," she said as she started to giggle. "No can do, GI. You not supposed to kiss me. I am proper Vietnam girl. Not butterfly girl…not Saigon-tea girl."

She glanced at the monk again and covered her mouth with her hand.

Thuy Van established the proper distance again and the two walked back to the cafe along the small path between the houses. Ruland felt good walking beside the young woman. He enjoyed watching her walk beside him, lightly stepping down the path, her white ao dai flowing behind her. It was hard for him to keep from looking at her.

Lieutenant Tram was sitting at Thuy Van's cafe with his wife when the couple arrived. Lieutenant Tram was wise enough to stay clear of the soldiers trying out their new rifles back at the compound, figuring that was a job for the sergeants. The small lieutenant would laugh and shake his head when a burst of fire could be heard from the direction of the compound. Ruland shook hands with his Vietnamese counterpart and bowed to Lieutenant Tram's wife. Thuy Van stood in the doorway and assumed an impatient look that Lieutenant Tram noticed. He immediately pushed Ruland in the direction of Thuy Van and shook his hand again. Lieutenant Tram's wife bowed politely.

Thuy Van led Ruland into the main living room. She disappeared into the smaller side room and returned with a large, elaborately embroidered pad and placed it beside the long wooden table. After gently pushing Ruland down on the pad she quietly knelt down and unlaced Ruland's jungle boots and removed them. Thuy Van then disappeared into the small room again and returned with three photo albums. She stacked them on the long table in front of Ruland and sat across from him.

"Here, Ruland. I will let you see my pictures." She opened one of the albums in front of Ruland and asked, "You like cold beer?"

Ruland had to touch her. He took Thuy Van's hand and carefully pulled her toward him. He gently held her and put her head on his shoulder. They stayed that way for a long time. The tinny sound of Vietnamese music was playing on her portable radio. He hadn't noticed it before.

"Thuy Van," Ruland said, breaking the silence. "I want to take you back with me. I've decided to extend my tour six months to make the arrangements. We'll have to go to Saigon or someplace for the final paperwork. I guess we go to the U.S. Embassy."

Ruland looked into Thuy Van's eyes. Then he sat up straight. "I just remembered. You never said you would go. Will you come with me?"

"I'll have to think about it," Thuy Van said as she sat up and pulled away, folding her hands in her lap. "You have six months extension: I have six months to think. That plenty of time for proper Vietnam girl." She smiled at Ruland as she opened the first photo album. "First you see my pictures. This is my history. Maybe you change your mind. Anyway, you look while I make dinner. We have all night to talk."

Thuy Van left Ruland in the room by himself as she prepared dinner. She returned once to bring him a beer and touch him on the back of the neck, then disappeared into the kitchen area.

Her photo album was mostly filled with schoolgirl pictures. There were scenes of Thuy Van and her friends at school and in the gardens and cafes of Hue. In the bottom album was a slightly yellowed photo of a Caucasian man in a French military uniform standing beside a beautiful Vietnamese woman. Ruland figured these people were Thuy Van's parents.

Ruland sipped his beer slowly and leafed through the album. Thuy Van returned and carefully placed blue and white dishes on the low table. She would occasionally sing along with the Vietnamese songs on the radio and would always touch Ruland on the shoulder or back of the neck as she passed by him.

Thuy Van had prepared a traditional Vietnamese meal of roasted chicken, ga xoi mo. She served Ruland the food and studied him while he ate. Thuy Van even managed to get Ruland to try a little nuoc mam on the noodles. To his surprise, he discovered he liked it. She would carefully fill his beer glass when it became half-empty, congratulating herself when the head of the beer came exactly to the top of the glass. They talked about many more meals like this one during the next six months. Thuy Van even mentioned she wanted to take Ruland to Hue and meet her friends. She also asked if he was interested in meeting her uncle, who was in hiding somewhere in the district. Ruland told her he wasn't that interested in visiting a Viet Cong stronghold to visit relatives, but he thanked her anyway.

After the meal, Thuy Van cleared the table and changed the radio station to the Armed Force Network. They danced to all the slow songs. When the American station went off the air, Thuy Van took Ruland by the hand and led him to the front door. She pushed him through the doorway and partially closed the door like a schoolgirl on a first date.

"Thank you, Ruland," she said. "I had very good time with you today. I see you tomorrow maybe."

Ruland leaned toward Thuy Van and kissed her for the first time. He moved closer to hold her but Thuy Van closed the door even more.

"Night, Ruland. See you tomorrow. I got work to do. You no go to Majestic. Go back to compound. I no butterfly girl." Thuy Van looked at Ruland and closed the door.

Ruland found himself alone on the dark street facing a long walk back to the compound. However, he was beginning to feel like he was a part of the village. Since he had made it known that he wasn't interested in getting involved in bothering the Viet Cong, and since the Popular Forces soldiers who were not Viet Cong didn't really want to bother the Viet Cong either, Ruland reckoned no one would bother him. With this confidence based on a shaky proposition, Ruland walked confidently down the dark main street back to the compound.

It was a rare clear night before the monsoon season arrived, so Ruland got a couple of beers to sip on and took his regular spot on the sandbag wall. The PFs on nightly guard duty were used to him now, sitting on the wall at night with beer in hand, staring off to the west.

Ruland found the soft, rolling hills that formed the western horizon very relaxing. He particularly enjoyed the nightly fireworks. H and I fire from Camp Evans artillery would light up the sky at the base camp, followed by a low boom when the noise reached the village. Even more spectacular were the B-52 strikes off in the west. The rolling fireballs would move slowly across the horizon line like summer lights in the northern midwest. Then, in ten or twelve seconds the thunder of the bombs would begin. Ruland wondered how anyone could survive these bombing runs. When he was in the 4th Infantry in the Central Highlands, these arclights, as they were called by the troops, would be within a couple of thousand meters of their night positions. The sky would light up and the ground would shake as the American troops cheered.

Tonight, Ruland watched the Camp Evans' big guns counter-attack a lone rocket attack from the hills just to the north of the camp. A lone rocket was fired from the top of one of the hills in a graceful arc than landed somewhere in the middle of Camp Evans with a dull thump. Immediately the Camp Evans siren would sound an alert and the American artillery would turn their pieces on the area where the rocket was launched. Ruland knew that whoever fired the rocket was long gone by the time the American rounds landed in the hills. He knew that the single rocket was the Viet Cong's version of H and I. It would provide some excitement for the base camp warriors, he thought, and something for the REMFs to write home about.

Ruland remembered the rocket launcher leaning against the wall in the corner of Thuy Van's warehouse and made a mental note to look for it the next time he was there. But when the artillery show at Camp Evans had ended, and Ruland had finished his beer, he had forgotten about Thuy Van's rocket launcher.

October 20, 1968

When Ruland arrived in the mess hall for breakfast the next morning, Lieutenant Blossom and Sergeant Montague were sitting at the long table drinking coffee. Lieutenant Blossom told Ruland everything was "all set on the rifle range."

"What do you mean, 'All set'," Ruland asked.

"It's all set, Trung-uy, not to worry. I got everything taken care of," Lieutenant Blossom answered.

Ruland didn't question what Lieutenant Blossom had set up so fast, because he knew it was probably illegal. Although Ruland was a very practical person, and didn't mind bending the rules a bit to get the job done, getting things done illegally made him feel uncomfortable now that he put in for a six-month extension.

Around nine o'clock that morning, Ruland, Lieutenant Blossom, and Sergeant Montague drove to the sandy, flat area immediately south of the compound that Ruland had picked for the firing range. It was the best area Ruland could find that was relatively near the compound. It was just off Highway One between the compound and Camp Evans. This way, Ruland thought, the American troops passing by on the highway would know that the area was some sort of official Vietnamese Army training facility and not mistake the trainees for Viet Cong. At least that's what Ruland hoped.

Sergeant Scroop wasn't with the team. He spent every Sunday morning tending his marijuana patch down near the river north of the bridge. He rented some land from Nguyen O'Bannon in exchange for unwanted C-rations salvaged from the supply warehouse at Camp

Evans. Sergeant Scroop didn't actually rent the land from Nguyen O'Bannon, the C-rations were essentially protection money to keep the local Viet Cong from harvesting the marijuana patch and to provide some measure of safety on Sunday mornings for Sergeant Scroop's agricultural efforts.

Ruland, Lieutenant Blossom, and Sergeant Montague drove the jeep around the sandy flats in an inspection tour, then parked the jeep in the middle of the sand flats. Ruland could see farmers working in the rice paddies off to the east. The farmers stood up briefly and looked at the Americans, then stooped over and continued their work. Lieutenant Blossom had a covered trailer hooked on the jeep. He lifted back the canvas covering the trailer and took out a cooler filled with beer. He handed each man a beer.

"You sure you know what you're doing?" Ruland asked.

"You need a rifle range before you can get on the good side of Major Hannah," Lieutenant Blossom said, smiling, "you've come to the right man, ol' buddy. I would have built you one sooner except that would have put you out of a job, then they would have sent you back to headquarters to shuffle papers until they could get you a flight back to the world. That would get you out of here too early and it appears that your priorities have changed since you now have your little VC girlfriend. And besides, we kind of like having you around to catch the shit from Major Hannah."

"With all due respect, Lieutenant, Lieutenant Blossom will probably get us all a court martial," Sergeant Montague said to Ruland under his breath.

"Not to worry," Lieutenant Blossom responded, "I know what I'm doing."

Lieutenant Blossom walked over to the side of the highway and took off his jungle fatigue jacket. He was wearing a T-shirt that had GREEK WEEK '66 printed on the front. He rubbed sun tan lotion on his arms as the villagers passed by, laughing at the blond American rubbing oil on his body for some strange reason. Lieutenant Blossom whistled at the young girls carrying their water pails to the village. The girls would glance at the tan young man and turn their eyes away in embarrassment, giggling as they continued down Highway One, chattering to each other.

As Lieutenant Blossom applied his sun tan lotion and sipped on his beer, a jeep approached from the direction of Camp Evans. The jeep stopped beside Lieutenant Blossom and the two MPs in the jeep began talking to Lieutenant Blossom so no one else could hear them. Ruland walked over to the MP's jeep just as a voice came over their radio.

"Four-six, four-six, this is four-one, over,"

"This is four-six, go," the MP sergeant in the jeep answered.

"They'll be on top of you in one minute, over."

"Roger, out," the MP sergeant answered.

The MPs moved their jeep to the center of the highway and parked it so it would block traffic. The two MPs jumped out of the jeep and put on their white MP helmets. Lieutenant Blossom quickly put on his fatigue jacket, then ran over to the MP's jeep, grabbed an MP helmet and put it on, then stood beside the jeep looking very official. The driver of the jeep then took a sawhorse with a sign on it out of the rear seat. He placed the sawhorse in the middle of the highway. The sign read: ROAD CLOSED- MINE CLEARING AHEAD.

In a matter of seconds a small convoy rumbled down Highway One from the north. The small convoy was from a Seabee detachment. The convoy was lead by a jeep, followed by a deuce-and-half, two five-ton trucks, and a flatbed truck with a bulldozer on it. Another jeep with an enormous chief petty officer sitting in the passenger's seat brought up the rear.

The leading jeep stopped in front of the MP's sign, and the trailing vehicles slowly came to a halt behind it. A peach-faced Navy ensign who looked about 16 years old was in the lead jeep. Lieutenant Blossom, now wearing one of the white MP helmets and apparently enjoying his new role in law enforcement, walked over to the young Navy officer and quietly spoke to him.

"Sorry, Lieutenant," Lieutenant Blossom said, not knowing the single gold bar of the Navy officer meant he was an ensign, not a lieutenant, "Highway One is closed down for mine clearing."

"But we got a job in Hue this afternoon," the ensign replied.

"I can't help that," Lieutenant Blossom countered. "You're going to have to hold up here for a couple of hours until were done. You don't want to take a chance getting your bulldozer blown up, do you?"

"No, but a couple of hours puts us behind schedule. My boss will have my ass for this." The Navy ensign looked worried and shook his head.

"Relax," Lieutenant Blossom said, "you'll be out of here in no time." Lieutenant Blossom walked closer to the jeep and spoke directly to the ensign. "You can do me a favor while you're waiting, Lieutenant," Lieutenant Blossom continued. "I need to go to the village you just past through for some business. Why don't you run me in there instead of waiting out here in this sun. It would be a big help to me."

After a moment of thought, the ensign told his driver to get out of the jeep. Lieutenant Blossom got in the driver's seat and turned the jeep around and headed back north on Highway One toward the village. The ensign motioned for Lieutenant Blossom to stop at the trailing jeep in the convoy. Lieutenant Blossom pulled up along the jeep and stopped on the driver's side. The ensign walked around to the passenger's side of the Navy jeep and told the chief petty officer to hold the convoy there until the road was cleared, and that he would be back in a few minutes. The ensign then jumped back in the jeep and he and Lieutenant Blossom continued on toward the village.

As soon as the jeep disappeared into the village, the Navy chief petty officer sitting in the last jeep directed his driver to pull to the head of the convoy. The jeep stopped at the MP's jeep and the chief petty officer rolled out of his seat with a groan. He walked over to Ruland as he surveyed the area, scanning back and forth with squinted eyes. The chief petty officer had a giant beer belly, and would scratch his belly as he evaluated the job site. He stopped in front of Ruland and offered what looked like some sort of salute with his right hand, all the time scratching his belly with his left hand.

"Where do you want this here rifle range?" the chief asked.

Ruland pointed over to the open field in back of him.

"Let's put it over there," Ruland said, pointing to the clearing to the east. "You see those farmers over there? We need to build some sort of berm to protect them."

The Navy chief nodded, rubbed his chin, and said: "No problem."

He then walked back to the convoy and started yelling incoherently. Instantly, Navy Seabees began jumping from the backs of the trucks carrying lumber and tools. Two Seabees quickly attached a ramp to the flatbed truck and the bulldozer creaked down the planks onto the ground. A wild-eyed young sailor revved the engine of the bulldozer when it hit the ground, sending a large cloud of black diesel exhaust from the pipe on top of the machine. The earthmover took off and rumbled at full speed past Ruland and the others with the wild-eyed sailor on board grinning from ear to ear. The bulldozer got to a spot pointed out by the chief petty officer and dropped its blade, pushing the white sand toward the edge of the rice paddies.

For the next half-hour the area was a flurry of activity. The Navy chief constantly paced the worksite yelling out in some strange language while scratching his over-sized belly. The Seabee on the bulldozer was creating a long pile of sand 10 feet high and nearly one hundred feet long that completely protected the farmers in the rice paddies behind it. When the berm was completed, the wild-eyed sailor roared back to the convoy in the giant earthmover and drove the bulldozer back up on the trailer of his truck at full speed. He stopped on the flatbed trailer exactly where the bulldozer had been tied down.

While the sand backdrop for the firing range was being formed, the other Seabees from the convoy were hammering and sawing away in what appeared to Ruland to be pure chaos. Then suddenly, the project all came together. They had constructed a twenty-foot high wooden tower to be used as a range tower. The sailors were just putting on the last touches of red paint as the bulldozer was chained down on the flatbed of the truck. The chief petty officer with the giant beer belly then climbed up the unpainted ladder of the wooden tower with great effort and secured a fifteen-foot flagpole in place on top of the tower. He lumbered down the wooden ladder, sweating profusely. The chief looked at his watch, then at Ruland.

"There you go, Lieutenant. That flagpole is for your red warning flag. It's probably a good idea to let those Army bozos from Camp Evans know this is some sort of training site so they don't shoot up your ARVNs. They understand that a red flag means a firing range."

"Good idea, Chief," Ruland said, still amazed at the speed with which they built the range. "You guys work fast."

"Hell, we got ten minutes to kill," the chief responded. Then he turned and yelled out to his Seabees. "Put all this shit back and take ten! Smoke 'em if you got 'em."

At the end of the ten-minute break, and right on schedule, Lieutenant Blossom arrived back at the range in the Navy jeep with the young Seabee officer-in-charge of the convoy sitting in the back seat. The young ensign was smiling and holding a plastic flower from one of the window boxes from The Majestic Steam Bath and Massage Parlor.

Meanwhile, the MPs had moved their jeep off to the side of the road. The warning sign was turned around to face the convoy. The other side of the sign read now facing the ensign read: ROAD CLEAR- PROCEED WITH CAUTION.

The MP sergeant stood in the middle of Highway One and yelled at the ensign. "You're clear to go, sir," motioning for the convoy to continue on.

Lieutenant Blossom jumped out of the ensign's jeep and was quickly replaced by a young seaman who spun the tires of the jeep as he drove back on the asphalt of the highway to take a position at the head of the convoy. The ensign's jeep began to move out slowly. Lieutenant Blossom saluted the Navy ensign, then returned to the MAT Team's jeep and scrambled under the canvas of the trailer. He pulled out a case of Jim Beam whiskey and ran back to the highway and handed a bottle to the driver of each truck in the convoy as they passed by. Lieutenant Blossom put the remainder of the case of whiskey in the back seat of the chief petty officer's jeep as it passed by and shook the hand of the giant man. The chief petty officer nodded as if the construction project was no big deal and directed his driver to keep up with the convoy.

When the convoy had gone past, Lieutenant Blossom returned to the trailer and took out a Chinese-made AK-47 rifle and gave it to the MP sergeant. The sergeant grinned broadly as the two MPs drove off. Lieutenant Blossom then removed his fatigue jacket and his Greek Week T-shirt, and walked back to where the other MAT Team members were standing. He rubbed sun tan lotion on his chest as he approached the men. When he reached Ruland, he smiled, and looked up at the bright red range tower.

"Piece of cake, Trung-uy," he said to Ruland. "I told you not to worry."

"Where'd you get the money for the whiskey?" Ruland asked.

"I didn't exactly pay for it. I traded for it. You see I bought a couple of televisions yesterday for Major Vien in exchange for half-price on his ghost soldier's M-16s. Old Major Vien even threw in that old AK-47 he had hanging in his mess hall," Lieutenant Blossom answered.

"Where did the new M-16s end up?" Ruland asked, not sure if he really wanted to know how all this came about.

"Oh…" Lieutenant Blossom moaned, as he looked down at the white sand and started to draw circles with his toe. "That's what I used for tradin'."

"Well, who'd you trade them to," Ruland continued the questioning, already anticipating the answer.

"Thuy Van," Lieutenant Blossom answered.

Ruland turned to Sergeant Montague. "And what will she do with them."

"Hell, she'll probably sell them to the Viet Cong, Lieutenant," Sergeant Montague answered in disbelief at Ruland's dumb question. "You know the girl's just trying to make a living."

Ruland shook his head and grunted a short laugh. "I just don't know what the hell's going on, but it doesn't matter. Let's go to town and celebrate the creation of the official Phong Dien Rifle Range and the Lieutenant Ronnie Blossom Memorial Observation Tower. We can tell Major Hannah and Major Vien the Ruff Puffs can begin qualifying on their M-16s tomorrow."

The Americans got in the jeep and drove back to the compound. The villagers on Highway One passed by the new red tower and long pile of sand and laughed at the latest American project. Then would pause a while and look at the strange red structure, then go on about their business, amused at another project of the Americans that meant absolutely nothing to them.

Ruland told Lieutenant Blossom to go tell Major Hannah that the range was completed. Ruland didn't want to talk with Major Hannah because he would ask too many questions, and he figured Lieutenant Blossom needed to get on the good side of Major Hannah since he still had a couple of months in-country. Lieutenant Blossom found Major Hannah in the mess hall and told him the news that the range was completed. Major Hannah grunted at the information and yelled for Lieutenant Fujita. He wanted Lieutenant Fujita to start preparing for the next day's opening of the range and the Ruff Puff's first qualifying session. Major Hannah wanted to make it a big deal so he could score some points with MACV. Major Hannah also had some news for Ruland that he gave to Lieutenant Blossom.

"By the way, Lieutenant," Major Hannah said as Lieutenant Blossom turned to leave the mess hall after delivering the news about the rifle range, "you can tell your buddy Lieutenant Ruland that his request for an extension was turned down." Major Hannah paused and smiled in satisfaction. "I guess headquarters paid attention to my recommendation."

Lieutenant Blossom nodded. "I'll inform him," he said.

"And one more thing, Lieutenant," Major Hannah said, his smile growing wider, "you can tell Ruland that I have booked him on a flight out of here tomorrow. I want him out of here ASAP. You can tell him that too."

Lieutenant Blossom nodded again without speaking and left the mess hall. He returned to the two Americans waiting in the jeep by the compound flagpole. He told Ruland the news about his request and Ruland just sighed and nodded in resignation.

The three Americans then drove down to Thuy Van's café. Sergeant Scroop joined them a little later, sunburned from working all morning in his marijuana patch. The men relaxed in the shade of the blue awning, out of the afternoon sun. Lieutenant Blossom, Sergeant Montague, and Sergeant Scroop repeated war stories they had all heard before, mostly to keep Ruland's mind off this new turn of events.

Some of the Vietnamese officers and NCOs from the compound joined the Americans at the café as the afternoon wore on. Lieutenant Blossom returned to the Majestic and brought back Yvonne and one of the other girls. Kate Maddock-Smythe also showed up, constantly taking pictures of the villagers who passed by in front of the café. Nguyen O'Bannon stopped in on his way to organize the nightly attack on the bridge and sat beside Ruland. Thuy Van arrived around six o'clock with no explanation of where she had been, and Ruland knew better that to try and press her for information. She took a chair beside Ruland when not serving her guests.

At around seven o'clock all of the small tables under the awning were pulled together to form one long table. Thuy Van's mother and grandmother brought out bowls of phu bo noodles. The main dish was a large bowl of bo nhung dam, a dish with meat Ruland was not familiar with, but guessed it was seasoned beef. Or at least Ruland hoped it was beef because he hadn't seen Stanley in a couple of days. Ruland placed fish sauce generously on his phu bo, getting accustomed to its taste. There was also a bowl of nuoc cham for dipping small, crispy, deep-fried crabs from the river.

The long table ran parallel to Highway One with Ruland and Thuy Van facing the villagers passing by. A group of children gathered outside the awning and looked in, squatting on their haunches. The villagers passed by but did little more than glance in at this strange gathering. It was getting dark as the group finished eating. At the end of the meal Sergeant Montague rose to his feet with some difficulty. He usually didn't drink a lot a beer because he needed to keep his head clear for any impromptu poker games.

"It's getting late and we all got to get someplace, but I just wanted to take a moment to say a few words," Sergeant Montague said as he looked at everyone sitting at the table. "First I would like to thank our gracious hosts for this wonderful meal."

Sergeant Montague nodded to Thuy Van's mother and winked. "And most importantly, we need to recognize Stanley for making this memorable meal possible."

Ruland was just reaching for another piece of meat in the bo nhung dam when Sergeant Montague said this. Ruland dropped his chopsticks in the bowl and gagged slightly.

"Thank Stanley for retrieving those ducks from the river Sergeant Scroop shot for raiding his special garden. Don't want good food to go to waste."

The group all raised their glasses in a toast to Stanley, the retriever.

"Let me continue with a few comments on this momentous day," Sergeant Montague said as he wiped the corners of his mouth with his index finger and thumb, his gold inlayed teeth glinting in the evening sun.

"Damn," Sergeant Scroop said. "We'll be here all night."

"I know we got stuck with kind of an off-the-wall assignment in this war," Sergeant Montague continued, ignoring Sergeant Scroop, "but once in a while something comes along to be proud of. Tomorrow we're going to open the best-goddamned rifle range west of Fort Benning goddamn Georgia. We're going to begin training our allies here, these brave freedom fighters of this lovely village, how to accurately and efficiently use their new M-16 rifles, hopefully without killing themselves."

Sergeant Montague weaved slightly, belched, then continued. "This is a gift from the people of the United States of America. And we're proud to say that this rifle range was constructed at no cost to the taxpayers…"

The quests politely applauded and Sergeant Scroop nodded like a rooster.

"But at the same time, at this hour of celebration," Sergeant Montague continued, pausing to observe a family of farmers passing by, "we gots to say farewell to Lieutenant Ruland. A good man…as officers go. We learned this afternoon that the Lieutenant's request for an extension was turned down, thanks to Major Hannah." Sergeant Montague looked at Ruland, and then Thuy Van. "Lieutenant Ruland will be leaving tomorrow after we open the firing range."

Ruland sat up straight as Thuy Van caught her breath and looked down at the table. She turned slowly toward Ruland and put her hand on his knee. Tears formed in her eyes when Ruland nodded his head to acknowledge what Sergeant Montague had just said.

"So tomorrow," Sergeant Montague continued, "the lieutenant here is going to have to leave this village and catch that great silver bird back to the real world."

All the people at the table looked down at their food, not knowing exactly what to say.

"Lieutenant," Sergeant Montague said as he raised his beer in a toast to break the silence, "you're all right."

That was as emotional as Sergeant Montague could get about officers and Ruland knew it. They both tipped their glasses toward each other and sipped their beer. The other men at the table stood up for the toast as best they could after an afternoon of drinking. Sergeant Scroop fell over backwards in his chair as he attempted to rise, but no one noticed.

"And," Sergeant Montague went on, "I know how you feel about that young lady there beside you, but not to worry, Lieutenant. We're going to fix everything."

"Ya, we'll fix everything," Lieutenant Blossom echoed.

Ruland didn't know what that meant, and was a little nervous about Lieutenant Blossom's comment, but raised his glass again with Sergeant Montague as Thuy Van blinked her eyes, locked her jaw, and sat up straight. She smiled bravely at Sergeant Montague and held her head proudly. She turned and smiled at Ruland. Her spirit had returned just as fast as Ruland's heart sank, knowing he must leave her the next day.

Sergeant Montague raised his bottle for one final toast as Sergeant Scroop attempted to get on his feet.

"You just got one more day, Lieutenant," Sergeant Montague said. "And we wish you the best of luck when you get back on the block. Good luck, sir."

That was the first time Sergeant Montague had called Ruland 'sir', and one on the few times he had ever addressed an officer with that honor. Ruland knew this as he rose to his feet for a response. He hadn't been drinking as much as the others because he knew he had to tell Thuy Van about his request being turned down. He wanted to be sober so he wouldn't say something stupid.

"I'll remember all of you," he said simply. "And I appreciate your offer to help Thuy Van and me get together, but I think it's too late. So for now, let's just say good-bye. We'll see what we can do after that."

"Well, ladies and gentlemens," Sergeant Montague interrupted, knowing it was time to stop Ruland. "I think the Lieutenant's got things to do tonight, and it's something we can't help him with. So let's get out of here and back to the compound…or wherever the hell you're headed," winking at Nguyen O'Bannon. "We got opening day at the range tomorrow." Sergeant Montague paused to reflect. "So life goes on in Phong Dien."

Sergeant Montague took a deep breath and placed his glass back on the table. He took a handful of money from his pocket and handed it to Thuy Van's mother. He winked at the middle-aged woman and patted her on the bottom. She squealed and swatted at his hand. Sergeant Montague then held out his arm in an exaggerated manner for Thuy Van's mother to take. She laughed and took his arm gracefully, and the couple began strolling down the street.

Lieutenant Blossom helped Sergeant Scroop to his feet and they left for the Majestic with Yvonne and the new girl giggling at their sides like the two teenagers they were. Kate Maddock-Smythe followed the foursome. The tall American woman strode down the street dragging the smaller Nguyen O'Bannon along behind her, intent on introducing the Viet Cong leader to the pleasures of a co-ed steam bath at The Majestic Steam Bath and Massage Parlor.

Thuy Van's grandmother quickly cleared the table as the partygoers left, then disappeared into the house. Ruland and Thuy Van remained at the table. They faced Highway One and did not speak for a long time. They watched the last villagers hurry back to their homes. Ruland broke the silence and reached into his pocket.

"I don't have anything real special for you, but here's something I'd like you to have."

Ruland took his dog tag chain from his pocket and put it on Thuy Van. The chain had only one of the two tags on it. Thuy Van held the dog tag in her hand and smiled.

"Ruland," she said. "You come back Vietnam someday?"

"Ya, maybe," Ruland answered, not committing himself again.

Thuy Van smiled and took Ruland's hand and led him toward the door of her house.

October 21, 1968

When Ruland woke up the next morning, Thuy Van was gone. He figured it was best that way. Thuy Van said she would go to Camp Evans to say good-bye, but Ruland had the feeling he would never see her again.

Ruland quietly got dressed and walked slowly down the street to the compound, oblivious to the chattering of the old women as they watched him from the cool shadows of their hooches. The whole village knew he had spent the night with Thuy Van. The Popular Forces soldiers on the sandbag wall yelled at Ruland and made the same obscene gestures with their hands when Ruland approached the compound, but he ignored them since it meant nothing now.

When Major Hannah radioed MACV about the opening of the firing range, the public information officers got real excited. They wanted Major Hannah to make the opening of the firing range a major event. So Major Hannah told Major Vien he wanted the ceremony to start at 1300, the hottest part of the day. This provided plenty of time for Lieutenant Fujita and Lieutenant Tram to organize the affair, and it would also provide time for public information officers to put together press releases for the five o'clock follies press briefing in Saigon.

It also gave time for General H.M.S. Cooley to fly to the district. He wanted to make sure he supplied plenty of quotes on the success of his Mobile Advisory Teams. The MACV staff thought the opening of the firing range would be a good example of the progress of the Vietnamization Program. They were excited about the prospect of news releases featuring their good work, and variations of the phrase "light at the end of the tunnel" were heard often that morning in MACV headquarters.

Lieutenant Fujita had booked Ruland for the flight from Camp Evans to Danang at 1400, so Ruland planned on attending the ceremony and leaving right after the affair. With the realization that his tour was up, Ruland spent the morning of his last day in-country gathering his things. His last official act as MAT Team leader was having Lieutenant Blossom sign the MAT Team's property book listing equipment belonging to the team. There were things in the property book that had been issued to the team that had just simply disappeared, or been traded for something more useful. The only thing on the property book that Ruland had actually seen was the MAT Team jeep, but that had the wrong serial number on it. Neither Ruland nor Lieutenant Blossom was concerned about this. They had been in the Army long enough to know that you could write off all the missing equipment as a combat loss.

At 1300, when it was time to begin the ceremony, the temperature on the white sand at the firing range was close to 100 degrees. Lieutenant Tram recruited a five-piece band of civilian musicians from throughout the district. The band was a motley crew of old men who served with the French in ceremonial bands and who kept the instruments when the French left. The band played a barely recognizable rendition of La Marseillaise to kick off the whole affair.

The ceremony began like most Army ceremonies with the traditional medals for people who were concerned about medals. All major events for any military organization of any country were mostly opportunities to give men medals for just doing their jobs. Although Major Hannah was not about to award a medal to Ruland, Major Vien wanted to give something to Ruland as a reward for his new television. So Lieutenant Fujita gathered up Ruland and three other Popular Forces soldiers who were receiving awards and had them stand in front of the new red range tower for the ceremony.

Major Vien, Major Hannah, and General H.M.S. Cooley stood at the edge of Highway One where their jeeps had dropped them off. They wanted to march to the ceremony spot at the base of the range tower like they had seen in newsreels. They wanted to symbolically signify this was a formal event of no small measure. General Cooley always liked these types of ceremonies, and he was particularly fond of making a grand entrance.

Major Vien led the procession of nobles, casually walking up to the men in front of the tower carrying a handful of Vietnamese military medals. Major General HMS Cooley and Major Hannah followed behind in their best marching cadence, trying to adjust their long strides with the shorter Vietnamese major sauntering ahead of them. Lieutenant Fujita was the fourth man in the line. He was carrying two blue boxes. One box held an Army Commendation Medal for Major Hannah as an award from headquarters for building the rifle range.

The Bronze Star for service normally awarded to officers as an end-of-tour award would not be given to Ruland. These last two weeks with Major Hannah apparently wiped out whatever Ruland had accomplished the first 50 weeks as an infantryman in the real war. The other blue box carried by Lieutenant Fujita was a Purple Heart for wounds Lieutenant Blossom received while fishing in action.

"Where is that goddamn woman reporter that's been snooping around town," Major Hannah yelled at Lieutenant Fujita. "This is the shit we want those goddamn commie reporters to write about."

"I don't know, sir," Lieutenant Fujita answered.

"And where the hell is Blossom?" Major Hannah yelled back at Lieutenant Fujita again as they marched closer to the tower.

"I don't know, sir," Lieutenant Fujita repeated.

"Well, piss on him, if he can't be here to get his damn Purple Heart, we'll give the goddamn thing to Ruland. I don't want it to look like we don't know what we're doing."

The officers stopped in front of each man and pinned a medal on his fatigue shirt. Ruland received a Vietnamese Honor Medal First Class from Major Vien, along with a Purple Heart for wounding Lieutenant Blossom. General H.M.S. Cooley pinned the Army Commendation

Medal on Major Hannah, then kissed him on both cheeks like a French general. The normally bright red face of Major Hannah turned purple and crowd of villagers howled hysterically.

Two Vietnamese soldiers received several colorful, but meaningless medals for not deserting during the past year. The third Ruff Puff who received an award was the man who lost part of his thumb when his new M-16 blew up in the middle of the inter-platoon firefight. He received the Vietnamese equivalent to the Purple Heart and another medal for bravery under fire. The medal for the wound meant a pension from the South Vietnam government for the rest of his life, or the life of the government, whichever ended first. The man beamed proudly at the thought of a steady income that unfortunately for him would be for only for a few years.

During the medal ceremony, there was a lot of noise and confusion in the crowd of villagers attending the ceremony. Most of this disturbance was caused by Mr. Dryman and Mr. Priorto. They mingled among the crowd, passing out propaganda leaflets. They were urging any Viet Cong locals in the audience to surrender and be repatriated through the Chieu Hoi, or Open Arms Program. The program was intended to encourage Viet Cong to defect to the Saigon government, but the word got around that if you pretended to be Viet Cong you could become a Hoi Chanh and receive immediate cash from the Americans. Sometimes whole families would take advantage of this easy money opportunity knowing that all they had to do was pledge allegiance to Saigon.

Mr. Dryman and Mr. Priorto were excited because they had recruited three young men as Hoi Chanh. The two American civilians could barely contain their joy at converting the three men. The three young men were equally excited about receiving as cash bonus for doing nothing. Mr. Dryman and Mr. Priorto scurried around the crowd side-by-side, elbow-to-elbow, never separating more that a few feet apart.

Ruland didn't know it, but the layout for the rifle range would become the standard training facility for local defense forces around the country and a hallmark of the Vietnamization effort. General Cooley had arranged for a public information officer from MACV and an enlisted photographer to fly in with him that morning and take pictures of the event. The information officer would write a press release, which along with the undeveloped film would be on a special plane from Camp Evans to Saigon that afternoon. This would give the public information officers time on the plane to rewrite and edit the news release until it described an event only slightly related to what actually happened.

The opening of the range would then be touted at the five o'clock follies that same day at the Rex Hotel as another example of the success of the American Vietnamization Program. And the day after this announcement in Saigon, it would be the lead item at the Pentagon briefing for the Joint Chiefs of Staff back in Washington, DC. One of the many general officers at the Pentagon briefing would wake up long enough to comment to his aide.

"Maybe we should look into this rifle range business," the general would say to the lieutenant colonel sitting behind him.

Then the ball would start rolling. The aide would interpret the general's off-hand comment as an order, and based solely on the pictures and press releases flown in that day, the aide would direct some senior Department of Defense to estimate the cost of building similar rifle ranges for the Popular Forces around the country. The bean counter would send his estimate up the chain-of-command. And in the manner of all Pentagon budget estimates, this original estimate would be doubled, then tripled, as the staff paper wound its way through the labyrinth of the Pentagon. So in the next year's budget for supporting the Popular Forces and the Vietnamization effort, the Pentagon planners would include a figure for constructing local rifle ranges many times the actual cost of the model in Phong Dien.

It would never be known that the actual cost of construction of the Phong Dien firing range was a lot less than the line item that would be presented to congress for approval. The rifle range at Phong Dien was constructed for a couple of black market M-16s, some American whiskey, and the first sexual experience for a young Navy ensign since a night with his roommate at the Naval Academy.

The Popular Forces soldiers stood patiently in formation while the ceremony was going on. When the medal-pinning formality was over, Major Vien shouted out a command, and his soldiers began to assemble on the firing line. The plan was to show General Cooley the soldiers' proficiency with their new weapons. Sergeant Montague picked out the best and the brightest of the Popular Forces soldiers and managed to instruct them on rudimentary marksmanship earlier that morning.

Major Hannah led the official party up the ladder on the red tower to the observation platform. General Cooley followed Major Hannah up the ladder too closely, so that when the red-faced Major stopped to catch his breath, General Cooley rammed his head against Major Hannah's rear end. Major Vien was last, and had the good sense to wait until the two overweight Americans made it onto the tower platform before he started climbing. When Major Vien reached the top of the overcrowded tower, the tower rocked slightly under the weight of the official party.

Lieutenant Fujita stayed on the ground to help pass out propaganda leaflets. Sergeant Montague and Captain Moss were already on the tower, not speaking or looking at each other. Captain Moss was scanning the rice paddies behind the long berm of sand with his binoculars.

Sergeant Montague noticed three people working in the fields behind the berm. He pointed the people out to the officers on the tower. Two men and a woman in the field were apparently working with shovels on a rice paddy dike. Major Vien yelled in the direction of the people and started flapping his arms. He then turned to the band and ordered them to stop playing so he could be heard. When it was quiet, Major

Vien yelled again. Captain Moss continued to look through the binoculars at the family of farmers.

"Fire a few rounds in the air," Major Hannah suggested. "That'll clear those slopes out of there."

Major Vien took out his pistol and fired it into the air. The farmers looked up, then went back to their work. Major Vien yelled for an M-16 from one of his soldiers to be passed up from below. One of the soldiers climbed the tower and handed his rifle to Major Vien. The major took the M-16 and fired a three-second burst in the air.

The two men and the woman looked up when they heard the rifle fire, but continued on with their work. They were dressed in black pajamas and straw hats. The two men each had a shovel digging furiously. The woman looked down so her face could not be seen from the tower. She was taller than most Vietnamese women. She was holding three bundles, each wrapped in black plastic sheets. She was obviously in a hurry to accomplish her task. Captain Moss studied the three people carefully with his binoculars, straining to see their faces clearly at that distance.

Back at the firing range, the crowd was silent. They waited for Major Vien's next move. Sensing the impatience of the crowd, the Major fired another burst with the M-16, this time high over the heads of the workers. The three people in black pajamas remained. They were hurrying to finish their job.

Then, apparently giving in to the fact that they could not finish their task, one of the men in the field took one of the plastic bundles from the woman and started to walk out of the area. The other two people followed, each carrying one of the bundles. Major Vien looked at Major Hannah and nodded, as if to indicate they could proceed with the training soon.

However, the lead man walked about ten yards along the rice paddy dike, then slipped and fell to one knee. As he caught himself, the black plastic package he was carrying suddenly became unwrapped and the stock of an M-16 rifle was uncovered. It had "PF" stenciled on the butt of the stock in bright yellow letters. The woman quickly reached down and covered up the rifle with the black plastic, and the three people continued toward the relative safety of a nearby cluster of tall brush.

Captain Moss wasn't sure what he had seen. He lowered the binoculars, raised them to his eyes again, and then lowered them slowly.

"Viet Cong!" He screamed. "They got our weapons! M-16s! VC! VC!"

Major Vien looked at Captain Moss, then out to the fields. Captain Moss dropped his binoculars and grabbed the rifle from Major Vien. He fired the last burst remaining in the magazine. The bullets struck behind the people as they ran to hide behind the tall brush. Captain Moss pointed the empty rifle at the bewildered Popular Forces soldiers standing on the firing line below him. The soldiers looked up at the men on the tower platform.

"Di di moi! Di di moi!" Captain Moss screamed at the soldiers, then pointed his rifle at the fleeing people in black pajamas.

"Shoot their ass! They're VC! They got your fucking rifles!"

The Ruff Puffs stood silently for a moment, then began to run down the range toward the long mound of sand. They were followed by the villagers, with the old men in the band straggling along behind. When the soldiers reached the berm, they struggled to the top of the sand pile and stood for a moment at the crest, puzzled at all the confusion. They looked back at the tower for further directions.

Major Hannah grabbed Major Vien's pistol and fired three shots over the heads of the Ruff Puffs at the three figures in black pajamas as they neared the brush. One of the Ruff Puffs then turned and fired a single shot over the heads of the fleeing people. Another soldier fired a burst from his new rifle in the same general direction. The force of the kickback caught him off balance and he tumbled back down the berm. The villagers howled in laughter. Then, almost in unison, all the Ruff Puffs on top of the berm began firing their weapons on full automatic at the fleeing people in black pajamas.

The white sand and dark water of the rice paddies around the three people shimmered as the bullets struck. All three people dropped quickly. The woman quivered slightly for a few seconds, then was still. The Ruff Puffs put in their second magazine and continued firing at the fallen figures for another ten seconds. Then it was quiet.

On the tower, Major Vien looked confused and shocked. Captain Moss was smiling as he took out his pipe and started to light it. Ruland stood at the base of the tower and yelled up at Captain Moss.

"What the hell you doing, you fucking creep! You didn't have to waste them just to clear them out of there!"

Captain Moss leaned on the railing of the tower platform and looked down at Ruland and smiled.

"They're VC, Lieutenant. They're Viet Cong and they got our rifles. Our job is to terminate the Viet Cong, Lieutenant, in case you didn't know. That's what we're here for."

Sergeant Montague climbed down the tower and took Ruland by the arm.

"Come on, Lieutenant. Your war's over. You got a plane to catch. Just put all this behind you like a bad dream. There's nothing you could have done."

Ruland was still staring up at Captain Moss, who was leaning on his elbows on the railing, watching the smoking bowl of his pipe.

"You're crazy, you know that, Captain Moss! You and your fucking Phoenix shit. This isn't a war of computer tapes. It's people. And it's people you just killed out there."

Captain Moss just looked down at Ruland and tamped the tobacco back into the bowl of his pipe with an M-16 shell casing he kept on the end of his dog tag chain.

Sergeant Montague pulled Ruland away. "There's a plane waiting for you, Lieutenant. Forget about it. It's not your war anymore. You're going home."

Sergeant Montague took Ruland by the arm and led him over to the MAT Team's jeep. Ruland's gray suitcase was on the back seat. The two men got into the jeep and drove off the white sand and on to Highway One as the band began playing their version of "Home on the Range".

Ruland never looked back at the officers on the tower or the soldiers and villagers standing on the berm. Sergeant Montague drove to Camp Evans as Ruland sat in silence, passing the farmers on the sides of the road hurrying somewhere. Then as they men neared the main gate, Ruland looked up and turned to Sergeant Montague.

"Where the hell is Thuy Van?" Ruland asked Sergeant Montague. "Last night she said she would go to Camp Evans with me."

"I think this is better, Lieutenant," Sergeant Montague said. "You said all you need to say last night. It's done with now. This is better, Lieutenant, believe me. It's time for you to go home."

Ruland looked off to his right at the beautiful green hills to the west for a moment, then took a deep breath. "Ya, you're probably right."

The gate guards at Camp Evans waved the familiar jeep into the base without leaving their guardhouse. They stayed out of the sun as much as possible at this time of day. Sergeant Montague drove past the helicopter landing pad next to the division headquarters and on to the metal runway used by the fixed wing aircraft. He stopped at a small Quonset hut that served as a terminal next to the landing strip. An Air Force C-130 cargo plane was waiting on the airstrip with the engine running, the pilots nervous about spending too much time as an easy target on a runway.

American soldiers at the end of their tour were standing in line to board the airplane. This was their last flight in-country before getting on the contracted civilian airliner waiting in Danang to take them home. The men passed by an Air Force crew chief carrying a clipboard with the manifest for the flight. The sergeant checked off the names of the soldiers as they stopped and showed their ID cards. The sergeant would carefully look at the ID cards, then motion for the soldier to board the plane. At the end of the line was the Red Cross worker who questioned Ruland at the Officers' Club. She had a large red suitcase sitting beside her and was carrying a large brown envelope with a red cross on it. The envelope had the words OFFICIAL RECORDS printed just below the red cross.

Ruland got out of the jeep and took his gray suitcase off the back seat. He turned to Sergeant Montague, knowing it was one of those uncomfortable times when he had to say goodbye to a friend.

"Well, Sergeant Montague," Ruland said. "I guess I'll see you around."

"So long, Lieutenant," Sergeant Montague said, remaining in the drivers seat and looking straight ahead. "Take care of yourself."

The two men shook hands quickly and saluted. Sergeant Montague had been in the Army too long to make lengthy good-byes. He drove off without looking back.

Ruland went to the end of the line and stood behind the Donut Dolly.

"They're letting you out of here, Lieutenant?" she asked. "I thought the Army had to clear up any venereal disease before they sent you folks back to your little sweethearts."

"Not all the time, honeybuns," Ruland said. "That's why they put us on the same plane. They figure you're immune by now."

The Donut Dolly turned around quickly and looked straight ahead.

Ruland sat his suitcase down on the tarmac and looked at the surrounding hills, and like all soldiers about to leave Vietnam, he really didn't comprehend the fact that he was leaving. He scanned the horizon of the hills and suddenly felt the loss of Thuy Van. Ruland looked back in the direction of the village and wondered what he was leaving behind. He then took a deep breath and looked back toward the green hills.

Ruland couldn't see it, but near the crest of one of the hills overlooking the airstrip, two men and a woman in black pajamas crawled through the bushes. One of the men carried an RPG-7 rocket launcher.

When the group reached the crest of the hill and had a clear view of the airstrip, the taller of the two men peered through binoculars at Camp Evans below them. The man with the binoculars guided the man with the rocket launcher until the weapon was pointed at the airstrip where Ruland's plane was warming up.

When the weapon was steady, the man squeezed the trigger of the launcher and the rocket arched gracefully toward the runway. It landed about twenty-five yards in front of the green airplane and exploded. The soldiers waiting in line fell to the ground and tried to hide behind their duffel bags.

The Air Force sergeant with the clipboard yelled at the crowd of waiting passengers now sprawled on the tarmac.

"Everyone on the plane! Let's get the hell out of here! Yell out your name as you go by!"

Meanwhile, on the small hill overlooking the airstrip, the two men who fired the rocket stood up and smiled at each other while the woman patted them on their backs. Lieutenant Blossom and Nguyen O'Bannon then shook hands as Kate Maddock-Smythe took a picture of the two men in black pajamas holding the RPG-7 rocket launcher for the next issue of Bold Challenge magazine. After the photo opportunity, Nguyen O'Bannon led the two Americans down the far side of the hill in an escape route very familiar to him. They would be safely off the hill before the counter-artillery could be called in on their position.

There was a lot of scrambling and confusion on the airstrip. The Camp Evans siren began to wail as the soldiers grabbed their duffel bags and got on their feet. The pilots revved up the engines of the plane and prepared for takeoff. The men shuffled quickly past the Air Force sergeant, yelling out their names as they passed. The sergeant shouted "Check"' as each man passed and stumbled up the ramp and into the plane.

Suddenly Sergeant Scroop appeared from behind the Quonset hut at the edge of the airstrip. He ran up to the Donut Dolly, now shuffling toward the airplane while trying to wipe the dirt off her knees. He grabbed her suitcase and took her arm and turned her around.

"You come with me, Ma'am," he said. "You're supposed to be under cover during an attack. We'll put you on the next plane when things cool down."

Sergeant Scroop dragged the confused woman toward the sand-bagged bunker beside the Quonset hut and grabbed her red suitcase and the brown envelope she was carrying. He then pushed her in the bunker headfirst. He looked around for a second, then ran back to the flight line with the woman's suitcase and brown envelope just as Sergeant Montague and Thuy Van, wearing her Red Cross uniform, appeared from behind the Quonset hut. Sergeant Montague and Thuy Van ran to the end of the line and stopped just behind Ruland. Sergeant Scroop arrived there at the same time and handed the brown envelope to Thuy Van and placed the red suitcase on the ground beside her.

"We forgot to give you your farewell gift!" Sergeant Montague yelled over the roar of the plane's engines. "See you around, Lieutenant." The veteran soldier stood at attention and saluted Lieutenant Ruland smartly. "You better hit the road, sir."

Ruland returned Sergeant Montague's salute and turned to Thuy Van. She smiled at Ruland. Ruland stood motionless in disbelief, not sure he believed what was happening.

"Come on, Ruland," she said. "Make up your mind."

Ruland grabbed his suitcase with one hand and the red suitcase with the other hand. He turned and ran to the Air Force sergeant.

"Are you Lieutenant Ruland?" The sergeant yelled over the noise of the engines.

"Roger," Ruland answered.

"Get onboard, sir. We're taking off." The Air Force sergeant turned to Thuy Van. "You must be Miss Pheeters, right?"

"Check," Thuy Van said.

The Air Force sergeant motioned for Ruland and Thuy Van to get on the plane. They ran up the ramp of the airplane and into the plane. The Air Force sergeant followed them and pulled the door shut behind him. The plane immediately taxied down the runway and turned around at the end of the field without pausing to rev up the engines for takeoff. Then the green plane roared down the airstrip past Sergeant Montague and Sergeant Scroop just as the Donut Dolly stuck her head out of the bunker. Her mouth dropped open as the plane lifted off the ground.

The aircraft rose slowly and began to circle around to the south, setting a course for Danang. There the passengers would be transferred to a chartered jet back to the world. Ruland looked at Thuy Van sitting on the canvas seat beside him. The half-French, half-Vietnamese woman smiled at Ruland and gave him the peace sign. After a few seconds, Ruland smiled back and returned the two-fingered symbol, not knowing what would happen next, or even caring.

As the plane passed over the village, Ruland looked out the small window at Highway One below them. He saw the Phong Dien rifle range passing underneath the aircraft as raindrops began to splatter the small passenger window. It was the beginning of the monsoon season. Within a couple of weeks the long mound of sand on the firing range would be slowly washed away by the rain. The range tower would disappear soon afterwards. The timber would provide a few villagers with the frames for new houses. And the flat, sandy area south of the compound would soon blend into the landscape like nothing was ever there.

Ruland looked at Thuy Van, then down again at the people on Highway One. They continued to move along the sides of the road, always in a hurry, but never seeming to go anywhere.

The end.

About the Author

James E. Davidson spent 1968 in Vietnam as an infantry platoon leader in the Central Highlands and as an advisor to the South Vietnamese Popular Forces. He is now a community college instructor in Indiana.

Printed in the United States
84319LV00003B/80/A

9 780595 196548